MW01529067

FREEZE FRAME

A Vicky Bauer Mystery

OTHER BOOKS BY LEONA GOM:

NOVELS

Housebroken
Zero Avenue
The Y Chromosome
After-Image
Double Negative

POETRY

Kindling
The Singletree
Land of the Peace
NorthBound
Private Properties
The Collected Poems

Mo. B.

FREEZE FRAME

A VICKY BAUER MYSTERY

by

LEONA GOM

SECOND STORY Press

CANADIAN CATALOGUING IN PUBLICATION DATA

Leona Gom, 1946–
Freeze frame : a Vicky Bauer mystery

ISBN 0-896764-26-6

I. Title.

PS8563.O83F73 1999   C813'.54   C99-931767-9
PR9199.3.G65F73 1999

Copyright © 1999 by Leona Gom

Edited by Charis Wahl
Copyedited by Rhea Tregebov

*Second Story Press gratefully acknowledges the assistance of the
Ontario Arts Council and the Canada Council for the Arts
for our publishing program. We acknowledge the financial
support of the Government of Canada through the
Book Publishing Industry Development Program.*

Canadä

Printed and bound in Canada

Published by
SECOND STORY PRESS
*720 Bathurst Street, Suite 301
Toronto, Ontario
M5S 2R4*

ACKNOWLEDGEMENTS

My gratitude, as always, to Dale Evoy for his assistance and advice.
Thanks also, for their ongoing support and rejuvenating e-mails,
to Maureen Shaw, Ranjini Mendis, Rita Patel, Emma Patel,
Herman Gom, Chris Olson, Aritha van Herk, Maureen Moore,
Florence McNeil, Heidi Greco, Murray Speer, and
Ken Long. And thanks to Charis Wahl and Rhea Tregebov
for their invaluable editorial aid.

I am also grateful to Sharon Velisek for her writings on
criminal harassment, to Allen Elliott for his paramedical
expertise, and to Sgt. Ron Paysen and Judge Elaine Ferbey
for their answers to my questions about RCMP procedure.
All errors are entirely my own, and this book is
entirely a work of fiction.

For Rita

PROLOGUE

S OMEONE WAS HAMMERING at the door. *Vicky, sitting in the study surfing the Net, went rigid. She clicked the modem closed; she would need the line free.*

She picked up the cordless phone, her finger ready to push 911, and moved cautiously to the living room, peeked out the window which gave her a partial view of the front steps.

It wasn't him.

It was Lois, her seven o'clock tutoring student. She was early, and something was clearly wrong.

When Vicky opened the door Lois almost fell into the room. Fourteen and small for her age, she was pale, her eyes huge. Her words came out in gasps, barely comprehensible.

"Someone—there's—" She gestured down the street. "By the side of the road—lying there—just lying there—"

"My God." Vicky closed the door. "What happened?"

Lois swallowed several times. "I don't know. I was walking here from the bus stop and I saw this jacket, that's all I thought it was, a jacket, just, like someone had thrown it away.... And then I got closer and it was a person. Just lying there." She leaned against the door, her book bag sliding unnoticed from her shoulder to the floor.

Vicky was dialling 911. A man answered before she could hear the first ring. She gave him her address, told him what Lois had said, surprised at how steady her voice was.

"They'll be right here," she told Lois, who was shaking now, her teeth starting to chatter. "The person, could you tell if—" Vicky stopped; she couldn't ask. The girl was traumatized enough.

"I don't know," Lois said. "I think I saw a hand move. I should have stayed, to check. But I got so scared, all I could think about was that I should go get help."

"You did the right thing. Now just stay here, stay calm. I'm going to run down there. When the ambulance comes, can you show them where to go? Can you do that?"

Lois nodded.

"Good. You're doing fine. Just wait for them and then show them where to go, if they haven't seen me already."

Vicky shoved her feet into a pair of sandals, the first thing she could find without laces, and then, because she could think of nothing more useful to take, she grabbed the comforter from the top of her sofa, bunched it under her arm, and began to run down her front walk. The sandals slapped clumsily against the cement; she should have taken the time to put on her runners. A light rain was falling, but the air was warm, promising spring.

She turned onto the street, kept running. There was a slight downward slope, making it easier. She shifted the comforter to the other arm without slowing her pace. It was dark, though; the sun had set an hour ago, and she had trouble seeing anything away from the circle of the sole streetlight at the end of the block. Why hadn't she thought to bring a flashlight?

A chained dog had been waiting until she was opposite it and then lunged towards her, silently, more threatening than if it were barking. She stumbled on the uneven pavement, moved closer to the centre of the street, pressing her hand into the ache starting in her side.

She ran. Behind her she could hear the faint cry of the siren.

CHAPTER ONE

*T*HE FIRST PICTURE came in the photograph album.
Vicky had just finished reading the morning paper when she'd heard the clatter of the mail arriving, followed by a thud that announced a parcel. She yawned, stretched, and went to the door.

The package was a brown bubble-padded envelope, with no return address. She was pressing her fingers under the flap when she realized the envelope wasn't addressed to her but to Rachel.

Curious, because Rachel had hardly ever received mail here, Vicky took it into the kitchen, to the top of the stairs, and called down, "Rachel! Parcel for you."

"Okay."

Vicky poured herself another coffee. She heard Rachel's door open, and then the creak of the steps.

"For me? Are you sure?" Rachel came into the kitchen.

She was wearing an old blue housecoat from the local Goodwill shop, and she had to hold it up, the way women used to do with long dresses, to keep it from dragging on the floor. Underneath, she was wearing the pink flannel pyjamas Vicky had given her. They were several sizes too large and needed to be turned up into thick cuffs on the sleeves and legs. With Rachel, who was barely over five feet tall, Vicky always felt conspicuously sturdy. Rachel had taken the day off work because she had a cold, but even red-nosed and rumpled, with her blond hair wadded up on one side of her head and the seam from the pillowcase etched into her cheek, she still looked gorgeous.

Vicky doubted if "gorgeous" would be the word people used to describe her, with her stocky body and her somewhat eccentric nose and her mouth developing a distinct droop at the corners; but she knew she probably wouldn't be called "plain," either, and that the thick black hair and large dark eyes and smooth complexion she'd inherited from her Native mother gave her a kind of distinction. Her white father had impressed his genes on her less noticeably, at most contributing to the look her best friend Amanda called Mediterranean.

Rachel pried up the flap of the package. "I can't imagine what it is," she said. Her voice matched her body: slight, delicate, tentative, something a breeze could flutter aside.

What she pulled out of the envelope was an album, the size to accommodate one photograph a page. It had a thick, padded pink cover with the word "Memories" embossed on it in a zealously italic script, and about a dozen cardboard-thick pages inside.

"How odd," Rachel said. "Why would anyone send me this?"

When she opened the cover, they saw it, on the first page, carefully centred and pressed under the attached acetate sheet. The picture looked to be old, a faintly yellowed black and white, with a white, serrated-edge border.

"Who is it?" Vicky asked.

The album had started to tremble in Rachel's hands. She set it down on the kitchen counter.

"It's me," Rachel said. "It's a baby picture of me. I recognize the cushion I'm sitting on. My mother embroidered it." Her finger reached out, touched the image, the cushion and then the tiny, infant face staring open-mouthed at the camera.

"Do you know where it's from, who took it?"

"It's from an album my mom kept. She took so many pictures of me. Especially later. When she was sick. When she knew."

Vicky nodded, kept her eyes on the photograph. Rachel's mother had died of cancer when Rachel was twelve. It was something they had in common, Vicky had thought when Rachel had told her: losing their mothers when both the mothers and daughters were far too young.

"But what's it doing here?" Vicky asked. "Who would be sending this to you now?"

Rachel made a soft fist and pressed her knuckles into the space above her upper lip. Her head began moving slowly from side to side, but whether it was in answer to Vicky's questions or not Vicky didn't know.

"Come sit down." Vicky closed the cover on the album, slid it away from Rachel. She put her other hand on the young woman's shoulder. Rachel cringed away. Vicky withdrew her hand, quickly; she should have remembered that Rachel didn't like to be touched.

They sat down at the dining-room table, Rachel facing the window with the view across Semiahmoo Bay of Washington State and the town of Blaine, gleaming today in unexpected February sunlight. Vicky's house was in the tiny city of White Rock, which was just across the border in Canada and clung to a crescent of oceanfront eyed with amalgamatory envy by the city of Surrey, which surrounded it on the other three sides.

"So tell me," Vicky said. "Who sent this to you?" She set the album on the table.

"Dennis," Rachel said. "It has to be."

Dennis.

When Vicky thought of him, it was always of the way she had first met him. She had been walking up Johnston Road on the way to the bank and was just opposite the gangly clock tower, whose main purpose seemed to be to impair the ocean view from higher up the hill, when she was aware of the couple walking towards her. They were young, in their thirties, dressed in similar blue and white jackets, the man tall, with a body-builder's physique, and the woman much smaller, with long blond hair that was being slowly unbraided both by the wind and by the man clutching it in sudden brief contractions in his fist.

As the couple got closer, Vicky could hear his words, loud and furious and repetitive. "Bitch. You stupid bitch. You goddamned useless bitch. Stupid goddamned *bitch*."

What should she do? It would be easy to avert her eyes, to let them pass, to tell herself it was none of her business. She looked at the woman, hoping for some sign of what she might want, some silent appeal either to intervene or to ignore them, but what Vicky saw on the woman's face was an utter emptiness, the look of a sleepwalker. It was a beautiful face, with perfectly symmetrical features, the large eyes and small nose giving it the innocent look of childhood, but its blankness was nothing that innocence could have produced.

They were just a few metres in front of Vicky now. The man's hand fisted suddenly again into the woman's hair. "You fucking *bitch*," he said, giving his hand a twist. The woman's head pulled towards him, but her face showed no expression of pain.

"Stop that," Vicky said. She stepped in front of the man, barring his way. Her heart was beating so hard it seemed to want to gallop away. What had she done?

The man stopped abruptly, his hand opening and falling from the hair of the woman, who also stopped. Vicky kept her eyes on the man, who up close seemed well over six feet tall and nearly as broad across the chest. His hair was thick and dark and curly, with matching heavy, mobile eyebrows, and his face was handsome in a large-featured, confident kind of way. He stood staring at Vicky, his mouth slightly open.

"This is none of your business," he said, in a surprisingly civilized voice.

"What you're doing is against the law," Vicky said. She

hoped it was true. "You don't have the right to treat anybody like that."

"She's my wife. I can treat her any goddamned way I want."

"No, you can't. She's not your property."

The man gave a harsh laugh. He took the woman's arm. "Come on," he said.

He stepped around Vicky, not so far that his shoulder didn't thrust into hers, forcing her to move back a few steps.

The woman didn't move. "Come *on*," the man said, taking a firmer grasp of her upper arm.

"You don't have to go with him," Vicky said, focusing on her.

The woman didn't answer, only lowered her eyes. She took a step forward, though Vicky couldn't tell whether it was of her own volition or because of her husband's pulling.

"There's a bench over there," Vicky said to her, gesturing to the one a few metres up the street. "We can sit down and talk a bit, if you'd like. He can leave. I'll see you get home. Or somewhere else."

"Oh, for Christ's *sake*," the man shouted. "Let's go!"

But there was a resistance in the woman now. She had moved her legs slightly apart and was leaning back, a posture that suggested the man would have to pull her off her feet to move her.

"Let her go," Vicky said. But she was frightened now at what she had done. It was the woman who would eventually pay for her meddling, she thought.

An older couple was coming up the street, looking at the three of them with alarm. Perhaps it was their presence that made the man suddenly release the woman, giving her a little shove into Vicky. They staggered backward, against the storefront of a used clothing store. The window rattled behind them.

"Oh, dear," exclaimed the elderly woman.

"Go then," the man was shouting. "Go! What the hell do I care, you useless bitch." He slammed his hand so hard onto the lamp post beside him that it shivered. Then he turned and strode away.

The elderly couple sidled by, staring at Vicky and the blond woman as though they were the frightening ones.

"Let's go sit down," Vicky said, trying not to let her voice shake. The woman followed her to the bench, sat down, keeping her eyes on her feet. Her hair fell forward, screening her face.

Now what, Vicky thought, sitting beside her. It began to rain. The traffic hummed loudly at her back, as it must have been doing all along.

"What's your name?" Vicky asked.

"Rachel," said the small voice at last.

◆

And that was how Rachel Cornelius Mandaro came to be living in Vicky's house. At first she was only going to stay for an hour or two, just until they figured out what to do, who to call; and then it was only going to be for that night, until they could get hold of Rachel's boss and uncle, John Harding, and his wife, Linda, who had taken her in before. Then it was supposed to be only for two weeks, until Linda's parents, who were visiting, went back to Seattle. But then, Linda explained to Vicky on the phone, "When she comes to us she ends up going back to Dennis. She feels we're just giving her charity, I guess, but she's so ... passive that she won't get a place of her own, and even if she did Dennis or her father would just convince her she couldn't disobey her husband."

"So what should I do?" Vicky demanded. "Keep her here forever?"

"I don't know," Linda said. "But she does seem to be happy there. You must be a good influence on her. John said she was actually humming at work yesterday. Humming! I wouldn't have thought the poor thing knew how."

Vicky smiled grimly. A snow job, that's what she was getting. But there was something in her that couldn't help being pleased: she had rescued someone, she was making a difference, she was a good influence. And, she had to admit, Rachel was as unobtrusive as she could want, coming upstairs only when invited, gently persisting in paying something equivalent to rent. Vicky had begun to be grateful for that quiet presence. It was comforting to hear, again, the small domestic sounds of another person in the house, to know herself not to be alone. It was only a year since Conrad, her husband, had died. She would not have thought she could bear to share their small, old house with anyone else, but Rachel was not an ordinary person. Not quite a tenant, not quite a friend: Vicky wasn't sure how to explain her growing attachment to Rachel.

She'd talked about it to Amanda, whom she had known long enough to know her opinions would be unflavoured by excessive tact. Or any tact at all, usually. "You just like playing God," Amanda had told her, more than a little jealously, but it was as good an explanation as any. And so Rachel had stayed on, about six weeks now.

Vicky knew, that first day, that the black Honda following them home must belong to Dennis, and she wasn't as surprised as he must have thought she would be when he came banging on her door later that evening. She played the tape Amanda had once given her called "Attack Dog," and it seemed to have dissuaded him from persevering that night. But he came again the next day, and this time she called the police. Not that it did any good. "If she doesn't even have a restraining order ...," said the officer, sounding too indifferent even to complete the sentence.

Rachel had, at the urging of the Hardings, apparently gotten at least two prior restraining orders when she'd left Dennis. But, she said, since she'd gone back to him each time she knew that the police would just consider it a joke if she asked for another one every time she left him. So despite Vicky's pleas, Rachel wouldn't consider it now. And maybe she was right: Vicky knew how ineffectual restraining orders were, anyway, and how they sometimes actually increased the harassment. A woman she'd taught with had called the police over forty times before the man stalking her was even arrested, and then he was promptly released.

"He'll quiet down," Rachel had promised, pleaded.

And it seemed she was right. Dennis hadn't come to the house for about three weeks now. He'd come to where Rachel worked, though, at her uncle's refrigeration plant, but if John Harding hadn't told Vicky about it when he drove Rachel home a few days later Vicky would probably never have known of it.

"I don't think he'd really hurt me," Rachel had said one unseasonably warm morning as they'd sat on the back step having coffee. "Not when it comes right down to it."

"Yeah. Sure." Vicky couldn't keep the sarcasm from her voice. She had heard this explanation from Rachel before, her excuses for Dennis, her refusal to be angry, to blame him. Rachel was intelligent, but she had a kind of willful meekness and self-denial that Vicky knew she was supposed to understand but that still irritated and frustrated her. Meekness, of course, was not a quality anyone had ever accused Vicky of possessing.

"He's disappointed that I didn't give him children. It upsets him when he sees his brother, they've got three kids already—"

"A lot of women can't have children. It doesn't give their husbands the right to abuse them. Besides, he knows you've got endometriosis, that it's likely damaged your Fallopian tubes. Or does he say that's all your fault, too?"

Rachel fidgeted on her seat, retied the knot in the belt of her robe. Her waist was so small the belt could go around it twice. A slim waist, Vicky recalled reading somewhere, was apparently, more than any other womanly feature, a universal symbol of sexiness, fertility. Vicky thought of her own waist, which had not exactly disappeared but had certainly broadened its horizons. Rachel's slim waist, though, had done her no good, either, attracting a man who felt he had been deceived and cheated.

"Dennis just needs me to respect him. Just to ... obey him."

"Just."

"I promised to, after all, when I married him. My father says—"

"Your father," Vicky snorted. "Your father thinks the world was made in seven days and that women are evil and should be beaten regularly. Why do you listen to him?"

"He's my father."

"I know." Vicky sighed. Her own father, whom she had loved and hated, had died six months ago. She missed him far more than she had expected to.

"I just don't think Dennis would really seriously hurt me. He never has. He wants to keep ... reminding me, that's all. That I belong to him. That he still has control over me."

Perhaps that was what the photograph album was about, Vicky thought now, sitting at the dining-room table with Rachel, the album in front of them. Vicky opened it again, leafed carefully through all the pages, but the first picture was the only one in it. She left it open at that page, the photograph of a baby wearing a lacy white dress and knitted booties, propped on a cushion and staring up at the camera. The hands were curled tidily into each other on her lap, as though the infant that would become Rachel had already learned to sit still and obey.

"Are you sure this is from Dennis?"

"Well, the album my mother kept was at my father's. But it would have been easy for Dennis to sneak a picture out of it or even take the whole thing. Dad never locks the door at that place when he goes down for meals. Maybe he even gave Dennis the picture. I imagine the two of them are friendlier than ever, now that they're sure how sinful I really am." Rachel allowed a faint smile. "To me, Dennis would laugh at all the religious stuff. But it was useful to him. The man as the head of everything."

"Even some atheists like that bit," Vicky said. She went into the kitchen and brought back the mailing envelope, handed it to Rachel. "Can you tell anything from the handwriting? Does it look like Dennis's?" The script was large block printing, with a black felt pen, careful, precise strokes.

"It's hard to tell. But, yes, it could be his. We had a black marker we sometimes used for addressing parcels." Rachel put her hand to her mouth, coughed.

"So why would he send this particular picture, do you think? Just to upset you?"

"I suppose so."

"Unless it's your dad who's done this. Is that possible?"

Rachel pulled the housecoat more closely around her, wadding up the pyjama collar around her neck. "It doesn't seem like the kind of thing he'd do. His way is more direct."

"Why don't you call him? See if his album is missing?"

Rachel picked at the flap of the envelope. "I guess that makes sense," she said halfheartedly. "But ..." She looked up at Vicky, pleadingly. "I just hate talking to him. He'll start shouting Scripture at me, tell me to go back to Dennis, tell me to be a dutiful wife."

"I could call him, ask if the album is missing."

"No! No, please. It would just make things worse, him thinking I'd brought someone else in, that I was talking about private family things to an outsider."

Vicky shrugged, trying not to let Rachel see how the word "outsider" had given her a slight sting. But it was what she was, after all, an outsider, someone who had lurched into the middle of someone else's life and expected her own answers to be Rachel's. And Vicky was hardly an expert on families, having come from one where her father had abandoned her mother and her when she was just fourteen and where her despairing mother subsequently more or less drank herself to death, a fate Vicky seemed destined for as well had she not been rescued by Conrad, her patient, sad, lost Conrad. What family Vicky did have were relatives on her mother's side, Blood Indians from southern Alberta, but it was a part of her ancestry she had never particularly pursued. A month ago when a teller at her bank, waiting for a balky computer, had commented on her nice tan, Vicky had only sighed and not bothered with the correction.

The cat, whom Vicky had never gotten around to naming, crawled out from under the sofa, yawned elaborately, then jumped into Rachel's lap. Rachel stroked his head, murmured fondly to him until he sank, eyes closed, into a purring ball on her lap.

"Good thing you haven't had a baby," Vicky said, watching them. "You'd spoil it rotten."

Rachel smiled, scratched the cat under the chin. He stretched his head up, blissful. He was a winter cat, Conrad had said of him once: user-friendly only when it was cold and rainy outside. "Maybe he has Seasonal Affection Disorder," Vicky had said.

The doorbell rang, a long, loud buzz. The women's eyes met, in some instant acknowledgement of fear or complicity, and then they looked to the door. Rachel closed the album, quickly. The cat caught their tension and jumped down, staring at the door, too, his tail bristling.

"Dennis." Rachel's voice was barely a whisper.

Vicky laughed, suddenly, in relief. "No, it's not. It's Rob." She gestured at the history textbook on the table. "My eleven o'clock tutoring student."

Rachel put her hand to her throat. "Just *Rob*," she said, relief flooding her voice, saying the name as though he were an old and dear friend.

Vicky went to the door, opened it, leaving the chain on. "Hiya," said Rob through the crack. "Am I early?"

"No, no, you're fine." Vicky let him in. With him came a smell of clean air, only slightly too ozone-rich from the unusual sunshine, as well as a small brown pancake of leaves on his soles from her front walk where she had been too lazy to rake in the fall.

Rob, although he'd only been with her a month or so, was her favourite of the six students she was tutoring now in Social Studies and English. He was older than the others, twenty or twenty-one, and a student not at high school but at the local college, where he was majoring in Psychology with a minor in History. His difficulties with writing came not from a lack of intelligence but from, apparently, a mild dyslexia and, probably, a dab of laziness. She'd arranged with his college instructors to proof and lightly edit his papers, but they seldom needed much work. Rob himself was cheerful and amiable, with a somewhat horsy Prince Charles kind of face but a grin that was hard to discourage. He had been grinning a lot lately, he'd told her, because he'd finally located his birth mother and she'd been delighted to meet him. He'd celebrated by having his right ear pierced and now wore a stud which he would fondle in a distracting manner that Vicky hoped wouldn't become a habit.

Rachel was sidling away through the kitchen, but Rob's, "Hi, there," caught her, so she had to murmur an acknowledgement before she could retreat downstairs.

"She's cute," Rob said.

Vicky made a face. "If you like those petite, blond, movie-star types."

"She's your tenant, right?"

"Well, sort of." It wasn't the first time Rob had expressed interest in Rachel, but Vicky didn't want to encourage it. She sat down at the dining-room table, set her hands on the college text. *Age of Conflict.* "Well," she said. "Let's see that essay on the Middle East."

Rob was looking at the album Rachel had left on the table. "Me-e-emories," he sang in a parodic tenor, looking at the cover. He opened it, looked at the photograph. "That you?" he asked.

"No. It's Rachel." She flipped the book shut, annoyed at his opening it without asking, and slid it back into its envelope. Then, afraid she had sounded too gruff, she said, making her voice light, "Now let's have that essay, college boy."

"*University* college boy, *please*," Rob said, referring to the college's recent upgrade to degree-granting status and equivalent pretensions. He swung his book bag from his shoulder onto the table and unzipped a pocket.

Vicky set the album on the floor where it wouldn't keep drawing her eyes and picked up her red pencil.

◆

Two days later, the second envelope arrived.

CHAPTER TWO

A S SOON AS Vicky saw the black printing on the birthday-card-sized envelope, she was pretty sure of what would be inside.

Rachel was at work and wouldn't be home until five o'clock so Vicky had to resist her urge to steam the envelope open. The postmark, she noted, carrying the envelope to the small table at the top of the stairs where she left things for Rachel, was Vancouver, as it had been for the album, but of course that wasn't terribly helpful. Dennis lived in Surrey but worked out of Vancouver as a bus driver.

Vicky spent the rest of the morning doing an overdue vacuuming. At least she didn't need to do the basement, which Rachel kept embarrassingly cleaner than it had ever been. The cat twitched his tail resentfully as the machine prodded him from one hiding place after another.

The house was less than a thousand square feet but seemed to be increasingly cluttered, although it was a mystery to her with what, since she hated buying anything new. But she could afford to do so now, she thought, remembering the money in the bank, the plump certificates and mutual funds that Conrad's insurance money had bought and that enabled her to take only six tutoring students instead of twice that many.

She rolled up the cord, glanced at her watch, sighed. School was out almost an hour ago, but Kristin was late, as usual. If Rob was her easiest student, Kristin was her hardest. Bright but lazy, she had begun coming to Vicky at the insistence of her mother, a grimly religious woman Vicky had talked to once or twice on the phone, and of her English 11 teacher who, according to Kristin, claimed she needed someone to "write her ideas down for her."

"Yeah, right," Vicky had replied. Having worked for two years as a sub had given her what Amanda called an enhanced olfactory capacity for smelling bullshit. "And can you give me your teacher's name so I can check on that?"

"Well, I don't mean that you write it all *for* me," Kristin said, although of course that was exactly what she *had* wanted.

Their relationship had improved since then, Kristin no longer assuming her tutor was an overeducated and gullible naif, but Vicky still found her less than endearing.

That was her at the door now, twenty minutes late.

"Sorry," Kristin said. "I think they must have changed the bus schedule."

She was an attractive girl, fair-skinned and fair-haired, with large blue eyes and the sensuous lips actresses injected collagen to achieve. But she was somewhat overweight, and Vicky imagined that she had suffered more than her share of taunts from her classmates and that compliments had been in the inadvertently cruel "oh, you have such a pretty *face*" category. Kristin's I-don't-care attitude may have developed in response. Vicky had been there, and would remind herself of it whenever she felt herself envying the young.

Kristin dropped her coat onto the sofa, pulled the scarf from around her neck. The first few times she had come she had kept the scarf on, to cover a purple birthmark the size and shape of a teacup. Either she trusted Vicky now or didn't care what she thought.

"Well," Vicky said, "have you finished reading *Hamlet*?"

"A bunch of us rented the movie. Branagh is sooo sexy."

"I suppose he is. But did you *read* the play?"

"We read some of it in class. Taking parts. You know." Kristin opened her book bag, took out the play and a battered notebook with "English" written on it in uneven and smudged italic.

"It'll be hard to write your test next week if you haven't actually *read* the play."

"It's a *play*. Shakespeare meant it to be seen, not read."

Vicky smiled. She would let Kristin's English teacher field that old one. "Well, let's anticipate some test questions. Theme, character, tragic flaw, that kind of thing. Write me a paragraph on Hamlet's character."

"Right now?"

Vicky handed her a pencil, looked at her watch. "Right now. You have ten minutes. It's the test. Focus."

Kristin sighed, opened her notebook. If she writes me a biography of Kenneth Branagh, Vicky thought, I will scream.

♦

The next student, Travis, arrived on time and before she had done all the work she wanted to with Kristin, but the young woman seemed only too happy to leave.

She had, Vicky noticed with a pang of sympathy, snatched up her scarf and wound it around her neck by the time Travis came into the room. She murmured a greeting, keeping her eyes down, and Vicky was certain she wouldn't have believed that Travis was looking at her with obvious interest. She was out the door before Travis had his jacket unzipped.

He was a gangly seventeen-year-old, so tall he had gotten into the habit of looking upwards whenever he walked through a room, especially one like hers, where his caution had prevented collisions with the archway between the living room and dining room. He had a pleasant if rather homely face dominated by a large and asymmetrical nose. Since his junior hockey coach was promising him a dazzling athletic career, Vicky told herself she should be impressed that he had any interest in academics at all. She knew the long road trips and practices expected of junior league players left little time for anything except hockey. Travis, like Rob, had been diagnosed once with mild dyslexia, but Vicky had found this label, for both of them, more annoying than useful. She couldn't help remembering a nasty British cartoon she had seen once, a principal telling a raggedly dressed boy, "You're not the right class to be dyslexic. You're just stupid."

Travis, she thought, whatever his social class, was neither dyslexic nor stupid, but his grades were abysmal. He had gotten a C+ on his last Socials exam, however, which Vicky allowed herself to think was in some part due to her help.

He sat down, banging his knees on the table, rattling Vicky's coffee cup. "Sorry," he said. He never got through a session without apologizing for bumping into something.

Vicky went into the kitchen, took the cluster of green grapes out of the fridge, set it on a plate, and held it in front of Travis. He grinned.

"They're delicious," Vicky said. "Now write down the European countries and their capitals." She took a grape, said, "Mmm," and set the plate out of reach in the kitchen.

"Does spelling count?" Travis took out a blue-lined notepad, eagerly.

"You betcha."

Vicky doubted her little bribery games with Travis, who was chronically ravenous, were pedagogically sound, but she didn't care.

He wrote his answers with great concentration, frowning, chewing at his lower lip. She went back into the kitchen, ate a few more grapes, then turned the porch light on for Rachel, feeling that familiar early-evening anxiety about her. She would be waiting by now, alone, probably, at the bus stop. Vicky's eyes went to the small table at the top of the basement stairs, to the envelope there.

"Okay," Travis said.

Vicky picked up the plate of grapes.

"I'm not sure about Brussels," Travis said. "If it's one 's' or two." His stomach rumbled.

Vicky took his paper, sat down across from him and set the plate of grapes in front of her. "Good, good, uh-huh. Brussels is right. You missed Austria, that's all, and Vienna."

"Oh, shit! I mean darn." Travis eyed the grapes morosely.

"This is good, Travis. A few months ago you didn't even know or care where Europe was." She broke off a twig of grapes, about the size of Austria, and pushed the remainder over to him.

He grinned. "I might be playing hockey there some day."

They spent the next hour reviewing the chapter on the Common Market. When he left, Vicky stood watching him through the front window until he got to the end of her walk and into his new mirror-sleek black sports car, the kind no teenager should ever own or what's a heaven for? She realized she had been watching to make sure he reached his car safely. Of course it was Rachel she was thinking of. Vicky felt the urge to get in her car and go to meet her at the bus stop; but she had done that once, and Rachel had been so embarrassed and uncomfortable that she knew she mustn't do it again. The last thing Rachel needed was to think someone else was form- ing an obsessive attachment to her.

She made herself draw the curtains, sit down in her loveseat and start reading ahead in Rob's textbook. *The Age of Conflict.* History was such a cheery subject.

It was almost six when Vicky heard a car turning into her driveway from the alley. She jumped up, peered through her kitchen window. A blue Mercedes: she felt a gush of relief. John Harding must have brought Rachel home from work. She would have to restrain herself from reprimanding them for not phoning, for making her worry, for being thoughtless children.

There were three people in the car. Rachel got out of the back, and then John Harding and a woman got out of the front. It was Linda, Harding's wife: Vicky had met her once and talked to her several times on the phone. She was a rather quiet, plain woman, with a sword-like nose. She looked older than she probably was, which must have been, considering she had a son in his mid-twenties, somewhere in her forties. Her most striking feature was her thick, black hair (probably dyed, Vicky thought unkindly) that she wore up, in a style somewhat too elaborate for the times. She had a lovely smile, Vicky remembered, but she didn't use it often.

Rachel was lifting an armful of clothes out of the car's back seat. Harding opened the other back door and took out a cardboard box, which he handed to Linda, and then he picked up another armful of clothes. They were all laughing, celebratory, and Vicky knew what must have happened. They had managed to get into the house Dennis had barricaded against Rachel, and they had collected some more of her things.

Rachel was coming up the back steps. Vicky opened the door for her. "Been shopping, have we?" she said.

Rachel laughed. Her face was flushed. "He forgot to change the lock on the side garage door! Can you believe it? We hadn't even intended to go in, we never imagined we could, not without breaking a window or something. We just thought we'd drive by and maybe talk to the neighbours, but then I tried my key and it worked!"

Linda was on the stairs now, too, carrying the box, which Vicky could see held underclothes and a few other personal things like a jewellery box and hair curlers and shoes. "We tried not to disturb things," Linda said. "And he'd moved her clothes to the second bedroom so he may never even notice we were there."

"That's great," Vicky said. Rachel was heading down to the basement with her armful of clothes, and Linda followed her, stepping carefully on the dimly lit stairs. Vicky resisted the impulse to say something apologetic about her house. She had been to the Hardings' once, and she knew her whole place must seem smaller to them than their kitchen.

John Harding was at the door now, with the second load of clothes. He handed them to Vicky, so she had to take them, but, not wanting to add to the congestion on her stairs, she draped the armful over the old ladderback kitchen chair on the landing and waited for Rachel to come up and get them.

"How are things going?" John Harding asked. He was a tall man, getting a bit paunchy and grey, with a receding hairline and a part far enough to the side to have been chosen for its comb-over possibilities. He had a nice, large-featured face, although his eyes were owlishly enlarged behind Hubble-thick glasses.

Vicky assumed he meant, how are things going with Rachel, so she answered, "Oh, fine. Rachel's an easy person to have in the house."

Harding gave a little awkward cough, and Vicky realized her remark must have sounded critical of him. She started to add something to cover her mistake, but Harding was already saying, "I'm glad she has a place where she feels okay." He glanced down the stairs to see if Rachel could hear him, but she and Linda were still both out of sight in the bedroom. "With us, well, I don't think she ever felt comfortable. Sure I'm her uncle, but on her mother's side, and her father, I guess you know how he is, he wouldn't have anything to do with anybody outside his church. I always thought I should've done more for Rachel, especially after her mother died."

"You gave her a job."

"Yeah, well. No big deal. I needed somebody anyway."

A small, grey spider descended from the ceiling and landed on Harding's arm. He took a step back out the door and, with more gentleness than Vicky would have used, brushed it away into the night.

"It must be a challenging time," she said, "converting from CFCs. But then I guess you haven't been using them since 1990."

Harding looked at her in surprise, blinking his magnified eyes. "I'm amazed you know about that. Most people couldn't care less about what's in their refrigerators, so long as they run."

"Oh, most people care, I think. They just feel powerless to improve things."

Harding sighed, scratched at his nose. "Well, I bet if I offered a hundred people a refrigerator with Freon at half the price of one with whatever HCFC we're supposed to be using tomorrow, ninety-nine of them would take the cheaper fridge."

"Maybe only because hydrochlorofluorocarbons are just about as bad. They've a shorter life-span in the atmosphere, but they still do damage."

She had really surprised him this time. "You *do* know your stuff," he said. "How'd you like to come work for me?"

Vicky laughed.

"You could be an education consultant, how's that? Most of my damned job these days seems to be convincing people we can't just sew shut the hole in the ozone. You think I'm kidding? I'm not."

Linda and Rachel were coming up from the basement now, so Vicky stepped up into her kitchen to make room on the cramped landing. Linda's heel caught on the top step, and she put her hand on Rachel's arm to steady herself. Rachel reached over quickly to turn out, unnecessarily, the downstairs light, pulling her arm away. Vicky felt a guilty satisfaction—her touch was not the only one Rachel shied from. If Linda noticed how Rachel had drawn away, she gave no sign of it beyond a slight twitch of her lips that might have been coincidental; but Vicky thought she saw John Harding tense, look too quickly away.

"Well," he said, "I guess we can go."

Should she have asked them in, for a coffee or something? It was too late now; the Hardings were already outside, going down the back steps. Besides, they were Rachel's guests, not hers.

"Thanks again," Rachel was saying. She closed the door and turned to the clothes Vicky had draped over the chair back. Her cheeks were still flushed, and she looked as excited as Vicky had ever seen her. Her smile had activated the reclusive dimple in her right cheek. She touched the blue embroidery on a long-sleeved white blouse on top of the pile. "It's so nice to have these back," she said.

"I can imagine."

Rachel slid her arm underneath the pile and lifted it. The swirl of a skirt knocked to the floor the envelope Vicky had set on the little table. In the flurry, she had forgotten about it. She picked it up, handed it to Rachel.

"What's that?"

"Mail for you. Looks as though it might be the same printing as on the package you got two days ago."

Rachel lowered the clothes slowly back onto the chair, took the envelope. Her fingers seemed so clumsy prying up the flap that Vicky had to resist snatching the envelope from her hands and doing it for her.

It was a card, with a picture on it of two white Persian kittens. When Rachel opened it, a photograph slid part-way out. She looked at it for several moments, then, without a word, handed it to Vicky.

The photograph, black-and-white, was of a child, about eight, standing in front of a small stucco house not unlike Vicky's own. The girl was holding a bread-loaf-sized lunch bucket in front of her with both hands, her shoulders hunched a little, perhaps with cold or perhaps with the awkwardness of the moment. Her blond hair hung in two braids down the front of her dark knee-length cloth coat.

"It's you?" Vicky said.

Rachel nodded. "My mother took it. In front of our house in Bellingham. It was my first day of school."

"It's from the same album as the other one?"

"It must be."

"And there's nothing written inside the card?"

"No." Rachel handed it to her. A regular-sized card, that's all it was, the two cute kittens some extra irony, perhaps. On the back of the card it said, in small type, "no greeting."

"This is so ..." creepy, Vicky wanted to say but caught herself in time, "... annoying. Look, why don't you phone your father? Just so you'll at least know for sure if these are from the album he has."

"My father." Rachel was turning the envelope in her fingers, looking down at it. She bit at her bottom lip. "It's just ... He overwhelms me. I want to hang up but I can't."

"Okay, then, how about if you gesture to me when you want the conversation to be over and I'll pick up the extension and say I need to make a call?"

Rachel thought about it for a minute. "All right. If you don't mind."

They went into the living room, and while Rachel dialled her father's number Vicky picked up the cordless extension phone and sat down on the sofa that stood at a right angle to the loveseat on which Rachel perched, looking as though she might leap up any moment and run.

"Dad?" Rachel's fingers tightened on the phone cord. "I have to ask you something.... No, I have to ask you something.... No, listen—" She threw a beseeching look at Vicky, then was silent for several moments, her eyes closed, her fingers twisted in the phone cord. Vicky could only imagine what she was hearing. Finally, Rachel managed, her voice raised and rushing, as if talking over her father's, to ask about the photograph album. She was silent again for several moments, her eyes closed, and then she put her hand over the receiver and whispered to Vicky, "He's gone to look."

"Good. See, I knew you could do it."

Rachel gave her a tense smile. "Yes?" she said into the phone. "It's gone? Are you sure?" She paused, apparently waiting for an answer. "Can you remember when you last saw it?" She listened for a while longer and then pointed to Vicky's extension phone.

Vicky pushed the "on" button.

The voice was pouring from the receiver, clearly audible even before she got it near her ear. "... who brings shame on the house of her father and her husband. If you thwart the Lord, there will be a reckoning, my girl, don't think you can play with the Devil and not pay a price—"

"Hello?" Vicky said loudly. "Rachel, are you on the line? I need to make a call."

There was silence. Then, "Who's that?" demanded the voice.

"That's my landlady, Dad. I have to get off the phone."

"That's right," Vicky said. Landlady? The word had thrown her for a minute, the way it came so easily to Rachel. It was probably the best word for her to use with her father. Still.

"Well, hey you, you landlady, maybe you can talk sense to my daughter. She thinks she can ignore what God planned for her. You don't let her stay in your house or the sin is yours, too. She belongs with her husband—"

"I have to make a call!" Vicky had to shout over his words, the rushing flood of them. "We're hanging up now. Goodbye!"

She made herself press the "off" button, hold her finger on it, hard, like pressure on a hemorrhage. Rachel hung up the other phone.

"Wow," Vicky said. "I see what you mean."

Rachel smiled weakly, ran the palms of her hands down

her corduroy skirt. "If I listen to him long enough, I feel myself ... drowning, giving in to him, being afraid, letting him make all my decisions again. Absurd, isn't it, someone my age thinking she has to obey her father?"

"No, it's not. Parents have this incredible hold over us, all our lives. Especially if they claim God on their side." She realized she was still pressing the "off" button, and she released it. "Anyway. The album. It's gone?"

Rachel nodded. "So it must be Dennis. Dad was all Dennis this, Dennis that. He goes to see Dad and gets him upset and then Dad puts pressure on me to go back to him."

"But you won't." She had intended to make it a question, to add "Will you?" at the end, but decided not to.

Rachel thought a minute, her eyes fixed on the corner of the room.

"So far," she said finally.

Perhaps if Vicky hadn't just spoken to Rachel's father she wouldn't have been satisfied with such an answer. But she had a better idea, now, of how far Rachel must already have come. Last week Rachel had said that when things "quieted down" she'd see about getting a divorce. "Quieted down" was about as vague as "so far," but for Rachel the very idea of divorce was progress.

Rachel picked up the photograph again, ran her finger gently over the small face. "I still don't understand what Dennis is doing. Why would he steal the album and then give me back little bits of it?"

"It must be just a power thing. He gives you something you want but only at his whim." Vicky stood up, stretched. "Look, you want something to eat? I've got a casserole that's too much for me and I'll be throwing out what's left."

It was how she had to word things or Rachel would refuse, would go back to the basement and heat a can of soup on her hot plate or nibble some peanuts and call it supper. She *had* gained a little weight since she'd moved in, but she still seemed to have the appetite of a minnow. But that was why Rachel was petite and Vicky, well, wasn't.

"If you're sure," Rachel said.

CHAPTER THREE

IT WAS NICE to get out of the house. Vicky rolled down the car window, let the wind flick some rain at her. She had grown up in Alberta, and she couldn't understand how people in BC could complain about rain in February, when the rest of the country was shovelling snow. Her car, a cranky Toyota, grunted as she prodded it off the King George Highway and onto the Surrey side street that led to Dulci's house.

She was charging ten dollars an hour more than usual for going to a student's house, but she felt a little ashamed about it because the parents usually urged food and drink upon her and the students likewise wanted to impress. Dulci Warner's house was not as elaborate as some she had visited—owned by clients Amanda, who had gotten her started in tutoring, called RAMs, Rich As Midas—but it was a cheerful split-level and immaculately tidy, smelling always of flowers because Dulci's mother was a florist.

It was creative writing that Dulci wanted help with today. She handed Vicky a note from her mother saying it would be okay. "It's not really my area of expertise," Vicky protested.

"I'm desperate. This story is due tomorrow and I just can't get any ideas," Dulci moaned, clutching her short reddish hair as they sat at the kitchen table. She was sixteen, already grown into the kind of tall, shapely woman people would call beautiful.

"Did your teacher assign a subject?"

Dulci shook her head. "No. So I don't know where to start."

"Would it be easier if I gave you a topic, made you write on that?"

"Sure. A first sentence. Why not give me a first sentence?"

Vicky thought for a moment. "Okay. 'Nobody knew why the strange photographs kept arriving at Victoria's house.'"

"Wait. Let me write that down."

Vicky laughed. "This will really make it easier for you?"

"Sure." Dulci was looking at the sentence she'd scribbled down, chewing her gum with so much animation she might have been afraid it was trying to escape. "I can see all kinds of ways the story can go."

Her father came in from the workshop; he was covered with a film of sawdust that drifted onto the kitchen table and counters. A small, heavy-set man with a baggy face who looked nothing like Dulci, he smiled shyly at Vicky.

"Da-ad. You're making a mess. Go dust yourself off."

"Okay," he said meekly, backing away into the workshop. Vicky could hear him slapping the sawdust off himself. Another father learning obedience to a teenage daughter.

"Well, why don't you get going on that story then?" Vicky said. "Let me see the first page when you've got one. Or maybe you should show me an outline first."

"I don't need an outline. This is creative writing, not an essay. Besides, I have to work on the computer. I can't compose anything unless I do it at the computer."

Vicky sighed. The new generation. "Well, print up something for me when you have it."

While Dulci worked in her room, Vicky sat restlessly at the kitchen table, flipping through the new Socials 10 text she'd fortunately thought to bring. It was a waste of her time, being here at all, she thought, to say nothing of the waste of the Warners' money.

Dulci's father came back into the kitchen, looked surprised to see her sitting there alone.

"Dulci's gone to work on her computer," Vicky said quickly. She felt like a workman who'd been caught napping.

"Good, good." Mr. Warner poured himself a coffee, held the pot questioningly towards Vicky. She shook her head. "How's she, you know, doing?"

"Fine," Vicky said. "She's an intelligent girl. She just needs to learn to concentrate."

"We spoil her," her father said, as though Vicky had chastised him. "She's our only child, you see."

"Only children have a lot of advantages. They don't have to go through all that sibling rivalry stuff."

"Da-ad." Dulci stood in the doorway. "Stop bothering Mrs. Bauer."

Vicky laughed, more loudly than she intended. "It's all right," she said. "I was just sitting here waiting for you."

"Well." Mr. Warner sidled back to the door into the workshop. "I'll let you two get on with it."

Dulci sighed. "I *guess.*"

Vicky couldn't help thinking of how her own father would have responded to such snottiness. A cuff on the head, probably. She wondered what Rachel's father would have done. Sibling rivalry would have been a piece of cake for both of them compared to coping with their fathers.

"Here's my first page," Dulci said, handing it to Vicky. "I'm really getting into this."

By the time Vicky was ready to leave, Dulci had finished almost a whole first draft, and she printed up a copy for Vicky to take home. The story, at least as far as Vicky had read, involved CIA spies and photographs of Victoria's husband with Another Woman (capitalized), who was a Russian agent. "It's usually better to write about what you know," Vicky had said halfheartedly at some point, not knowing if it was what one still told young writers. What students knew, after all, was pretty boring.

She wondered, as she got in the car, if she dared show the story to Rachel, but decided against it; it was unlikely Rachel would be amused at her life being used as an assignment.

She was picking Rachel up after work today, since she was in the neighbourhood. The rain had stopped, and the sun was slanting now through her windshield. She was glad when she could turn away from the glare, into the commercial strip where Harding Refrigeration was.

The plant consisted of a front office, a showroom, and a big, windowless warehouse used for storage and repair. A large tank, which Vicky imagined stored the coolant, was connected to one end of the building by several big pipes.

She parked at the side, beside the small, red pick-up that Junior, the Hardings' son, often drove. Junior was, Rachel said, very good at his job, which was mostly in sales but also in the commercial repair and maintenance the business specialized in. It was probably because of Junior that the company had been growing, that they had hired three more technicians in the last year.

She went around to the front. Through the window she could see Rachel at her desk, adding something up on the calculator, the white tape spooling out of it, and Junior sitting on the chair at the desk behind her, on the phone. She could hear his voice right through the door.

She went in. Rachel looked up, smiled. She was wearing a prim blue dress with rickrack around the collar and down the front: something from her newly replenished wardrobe.

"Hi," Rachel said. "Just give me a few more minutes."

"No rush."

Junior hung up the phone, grinned at her. "Hiya," he said, shoving a folder into one of the four floor-to-ceiling filing cabinets that took up a good portion of the office's space.

"Hi, Junior," Vicky said.

She felt silly calling him "Junior" when his real name was

Vance, but it was what he preferred; maybe it made him feel boyish and doted upon by indulgent parents. He was somewhere in his mid-twenties but was starting already to add that heaviness of his father's, that flesh at the jaw that would be a double chin by the time he was thirty. His features were small and plain, but if he lacked a memorable face he made up for it in ambition and enthusiasm. Vicky had only met him twice before this, but each time he seemed like someone who had just had new batteries installed. Perhaps it was because he had recently been divorced. Rachel was quite fond of him, and while she still seemed nervous around his father, even though he was her uncle, she seemed on more equal and comfortable terms with Junior.

"So how's business?" Vicky asked him.

"Great!" He actually rubbed his hands together, gleeful, then pointed at the phone. "That was our lawyer. He just signed a preventive-maintenance contract with the Nippon House restaurant chain."

"That's wonderful," Rachel exclaimed. She turned to Vicky. "Junior's been working on getting that contract for a month."

"I put away a lot of Japanese food to schmooze this one around, let me tell you," Junior said, patting his slightly round stomach. "I'm going down to the club to tell Dad." He grabbed his suit jacket from the coat rack and trotted out the front door, whistling.

Vicky raised an eyebrow at Rachel. "He seems pleased with himself."

"He has a right to be. I just hope his father appreciates it." Rachel stretched her arms up over her head. "Well, his day has to have been better than mine. This morning I was mostly calling overdue accounts. You wouldn't believe how some people can treat you when they owe you money. One woman swore at me in what I think was Spanish, and then she told me it meant, 'I hope your children become maggots.'"

"It loses something in the translation."

"Well, now I can hand her over to the collection agency. I imagine they've heard worse things." She scribbled a number on the invoice she had been working on, then put the calculator into her desk drawer, punched a few buttons on the computer and turned it off. It made a sound like a long sigh, making them both laugh.

It wasn't until they were almost home that Rachel asked, trying to sound casual, "Anything in the mail for me today?"

Vicky had been as curious about that as Rachel. "I don't know," she said. "I went out before the mail came."

They crossed North Bluff Road into White Rock, started the downward slope that eventually ended at the beach. It was overcast and getting dark; Vicky put on her lights. She turned off at Pacific Avenue, the sea below them flat as the prairie. She remembered her surprise when she had first seen the ocean here, how she had expected waves and surf, but the tides were gentled by the long protective arm of Vancouver Island and the other Gulf Islands in the Georgia Strait; she could see their misty backs now, in the bluing distance. She pulled into the lane that ran behind her house.

And slammed her foot on the brake. Blocking both the alley and her driveway was a black Honda.

"Dennis," Rachel breathed.

Vicky pulled to the right, against her neighbour Birdy's hedge.

"What should we do?" whispered Rachel.

"I don't know," Vicky said. "But I don't think we should get out of the car."

The driver's door of the Honda opened. Dennis was wearing jeans and the blue and white jacket he'd had on when Vicky had first seen him, and he looked at least as big and muscular as she remembered. He started to move towards them, a slightly bow-legged walk, as though his legs had had to adjust to carrying such a large torso.

"Oh, God," Rachel said.

"I can back up and be out of the alley before he reaches us."

"That might just provoke him."

"Anything we do will provoke him."

Dennis was at Vicky's window. He would probably have gone to Rachel's except that the passenger side of the car was pressed too closely against Birdy's hedge. Vicky found herself watching his hands, his pockets, looking for a weapon. There was a bulge in his jacket pocket; please let it just be gloves, she prayed. Her heart was hammering. She put the Toyota into reverse, checked the rearview mirror, ready to jerk her foot from the clutch.

Dennis tapped on the window. Not banged, tapped. Politely. But his face was tense, unsmiling, made even more unwelcoming by a good day's growth of stubble. His posture held the latent power of a closed umbrella.

She rolled her window down, slowly, about two inches. "Hi, Dennis," she said, trying to make her voice calm, unafraid.

"I want to talk to *her*," Dennis said, nodding at Rachel, who had shrivelled down into her seat, not looking at him.

"We don't want any trouble," Vicky said. "Please move your car."

Dennis kept his eyes on Rachel. "I know you were in my house," he said, anger rising into his voice. "You stupid bitch. I never said you could come into my house."

"She just took some of her personal things," Vicky said. What was the right way to talk to someone like Dennis? The only thing she knew how to do was to reason with him, but she knew also that harassers were not reasonable people. But what else could she do? Threaten him?

"I see you sneaking in there again I'll fucking kill you," Dennis said, his voice rising. "You don't come in my house again unless you're ready to stay there. You got that? You got that?"

"All right," Vicky said. "Now move your car, please."

"And *you* keep your big nose out of it!"

Vicky could understand why Rachel couldn't look at him. His dark eyes seemed to force their will into her. His thick brows were not, as she might have expected, pulled down, but slightly up, making his eyes huge, glaring. A scar cut into his right eyebrow, as though he had shaved out a small triangle.

Vicky looked away, perhaps to appease him, perhaps because she couldn't meet his ferocious gaze any longer. "All right," she said quietly.

"And you" —Dennis pointed his finger through the crack in the window at Rachel— "you're my wife. You promised to love, honour and obey. *Obey*. Don't you bloody forget it."

Vicky had to stop herself from rolling the window up, fast, snapping his accusatory finger right off. "Let us alone, Dennis," she said. "Please. Go home."

"Shut up! I wouldn't have to be here if it weren't for you, you fucking dyke!"

Well. "Get out of here, Dennis," she said. "Right now."

Dennis slammed his palm onto the roof of her Toyota. The car shook. Rachel cried out, huddled deeper into her seat.

"Don't you tell *me* what—"

"Leave them alone! And get that car out of my hedge!"

They were all startled by the loud voice practically at Dennis's elbow. Birdy. Oh, God, Vicky thought; now she was going to be responsible for having her elderly neighbour beaten up. She should have realized that when Birdy's industrial-strength outside light blazed on shortly after they drove into the alley it meant the woman was watching them. Birdy was standing, legs apart, holding a broom against her chest like a rifle she might any minute swing to her shoulder, aim, and fire. She was a short, stout woman, coming barely to Dennis's chest, with a perpetually flushed face that was convenient for looking belligerent. She had just turned seventy, but she was as robust as a twenty-year-old and considerably more self-assured.

"This is none of your business, old woman." But Dennis's voice was barely a mumble.

"Everything is my business. Now get in that car of yours and stop making a nuisance." She bounced the broom on the pavement, hard, the bristles grating.

Dennis simply stood there. His mouth was moving but no words were coming out. Vicky held her breath, watching his hands.

Finally he turned back to Rachel, said through the window crack, his voice low, so that Birdy wouldn't hear, "This isn't over." And then he strode back to his car, got in, slammed the door and drove away, tires screeching, leaving a last warning of rubber on the pavement.

Vicky began to laugh. She opened the door, would have given Birdy a hug except for the broom. "That was lovely," she said. "Thanks."

"I was just protecting my hedge," Birdy grinned. "He thought it was you I was mad at as much as him."

"We'll have to call you next time he shows up," Vicky said.

"Sure. Not many bullies can stand up to an old woman with a broom. People don't know that, but it's true."

"That sounds positively quotable," Vicky said.

Birdy was squinting into the car. "How're you doing, Rachel?"

When Rachel had moved in, Birdy had wasted no time in ambushing her in the alley when she came home from work and introducing herself. Her intrusiveness had annoyed Vicky then, but she was grateful for it now.

"Hello, Mrs. Birdsell."

"Don't you have a restraining order on that guy?" Birdy asked.

"Well, not exactly," Rachel said vaguely.

"You better get *some*thing. He sounds nuts."

"The way he sees it, I broke into his house and stole things."

"*Her* house, too," Vicky couldn't help adding, "and *her* things."

"Well, you know where me and my broom are if you need us," Birdy said. She headed back down her driveway.

Vicky put the car in gear and turned into her own driveway, half expecting the house to show some evidence of Dennis's visit, but nothing was unusual, except for an empty beer can that a gust of cold wind rattled towards her. She picked it up, wondering if Dennis had thrown it there.

The neighbours on the west side of her house were just leaving, and the woman nodded at her. Vicky raised the beer can in what was likely a poorly chosen wave. The woman had cooled towards her considerably since the day, shortly after they'd moved in, when Vicky, after having said the obligatory things about how charming the couple's child was, had declined, with perhaps an audible panic in her voice, the woman's invitation to babysit. "I thought you might *enjoy* it," the woman had said stiffly, and somehow there didn't seem to be any way back for either of them after that. Still, the family was a great improvement over her previous neighbour in that house. Richard. It was still hard for her to look at the place without remembering him there, remembering her intense and foolish and disastrous involvement with him. After Richard, the couple wanting a free babysitter were at least in a category she could consider normal.

Rachel followed her into the house, where Vicky set the beer can into the recycling box at the top of the basement stairs, gingerly, as though it might be a live grenade.

"Well," Vicky said. "Should we call the police?"

Rachel didn't answer for several minutes. "They won't do anything without a restraining order."

"So—are you going to get one?"

"They won't do anything with one, either."

Vicky had to bite back an exasperated reply. But it wasn't Rachel she was annoyed with; it was the police, the system, for making what Rachel said true.

"I'd hoped it was over," Rachel said. "He seemed to be leaving me alone. I know this time he was mad because I took my clothes, but there was all the other old stuff, too. How I had to come back and obey him, all that."

Vicky sighed. "Yeah, I heard. Look, I think you should get that restraining order. It's better than nothing. It tells him you're serious."

"Like I was serious the other times? The times I went back to him?"

"This time is different," Vicky insisted, feeling a little nervous at the way the conversation was going. "This time you've really left him."

"I hope so."

"If he comes around here again *I'll* get a restraining order. I've enough cause, and the cops can't dismiss me as easily as they can you."

Rachel gave her a small smile. "You'd be surprised."

"Why? You think Dennis will tell them I'm gay and that I've kidnapped you?"

Rachel picked at her fingernails, wouldn't meet Vicky's eyes. "I'm sorry he said that. You know, calling you a ... dyke."

Vicky laughed. "I took it as a compliment."

By the time Vicky had taken off her coat and picked up the mail at the front door Rachel had gone downstairs to her room. Vicky called her back.

Rachel looked at the envelope in Vicky's hand. Her fingers went to her lips, pressed against them, making them white and flat. Vicky held out the envelope.

Rachel shook her head. "You open it," she said.

The picture was enclosed in the same kind of card as the last time: two kittens on the cover. The photograph, again in black-and-white, was, Vicky could tell immediately, of Rachel, about age eleven. She was wearing a frilly white dress, and she was sitting on a large chunk of driftwood at a beach, holding a piece of bread out to two large, grey seagulls. She was smiling, but her posture was rigid, as though she were ready to leap up and run.

Rachel took the picture gently from Vicky's hand. "Mom said to be careful. She said they might peck me. I was careful. But one of them nipped me, anyway." She rubbed the forefinger of her right hand. "It didn't even break the skin, but I can still feel it. The surprise of it."

◆

Another envelope arrived the next day, Friday. Vicky recognized the handwriting by now, the shape of the greeting card inside. She wondered if Dennis would keep doing this until he'd emptied Rachel's father's whole album. She left the envelope on the landing table on her way downstairs to put in a load of laundry. The door to Rachel's room, which adjoined the laundry and furnace room, was closed, as it always was, and Vicky had to resist the urge to go in and snoop. She had not been inside the room since Rachel had moved in, but she could imagine its condition. The exterior of the washing machine had never been as clean as it was now. And the small windows above the laundry sink, Vicky realized, were actually made of clear glass. Even the cobwebby furnace looked as though it had been scrubbed, and the downstairs bathroom couldn't have been scoured cleaner by a detailing shop. It had been tempting to accept Rachel's offer to clean upstairs as well, but Vicky had unearthed enough pride to say no.

She had two tutoring sessions today. The first, which went as smoothly as always, was with Ajit, an earnest young Indian immigrant who was two years ahead of his peers in the sciences but who wanted to improve his English skills. The second was with Kristin, who wanted Vicky to rewrite an English assignment on Wordsworth to raise its grade.

"I can't do it *for* you," Vicky explained for about the tenth time. If the girl replied with some version of that's-what-I-pay-you-for, Vicky thought angrily, she would say goodbye.

Kristin surprised her. "I know," she said. "I'm just too lazy to do it myself."

Vicky laughed. "That's exactly right. You're very clever, you know" —a little snake oil to lubricate the self-esteem— "and when you talk to me I can see you understand what Wordsworth means. You just have to sit down and write."

Kristin sighed, rubbed at her neck, which made the birthmark there darken. Her hands seemed to have developed a rash, dozens of small red spots covering the backs. "I know."

"Okay. Now expand on what you mean here: 'People who don't like London have dull souls.' You know the sonnet is more complex and interesting than that."

Kristin picked up her pencil, writhed on her seat, sighed, and finally began to write.

When the session was over and Kristin was leaving, Rachel was just coming home and bumped the door into her. The fluttering of excessive apologies from both of them made Vicky simultaneously amused and annoyed. She had grown up in a tougher world, where one saved such apologies for injuries that drew blood.

Vicky waved at the girl as she turned to go up the walk; from Kristin's sickly answering smile one would have thought Vicky had just accused her of cheating on her finals. She pulled her hood over her head against the light rain and hurried away.

"What is this allergy the young have to umbrellas?" Vicky asked, before she realized Rachel didn't have one with her, either.

"It's not cool," Rachel said.

She took off her jacket, the blue and white one that matched Dennis's. She was wearing a navy blazer and skirt with a grey blouse and matching pumps. With her hair pulled back and tied at the neck, she looked far more the professional business woman than the waif Vicky had first met.

"There's another letter for you."

Rachel was already heading for the little table at the top of the stairs. As she opened the envelope Vicky was surprised to see she was actually smiling a little, as if expecting something pleasant. She opened the card, another with two kittens on the cover, and looked at the picture inside for a moment before handing it to Vicky.

"It's you?"

Obviously it was. The photograph, unlike the others, was in colour, of a girl about fifteen, sitting on a sofa with a Christmas tree half visible to the right. She was wearing a red high-necked dress of some shiny fabric, and she had the newly beautiful face of the adult Rachel. Vicky was unexpectedly moved, seeing the young woman with so much to look forward to, with so much that would disappoint and betray her. Rachel finally had to reach out for the picture.

"This is four now, isn't it?" Vicky asked.

Rachel nodded. "I'm older in every one. This is just ... such a strange thing for Dennis to be doing."

"It does seem a bit, well, Byzantine for someone as confrontational as he is."

"I wonder how much farther he'll go."

"You said your mother kept the original album and she died when you were twelve, so is this from somewhere else?"

"No. My dad took it. I kept the album up, for a while,

until I was married, and I guess a little beyond that. The last picture in it was of my first wedding anniversary. Dad took that one, too." She paused. "I remember how when he handed the camera back to me he said he couldn't believe I wasn't pregnant yet. And I think it was after that that Dennis started to get fixated on the fact I wasn't, too."

"How old were you then?"

"Twenty-one."

"So maybe, since you seem to be more or less five years older in each picture, there'll be only one more."

Rachel slid the photograph back into the card. "It won't be much to have left of my mother's album, five pictures."

Another tutoring student, Lois, arrived then, and Rachel hurried away downstairs. Vicky wondered if she would open the little album she had been sent, the one that said "Memories" on the cover, and slide this last picture, lovingly, behind the fourth acetate sheet, just as Dennis must have expected her to do.

Lois was fourteen, a hand-me-down from Amanda, who had tutored her in French. A classic overachiever, Lois was urged on by a mother who, Amanda said, wanted to make sure her daughter had all the talent that money could buy. During their sessions Vicky had to work almost as hard as Lois did. *Why did I get only A, not A+, on this test? Can you give me more exercises using the growing-season map? Can you quiz me on the names of the major rivers in each drainage basin? Can you give me another example of a trellis river pattern?* After Kristin, who would have preferred to talk about Kenneth Branagh, Lois was, well, bracing.

Her session was almost over when the phone rang. Vicky let the machine take it. But she recognized the voice immediately, its loud, hectoring tone. Rachel's father. She strained to listen, making Lois impatient enough to begin beating her pencil lightly on the table.

"... I don't know how it happened, but here it is," the voice on the machine was saying. "I know it was gone, but today I came back from lunch and there it is on the shelf where it's always been. So I don't know." He coughed, and his voice changed a little, became suddenly sly, as though something clever had just occurred to him. "You can have it, if you want. You can come over and get it. I got no use for it anyway. So, Rachel, you there? You there, huh? These machines, I never know about these machines." There was a protracted clattering noise, the sudden blare of a radio or TV, and then the line went dead.

Lois had not even closed the door behind her after her session before Vicky was trotting down the stairs, knocking on Rachel's door.

◆

They had just turned onto the Steveston Highway. On the right was Fantasy Gardens, expanded into a Christian theme park by a former provincial premier. They passed the farms, the huge Buddhist temple, and, because Rachel forgot to tell Vicky when to turn off, the BC Packers Plant. Downtown Steveston, which occupied the southwestern edge of the Vancouver suburb of Richmond, was an uneven mix of thrift shops, fishing-supply stores and a few gentrifying restaurants that might have been going for "quaint." The area originally had been a thriving Japanese fishing village, but during the war the government had seized all the Japanese boats and fishing equipment and sold them off, never making any restitution, during or after the war, to the owners. It was a legacy that still clung unpleasantly to Steveston.

"I think it's off Trites Road," Rachel was saying, peering at the map. Her father had not been in the retirement home long, she said, explaining her uncertainty. He had moved there from Bellingham in Washington State, where Rachel was born and grew up and probably would have stayed if she hadn't married Dennis, who had wanted to move to Canada because it wasn't as full of foreigners as the US was. Foreigners, he'd explained to Rachel, were people who weren't white.

They were on Westwater now, winding along the shore, the old unpainted buildings of the Britannia Shipyard on their right. A big redevelopment sign stood at the entrance, promising more of the upscale condos taking over the waterfront. No developer, of course, was talking about what would happen to Richmond when The Big One hit, when the rich delta soil might, as geologists believed had happened there in previous earthquakes, more or less liquefy.

"There it is," Rachel said. "I remember the small-craft harbour at the south end."

Vicky turned left, letting the muscle car that had been tailgating her rocket past. Hillcrest Retirement Village was a two-storey complex, new and not cheap, which looked to have about fifty rooms and several large circular outgrowths that were probably dining rooms or recreational areas. Tall iron gates at the entrance stood open, but Vicky could see a security booth and a security camera keeping its beady eye on them. She parked in a visitor's spot, and followed Rachel inside.

The foyer was large and airy, with comfortable sofas and ficus plants satisfied enough to keep a healthy foliage. At the front desk a man with a white beard and front teeth the size of tombstones took both their names, Vicky's license and phone numbers, the guest they would be visiting, and the approximate length of their stay. Vicky was at the point of asking if he'd like to strip-search them, too, but she made herself smile politely and remind herself that when she got old she might be grateful to live in such a protective place. Besides, the man looked less like a prison guard than like St. Peter, inspecting them for a tour of the afterlife, which must lie beyond the thick and over-panelled double doors to which he was now directing them with an archangelic smile.

The hallway on the other side of the doors was noticeably less grand than the lobby; that was probably how it was in the afterlife, too, Vicky thought. They walked down the hall, past numerous doors, some of them half open, perhaps to encourage visitors, and past one of the circular outcroppings she had noticed from outside and which was indeed the dining room. Two doors beyond it Rachel stopped.

"This is it," she said. Her voice was a whisper.

"Don't worry. We won't have to stay long."

"He just ... I find it so hard to face him." Her cheeks were pale, and she was holding onto her purse strap as though she were approaching a mugger. Her hand shook as she knocked at the door.

"Come in."

They did. It was a larger space than Vicky expected, and the window let in the southern light and a view of the cedar trees at the building's entrance; but, still, it was just one room, with an adjoining bath. A single bed stood against one wall, and the rest of the room was filled with armchairs, end tables, an immense TV, and a ceiling-high bookcase crammed beyond capacity with religious books and tracts.

Jacob Cornelius was sitting on the bed. Beside him, open, as though he had been leafing through it, was a photograph album, the old-fashioned kind, with felty black pages, a string binding and silver photo corners. Vicky could see Rachel's eyes fix on it, hungrily. She turned her own eyes to the man. She had expected someone to match the loud and aggressive voice, but Jacob Cornelius was a small man, shorter than she was, with a slight build and a humped osteoporotic posture. He had a full head of enthusiastic grey hair, but his face was heavily lined, sagging into and over the shirt collar that seemed to be buttoned right into his neck and that encircled the top of his blue striped necktie. His white shirt, freshly ironed, hung over flowered flannel pyjama bottoms.

When she made herself look back to his face, it was his eyes she was drawn to. Whatever his mismatched clothing may have suggested, the sharp blue eyes focused on Rachel showed he was not someone to whom senility gave excuses.

"This the landlady?" His voice was the way Vicky remembered, loud, harsh, accustomed to getting the answers it wanted. His eyes barely flicked to Vicky before going back to Rachel.

Rachel had to clear her throat before her voice would come. "Yes," she said. The silence that followed made Vicky aware this was probably the extent of Rachel's ability to do introductions. Her eyes hadn't left the open album.

"Well," her father said, patting it. "Like I said, it was just here one day. It was gone and then it was back."

"Are there pictures missing?" Rachel's voice was high-pitched, that of an anxious child.

"Some." He closed the album, set it on his lap.

Vicky could tell Rachel was trying to say something but seemed unable to form the words. Her face was white, almost nacreous, her hands twisting into themselves in front of her.

"We can't stay," Vicky said. "We just came to get the album."

Jacob Cornelius clasped his hands on either end of it. A small, sly smile pulled onto his crumpled lips. "I changed my mind," he said, watching Rachel. "I've decided to keep it until you go back to Dennis."

"You can't do that," Vicky protested. "That's why we came here, to get it. You said Rachel could have it."

Rachel's father looked at Vicky then. It was almost impossible to meet those eyes, their arctic blue glitter. "I said, she has to go back to her husband! Are you deaf, woman? 'Wives, submit yourselves unto your own husbands.' Is she so heathen now she can't remember the Bible? She's my daughter and I gave her to Dennis. And now she shames me, she shames herself, she shames God. She has a duty! A duty! 'The husband is head of the wife.' It can't be plainer!"

Vicky laughed. "'Ephesians,'" she said, surprising herself with the memory of an ancient argument she'd once had with a religious classmate. "And the next verses say wives and husbands should submit themselves one to the other, and that husbands should love their wives as they love themselves. Well, I sure haven't seen Dennis do any of that, have you?"

The old man's eyes narrowed; he was taken aback, but not as much as Vicky had hoped. "The Devil can quote Scripture," he hissed. He pressed the album to his chest, as though he needed it to ward her off. He was a caricature, Vicky thought, staring at him: an actor gone way over the top. Except that he was real, Rachel's very real father.

"Well, give us the album as you promised and I won't contaminate your room any longer," Vicky said.

Rachel started to cry. "Don't," she whimpered. "Don't."

"See what you done," her father said, triumphantly.

Vicky looked at Rachel in dismay. "It's okay," she said softly.

"It's you who turned her against God!" her father exclaimed. "You're the one making her do this, making her not honour her husband or her father! What kind of a woman are you?"

"I'm a simple widow woman," Vicky said, the first stupid words that came into her mind.

"A widow!" He shuddered, as though it were even worse than he expected. "A widow that liveth in pleasure is dead while she liveth.'"

There were a lot of smart answers to that one, but Vicky realized now she couldn't win at this game, his game, so she said nothing. He wasn't going to relinquish the damned album, and he had done to Rachel exactly what he must have intended.

Jacob Cornelius leaned forward, so far that his torso and the album were almost parallel to the floor, then grunted to his feet. He turned to his daughter and pointed dramatically at Vicky with his free hand. "Tell this ... this *woman* to go!"

"Give us the album and we'll both leave," Vicky said, but she knew he must hear in her voice that she had little hope.

"Go!" He pointed at the door.

The album was sliding down a little, and Vicky considered making a grab for it. The muscles in her legs tightened, anticipating the sprint down the hallway, dodging St. Peter in the lobby, Vicky the quarterback for the secular humanists, through the front doors, touchdown. If she hadn't been with Rachel she might have gone for it.

"Do you want to leave?" Vicky asked her, trying not to think about what she would do if Rachel said no.

But Rachel nodded. They turned, and Vicky opened the door. She felt prickles on the back of her neck, as though the man behind her might be throwing something at her. Holy water, maybe. Although that might be a little high-church for him.

In the hallway a woman in a wheelchair was coming towards them. She smiled, clearly intending to say something, but when she saw Rachel's face she dropped her eyes to her lap and passed them without a word.

CHAPTER FOUR

ICKY AND AMANDA had gone to a small art gallery/ theatre in Vancouver Sunday to see the restored version of *Vertigo*. Vicky had asked Rachel to come, too, but was relieved when Rachel said no. They were a little uncomfortable around each other after what had happened at her father's, as though it were they, not her father, who had behaved badly.

After the movie Amanda wanted to go to a new French restaurant called Le Parvenu, but the line-up outside dissuaded her.

"I wasn't dressed, anyway," she said. She was wearing sweatpants and a navy cloth coat whose better days had been lived with a previous owner. Amanda taught full-time now and had assembled a professional wardrobe, but on weekends, she said, she wanted to remember her humble beginnings. It was as impoverished substitute teachers that she and Vicky had met years ago.

They found a small but noisy restaurant on Robson Street and ordered salads with rice and shrimp and a riveting curry sauce.

"Glad I didn't need those tastebuds," Amanda said, waving her hand in front of her mouth, which was large and expressive and to which she gave even more prominence with dark red lipsticks. She had a plump, round face that freckled in summer but that was well-suited to her new short haircut with the blond streaks. She had gained weight since they had last met; Vicky was annoyed at herself for having noticed. The pot-bellied calling the kettle round.

"So how'd you like the movie?" she asked.

Amanda took a long drink of water. "Oh, I dunno. Yeah, sure, maybe *Vertigo* really *is* a great surrealist film and one of the masterpieces of the century, but, well, it has this mechanical feel. Everything is so ... dead, somehow, the characters are like these wax dolls, their line readings so stiff—"

"But that's the point!" Vicky couldn't stop herself from interjecting. "It's the way San Francisco seems to be dead that shows Scottie's doomed obsession. He's in this spiral, he and Madeleine both, never seeing any way out. The Madeleine who could have brought one about no longer exists and actually never did exist. Scottie's surveillance may start out in a straight line, but gradually it begins to curve, until it becomes a perfect circle. Which is the shape of romantic compulsion, right? It's quite brilliant."

"If you say so, Professor Pedant."

Vicky made a face. "*Mean*," she said, although she'd probably deserved it. She was aware of her tendency to lecture when it came to film.

"Anyway," Amanda said, "I kept thinking what it must be like to be Judy, plain old Judy the shopgirl, whom Scottie is so grimly determined to transform into Madeleine."

"The object of obsession," Vicky said, suddenly seeing Rachel's face in Kim Novak's, in that same passive, pale beauty.

"How are things going with Rachel?" Amanda asked, as though she had followed Vicky's thoughts, which she probably had.

Vicky told her about the visit to Rachel's father, making Amanda shudder. "You both better be careful," she said. "The crazy father sounds almost as bad as the crazy husband."

"Rachel keeps saying Dennis wouldn't really hurt her."

Amanda snorted. "And of course you believe her. Wake up."

"I'm not the innocent here," Vicky replied, stung. "But if Rachel won't do anything I can't force her."

"Look, I just read an article by a stalking victim who said her primary emotions were not only fear and guilt—guilt because, hey, it must be her fault this poor guy is driven to this—but also denial. She had to deny she was in as much danger as she was or she'd have been unable to function. Maybe that's happening to Rachel. Maybe that's happening to you."

"It's not," Vicky said. But if Amanda's tone hadn't annoyed her she might have been less abrupt in her disagreement.

"Okay, here's a stat for you: in North America one in four women who are murdered dies after being stalked by a man she once loved."

One in four: Vicky had to stare hard at the tabletop to stop herself from seeing them, all the murdered women, every fourth face Rachel's. Statistics, she had once heard a doctor say, are just people with the tears rubbed away.

"And when these guys lose it," Amanda continued, "they sometimes don't just take out that woman. They take out anyone who might have helped her."

Vicky poked at her salad. The curry suddenly seemed to have turned the shrimp too vividly yellow to be edible.

"Right now this guy's amusing himself with sending Rachel those pictures," Amanda said. "But you say he could be running out of them. So that game might almost be over. He'll need some new way to scare her, to make himself feel in control."

"Well," Vicky said, "Birdy has offered to help. She has this theory about old women and brooms."

Amanda sighed. "I'm serious, kid."

"I know you are. But what can I do? Throw Rachel out?"

"Of course not," Amanda said impatiently. "But you should insist on the restraining order, at least."

"Since you know your stats you know we can't count on that. Especially with Rachel's history of going back to Dennis. The police would either do nothing or make Dennis even more nuts. Besides, aren't some shrinks even advising against restraining orders because they just provoke the guy?"

"I know, I know." Amanda jabbed the tines of her fork into the little serviette under her water glass. "Well, here's another stat for you: the first four months after a woman leaves a relationship are the most dangerous. You just need to wait it out. And be really careful. Don't leave anything unlocked."

"I locked up my VCR with the electronic child-proof function. Does that count?"

"Vicky."

"Okay. Sorry. Careful. Right."

◆

The next picture arrived on Monday.

Rachel was home when it came. Harding had told her not to come in until after lunch because the painters were doing the office. She must have heard the thud of the package of CDs for Vicky (who had given in once to the 11-CDs-for-1-cent seduction and now seemed trapped into endless deliveries, few of which she could remember ordering). Rachel had come up the stairs, dressed for work, and stood waiting by the front door by the time Vicky wandered over from the study. They looked at each other, not speaking, and then Vicky bent down and picked up the square envelope they both knew would be addressed to Rachel.

Rachel took a deep breath, slid her nail under the flap, and nudged it carefully open, as though it was important not to tear the envelope.

The card she pulled out this time did not have kittens on the cover. Instead, there was a reproduction of Munch's *The Scream*. When she opened it and looked at the photograph inside she bit at her bottom lip, hard, until Vicky could see it go white.

"What's wrong?" she asked. "Isn't this one like the others?"

Rachel shook her head slowly, her eyes not leaving the photograph. Vicky gave up waiting for Rachel to hand it to her and leaned her face close to Rachel's, peered down.

The picture was a formal, posed colour portrait of a group of eight people, half of them seated on a bench and the others standing behind them. All but two were women, who wore similar long, dark-coloured dresses. Their hairstyles might have been fashionable twenty years ago. The two men, who stood in the middle at the back, wore suits and ties and serious expressions. The group ranged in age from about thirty to sixty, and, from the bit of visible background, which may have been a blackboard or a bulletin board, appeared to be the staff at a school or some other institution.

A circle was drawn lightly in red pen around the head of one of the men. What must have upset Rachel most, though, Vicky thought, were the words printed, also in red ink, on the inside of the card cover: *Don't you know what he did?*

Vicky felt the goosebumps run up her arms.

"Isn't this one from your mother's album?" she asked. "Do you know who the man is? Or where the picture was taken?"

It took Rachel a long time to answer. When she did, her voice was so low Vicky had to strain to hear. "I know where it is."

Vicky supposed it might be unwise to keep pressing, but she couldn't stop herself. "And? Where is it?"

Rachel closed the card. Her fingers were shaking. "Let's go sit down," she said.

"Sure."

Vicky led her to the dining-room table, and they sat in the same chairs they'd chosen after the first picture had arrived. It was brilliantly sunny outside, as it had been that other day, the light glittering on the waters of Semiahmoo Bay. Rachel kept squinting so intently out the window that

Vicky finally reached over and gave the rod of the venetian blinds a twist to close the slats.

Rachel blinked several times, and then she lowered her gaze to the card in her hand. She propped it open, the way one did with greeting cards, on the table in front of her. The photograph slid out, face up.

"This isn't from my mother's album. I don't know where it came from." She paused. "But I ... But I know who the people are. Where it was taken. When it was, when it must have been, taken." She paused again.

Vicky crossed her legs, uncrossed them. This was harder than prying answers from a student.

"When I was sixteen," Rachel went on at last, "my father decided I was becoming too ... wild, that I was ... making bad friends, and so he sent me to this school." She gestured at the picture. "It was run by his church, and it was called The Hammond Christian School for Girls. It was just over there—" She pointed at the closed blinds. "Near Blaine. We could see White Rock. We used to joke that we could make a break for it, swim across the bay, and escape over the border." She smiled faintly.

"Were they hard on you? Fire and brimstone stuff?"

"Yes. There was ... discipline." Rachel looked away from the picture. "But sometimes, well, some of the teachers could be nice. Miss Butler, for instance, I remember her." Rachel pointed at one of the faces. "But most of the others were very severe. They were there to make us fear and obey God, after all. Obedience training, one of the girls called it. There was a lot of religious study, and we were watched all the time. Maybe that was the worst of it, the way we felt so imprisoned. We could never leave the place. Even when parents came to visit we couldn't go anywhere with them."

"And this man? The one with the circled face?"

"I don't *know*!" Rachel cried. "I don't *know*!"

The vehemence of her response made Vicky pull back in her chair. "It looks as though he was on the staff there," she said carefully.

"The other man was some administrator, the principal, maybe, a minister, but I don't know this one. I don't!"

"Do you have any idea what he was supposed to have done?"

Rachel shook her head. She got up abruptly, went into the kitchen. Vicky could hear her running the tap. When she came back she was holding a glass of water which, when she sat down, she drank almost to the bottom. "I suppose the man was on staff somehow, a janitor, maybe, but I don't recognize him."

"Have you any idea where Dennis might have gotten this picture?"

"My father probably had it somewhere. As I said, the school was run by his church."

"Well," Vicky said briskly. "It's just Dennis wanting to keep you off balance." She glanced at her watch. "Maybe we should leave." She was dropping Rachel at work on her way to taking her VCR to a repair shop. The electronic child-proof lock had defeated her.

Rachel checked her watch, jumped to her feet. "Oh. Yes. I said I'd be in by one o'clock." She was relieved, Vicky could tell, not to have to talk any more about the photograph, about the question in red ink on the card.

It was only a few minutes after one when Vicky pulled up in front of Harding Refrigeration, but Rachel hurried inside as though she were hours late. Vicky had just put the car into reverse when John Harding pulled up close beside her in his blue Mercedes. He waved, and, perhaps since Vicky was slow in backing out to make sure she wouldn't bump his car, when he got out he came over to her. She rolled down the window.

"Thanks for dropping Rachel off," he said, running his

hand over his head to smooth the lost hair he might have thought was being ruffled by the wind.

"No problem. You'll have to forgive her if she's a bit distracted today. She got another one of those photos."

"Photos?"

What had she done? She had just assumed Rachel had been telling the Hardings about what Dennis was doing.

"Oh, dear," she fumbled. "I shouldn't have— But Dennis, we assume it's Dennis, has been sending Rachel these pictures taken from her mother's album. Except today's picture was of some religious school she'd been sent to when she was sixteen. I suppose you know about that."

"Religious school?"

Something about the way he said it, the way he answered too quickly, with a kind of excessive surprise, made Vicky look up at him. His enlarged eyes behind his glasses were staring at the top of her car window, which protruded about an inch above the sill, and he ran his forefinger back and forth over it, then rubbed the dirt away between his fingers.

"Rachel's father didn't have much to do with us," Harding said. "Especially after Rachel's mother died. I remember old Cornelius telling me I would burn in hell for my secular ways." He laughed, but it sounded awkward. "So by the time Rachel was a teenager we were all pretty estranged. But Rachel could have used more support then, that's for sure. Maybe she wouldn't have married somebody just as bad as her father."

Vicky had been watching him, but that uneasy sense that he had been editing the truth had left her now. Why should he have lied, after all? What difference would it make if he had known about the school? It wasn't he, surely, who had sent Rachel the photograph.

"Well, " Vicky said. "I guess Dennis is still trying to upset her any way he can."

Harding sighed. "He's such a thug. Once he was waiting

for her here when she came back from lunch with Junior, and he said if he ever caught Junior with her again he'd make sure Junior learned his lesson." He shook his head. "Learned his lesson. Because he went for lunch with his own cousin. There's no way to reason with someone like Dennis."

"Rachel is pretty brave. I'd be a nervous wreck by now."

"Well. Be careful yourself, Vicky. Dennis hates anyone who's helped her."

Be careful. Amanda had told her the same thing. She said goodbye to Harding, waved at Rachel through the window, and pulled back out into the street.

Be careful. Were she and Rachel really in danger? Or was Rachel right, that Dennis was all bluff and bluster? Most men whose wives left them would be angry, after all, but not many of them would try to harm their wives. Or their wives' friends. Besides, Vicky couldn't watch herself every second. Did that mean, as Amanda had put it, that she was in denial? Was it denial to acknowledge that if Dennis really wanted to injure her there was damned little she could do to stop him?

She dropped off the VCR and headed home, turning the radio up loud, shutting out everything but the tough-love lyrics of Alanis Morissette. Her life was supposed to be getting easier now, she thought. She had almost gotten used to being without Conrad; whole days went by now when she didn't miss him. She was enjoying the tutoring, enjoying the fact that for the first time in her life she had more money than she needed. And then Rachel had to come along. Rachel and Dennis.

When she got home she saw Rob sitting on her front steps, his legs splayed out and his face uplifted, eyes closed, to the sun. He was early.

"Sorry you had to wait," she said.

"That's okay." He dropped his book bag onto the coffee table. "I was hoping to catch that sexy tenant of yours."

"She has enough men stalking her, thanks," Vicky said,

and immediately wished she hadn't. She couldn't seem to keep her mouth shut today about Rachel's private life.

"Stalking her?"

Well, she might as well tell him. Rob was in college now, after all, an adult. Another pair of watchful eyes around her place might be useful. "It's her husband. He doesn't want to accept that she's left him. So if you see someone skulking around, tell me."

"God. Poor woman. I had a girlfriend in Grade Eleven whose old boyfriend was like that. She was really afraid of him."

"Did he ever, you know, do anything?"

"Creepy phone calls, mostly. Then her dad went and had a talk with him, and it stopped. Maybe Rachel's dad should go have a talk with her husband."

Vicky laughed, resisted telling him Rachel's father was part of the problem. "Well" —she gestured at his book bag— "let's see that revised paper on the Middle East."

Rob unzipped a corner of the bag and pulled out half a dozen pages folded over twice into a crumply wad. Vicky made a face. "You better not submit it to your prof like that. It would be like going out on a date wearing stinky underwear."

Rob laughed, opened up the pages and smoothed them down. "It's just a rough draft, Mom."

"Don't be cheeky."

"Cheeky!" He puffed out his cheeks. "What kind of old-timey word is that?"

Vicky took the papers, slapped him with them. "Respect your elders," she said.

◆

Rachel stayed late at work, making up the time she had lost in the morning, so it was late when Vicky heard Junior's car bringing her back. They sat outside for some time before

Vicky heard the key in the lock, and she couldn't stop herself from saying, as Rachel came up the stairs, something that sounded entirely too nosy and insinuative about how Junior certainly liked her company.

Rachel blushed. "We were just talking about work," she said, taking off her coat.

"Of course." The words sounded ironic, although Vicky hadn't intended them to.

"Junior ... well, I worry about him." Rachel sighed. "He works too hard. He needs to be successful, needs everything to go just right."

"You don't have to explain. Just tell me to mind my own damn business."

Rachel smiled. "If you'd minded your own business I wouldn't be here."

Vicky laughed. "Come up and have a hot chocolate and watch *The Outer Limits* with me. Just what you need to empty your brain."

But Vicky wasn't surprised when Rachel said no, that she'd rather finish the novel she was reading. Dennis, she'd explained, had always expected her to watch TV with him, programs he chose, police shows and hockey games and the more moronic sitcoms, so when she'd seen Vicky's bookcases she was like a deprived prisoner released into luxury. She read quickly, eagerly, eclectically; the only order, Vicky concluded, was alphabetical, which explained why Rachel was now reading a D. H. Lawrence after finishing a Margaret Laurence.

"*Sons and Lovers*, right?" Vicky said.

Rachel nodded. "It's nothing like *A Jest of God*."

"I don't suppose so. They're not the same Laurence."

"I know." Was that an actual flicker of annoyance in her voice? Rachel had not finished high school, but Vicky should have known better, all the same, especially given Rachel's reading appetite, than to be patronizing.

"It used to be a test of our Canadianness," Vicky went on, quickly. "To see if we spelled 'Laurence' with a 'u' instead of a 'w.'"

"Well, I got impatient with the woman in her novel. The way she let her mother control her. In *Sons and Lovers* the mother wants to control the main character, too, but he doesn't really let her."

"To the point where he actually kills her." It occurred to Vicky that Rachel might not have gotten to that part of the book yet. Oh oh.

But Rachel said, "Well, yes, that's pretty awful. But it might have been better for Laurence's character to do the same." She must have seen Vicky's surprised expression because she continued, quickly, "I mean, not *really*, not like in real life. But isn't that what novels are supposed to do? Let us imagine solutions we couldn't try in real life?"

"That's an interesting theory," Vicky said.

She was trying to think of something more to say to encourage the conversation when Rachel yawned and said she'd better go or she'd be asleep after the first two pages. Vicky watched her go down the stairs and thought, as she had more than once, that Rachel was more complicated than she appeared. Like a book Vicky herself was reading, but with pages missing.

She made herself a hot chocolate, and flicked on the TV. She watched too much of it, she knew she did, but she had been grateful for it many nights, when the small talking faces and the car chases and the rock videos and the geographic specials made her not think of Conrad, of her aloneness, of her trembling desire for just one drink, just one, please, to get through the wheedling night. But she knew if she gave in to just-one-drink she would be back to hell. Television was the lesser addiction.

The Outer Limits episode was disappointing, predictable monsters with bad make-up, and she was just getting ready to turn it off when she thought she heard someone cry out in the basement. The cat sat up, his ears pointing towards the stairs, his tail going bristly. Vicky jabbed the mute button. Silence.

She went to the top of the stairs, said, "Rachel?"

There was no answer. She flicked the light on and went down the steps, cautiously. If someone had come into the house through either the front or back doors surely she would have heard him, even with the TV on. But if someone had broken in earlier, been hiding in the basement—

She stopped at the bottom of the stairs, her heart pounding. The bare bulb illuminated the washing machine and dryer, the hulk of the furnace, the pile of boxes and suitcases piled against the far wall, the uncarpeted corner where Conrad had built a workbench and hung his tools. The door to the small bathroom was open, and she could see inside. Nothing unusual.

The door to Rachel's room was only a few feet in front of her. She held her breath, straining to hear.

"Rachel?" she said softly.

There was a sound in the room, a bedspring creaking, a footstep. Vicky took a step up the stairs, half turned, ready to run, her hand as far up on the bannister as it could reach. The door opened. Rachel stood there, wearing her pink flowered pyjamas, her hair in an untidy braid, her eyes squinty.

"Are you all right?" Vicky asked in relief. "I thought I heard something."

"I'm sorry. I had this dream. This nightmare. This horrible nightmare. Then I was awake and sitting up in bed. I must have shouted or screamed or something. I'm sorry. It was so ... just so awful."

"Come up and have a glass of warm milk. It'll get you back to sleep."

"All right."

Rachel waited in the dining room while Vicky heated the

milk in the microwave. When she brought it out, Rachel was standing at the window. She had opened the blind and was staring out at the moon's broken reflection in Semiahmoo Bay, at the lights of Blaine on the other side.

"What was the dream about?"

Rachel started, turned around. She picked up the cup of milk but didn't sit down. "It was ..." She closed her eyes. "It was about that picture. About that man."

"Did you remember who he was?"

"In the dream ..."

Vicky waited, tried not to be impatient. Rachel was like this sometimes, slow to put words to her thoughts.

"In the dream the man is ... He has something hiding his face, a mask, but I know it's the man in the picture. He's standing over me and then he's ... raping me."

Vicky leaned back a little, as though Rachel had pushed against her chest. "Do you think," she said carefully, "that this might actually have happened?"

Rachel sat down. Her hands were clenched around her mug, from which she had yet to take a sip. "It's just too horrible. Surely it didn't. I mean, it *couldn't*. I couldn't have forgotten something like that, could I? This was just a dream, a silly dream."

"I'm sure it was. But sometimes, well, dreams are worth examining—"

Rachel took her hands from the cup, spread them flat on the table. Her nails were cut as close to the quick as they could be. "Repressed memories, is that what you're talking about? I've read about them. How they're saying now that it's therapists who implant these ... these false memories, that they aren't real."

"Well, I don't think that happens very often. Besides, no therapists could have implanted this memory in you, could they?"

"Well ... no. But it's from a dream! If I can't trust a therapist I certainly can't trust a dream."

"No, no, of course not. Still, suddenly recalling forgotten memories can happen. Sometimes people who have a trauma survive by 'forgetting' until they're able to deal with it. I had a car accident once in Alberta, somebody broadsiding me at a stop sign, and for a long time I couldn't remember what happened. I'd recall driving along, reaching over to change the radio station, and then I was sitting in this strange woman's kitchen as she phoned the police. It was six months later that, suddenly, I remembered the details of being hit."

"Still. You *remembered.* You didn't *dream* it."

"True," Vicky said. "But some studies have shown that traumatic memories are stored in a different part of the brain than more normal memories, and that when they do surface there can be a kind of hallucinatory quality to them."

"But ..." Rachel shook her head. "Sometimes people remember things wrong, remember things that didn't happen. They say that's why hypnosis isn't reliable, because people can be made to remember and believe imaginary things. And there was that note, asking me if I know what he did. It was so ... suggestive. Making me think, *what, what* did he do? Even if there was nothing, even if there's nothing to remember. Now my mind is trying to make something up to fit. Dennis went to a counsellor once, the police made him go, so maybe he knows how to do it, how to make my mind think something happened when it didn't."

"I wouldn't give Dennis that much credit," Vicky said. But what did she know? Maybe this was exactly what Dennis was doing. And maybe she had better shut up about repressed memories or she would become just as manipulative as he was. "Well, it might just have been a bad dream, as you say. Dreams are great opportunists. They use the day's most convenient anxiety and make you wrestle with it the whole night."

Vicky had had her share of those.

"Just a bad dream," Rachel said, sighing. "I hope so." She took a sip of her milk, which must have been cold by now. She wrinkled her face when she swallowed. "I'm sorry," she said.

"Why?"

"I think it's gone sour."

CHAPTER FIVE

*V*ICKY WAS IN THE KITCHEN trying to stir some appeal into a bowl of mucilaginous cream of wheat when Rachel came up the stairs on her way to work. Her eyes were red, the skin under them an unpleasant mauve, and everything about her seemed a little rumpled, as though she had been dressed by someone else, someone careless and in a hurry.

When Rachel poured herself a coffee at the kitchen counter, Vicky reached over and untucked the right collar tab of her blouse, which was folded in instead of out. She expected Rachel to pull away, but she only said, "Thank you," in a distracted voice and took a sip of her coffee, apparently not noticing until Vicky handed her the cream that she did not take it black.

"How did you sleep?" Vicky asked, as though the answer weren't obvious.

"I had that dream again. Every time I fell asleep there it would be." She kept folding in and reopening the spout in the cream container.

"Oh, Rachel."

"That man. His face was hidden, but I know it's him, I know it's the man in the photograph."

"I do think it might help to talk to a counsellor. There's this woman I went to, she could probably help sort this out, see if there's more to it than just a dream—"

Rachel shook her head vehemently. "No, no. I don't want anyone putting false memories into my head. I need to figure it out on my own."

Vicky had to stop herself from saying something impatient. "What can I do to help you?" she asked instead.

Rachel rubbed at her right eye, making it even more red and scattering a dismaying number of eyelashes onto her cheek.

"Oh, Vicky, I don't know. I shouldn't be bothering you with this."

"Pish. It's important. And I don't think Dennis is through playing his little mind games yet."

"I wonder what he'll send me next."

They both glanced at the front door, as though another missive had just clattered through the slot.

◆

But nothing came for Rachel that day, even though when the mail arrived Vicky jumped up in the middle of a stumbling answer from Kristin about the differences between Shakespearean and Petrarchan sonnets and trotted to the door with unseemly eagerness. She picked up the Hydro bill and Safeway flyer and went back to the table.

"You're lucky you still get home delivery," Kristin said. "Everywhere around us it's those awful supermailboxes."

"An advantage to having an old house," Vicky said.

"But it's not fair."

"Of course it's not! The post office is *making* money—it doesn't need to reduce service. It's just part of another privatization scheme."

Kristin was smiling. Vicky didn't know whether to be annoyed or amused that she had let herself be nudged towards a lecture. If she were still teaching, Vicky thought, she'd find it impossible to dress in that apolitical personality teachers were expected to wear to class.

"If my dad could hear you," Kristin said, "he'd say you sounded like a communist."

"And what would you say?"

Kristin shrugged. "I don't know. We haven't got to that part yet in school."

Vicky laughed. "I'm glad you have such faith in education."

"I don't think there are any communists any more, anyway."

"Maybe there never were," Vicky said. "Maybe they were all just a dream." Merrily, merrily, merrily, merrily, life is but a dream. She poked her pencil at Kristin's notebook, made herself concentrate on what Kristin's capitalist father was paying her to teach his daughter. "Well. Back to Shakespeare. Have you got that rhyme scheme down yet?"

Kristin scrunched up her face, twisted her mouth to one side, as though preparing to have something amputated without anesthetic. "A, B, B, A—"

"No, no. Look, why don't you just memorize one of the sonnets? Then you'll always know the rhyme scheme."

"*Memorize*? Like, the whole *thing*?"

Vicky sighed. "Forgive me. Whatever was I thinking?"

As Kristin was leaving, Travis was arriving for his two o'clock session. Vicky couldn't help peeking through the front window as they manoeuvred around each other on the front step, Kristin with her eyes cast down, her cheeks flushed, saying something giggly, Travis with his awkward height and long arms flapping like a confused bird grown too large to fly. Ah, youth, the flutters and peckings of hormones. It had been a long time since Vicky had felt her own hormones flutter, and it was something she told herself she did not miss. But looking at the two young people on her front step, what she felt, what she couldn't deny, was loss and envy and sadness so sudden and acute it misted her eyes.

She blinked, hard, several times and went to the door, prepared her smile for Travis, for her hour with him, for when she would bring out the cheese and crackers and watch him grin, both of them thinking only about getting the right names on the right countries and continents, no hormones allowed.

◆

Rachel was slightly early; Vicky could see her coming down the alley, almost at a run, the strap of her purse across her chest to allow a faster pace. She was eager to find out if there had been another picture, Vicky was sure, going down to the landing to unlock the back door. Rachel could have phoned from work to ask, but she seemed to have some odd rules about "bothering" Vicky unnecessarily.

"Hi," Vicky said. She had gone back into the kitchen and begun unloading the dishwasher, to dissuade Rachel from thinking she had been hovering about waiting for her.

"Hi." Rachel rubbed her hands together. "Cold today." She took off her coat. "Any mail for me?" She had managed an impressively casual tone.

"Nope."

Rachel came up the four steps into the kitchen. She smelled of the outside, crisp and fresh and slightly damp.

"I should be relieved, I suppose," she said. She began to put away dishes, nesting the pots tidily inside each other in the cupboard that usually looked as though things had been thrown in from across the room. "But it just makes me more anxious. Wondering what there'll be next. And when. I couldn't stop thinking about that last picture, that man, all day."

Vicky handed her some coffee mugs. "I wish there were someone we could ask. Your father?" At Rachel's stricken look she hastened to add, "Okay, okay, I know, that's out." She straightened up. "Is the school still there?"

"What school?"

"The one in the picture. The Hamilton Christian School."

"Hammond." Rachel was looking at her, her eyes wide.

"The Hammond Christian School. If it's still there maybe we could go down to see it, talk to someone, show them the picture. Some of the same staff might even still be there."

Rachel just kept staring at her. But Vicky could tell she was going to say yes.

◆

They decided to go the next day if nothing illuminating arrived in the mail. Nothing did. Vicky picked Rachel up at two o'clock from the plant, where she had arranged to work through her lunch hour for the next two days to make up for the time off, although Vicky was sure the Hardings didn't expect it.

"Did you tell them where you were going?" Vicky asked as Rachel got into the car. Rachel had her hair in a kind of French twist that made Vicky envious; she had seen Rachel put up her hair in a minute or two, a task that would take Vicky an hour and even then require the intervention of a salon. Vicky had her mother's thick black hair, and it turned surly at attempts at refinement. The last time she had curled it Amanda had said it looked pretty, which they both knew was not a compliment.

Rachel shook her head. "I should have, I guess. I just, well, don't want them to get involved." She paused. "They're too busy to worry about me." There was something a little evasive in her tone. Vicky had to stop herself from commenting on it.

Through the window she could see Junior and John Harding in the front office. She waved, but they were too engrossed in a gesture-filled conversation with two small Japanese men to notice. All four wore charcoal-grey suits with white shirts and blue ties. Looking at them and then at

Rachel, who was wearing black slacks and a silvery cotton blouse, made Vicky think she should have dressed better herself today. Her fleece sweatpants were pilling to transparency in spots and her red sweatshirt had half a dozen widening puncture wounds inflicted by the claws of the cat. Working at home had made her, well, a tad careless about how she dressed. And they were going to the United States today, after all. She should show some respect.

They had less than a five-minute wait at the border, the guard waving them through without any apparent concern about Vicky's indigent appearance, and then it was easy to take the turn onto Peace Portal Drive. It was a waterfront road, the ocean visible on the right, but the street had the seedy look, with its second-hand stores and taverns and run-down diners and uncared-for lots, of expensive real estate waiting for the developers.

"What was this like when you lived down here?" Vicky asked.

"What?" Rachel had been staring out the windshield, biting at her lower lip. "Oh. This road. I don't know. We weren't allowed to leave the school. In the whole year I was there I don't think I left the grounds more than once or twice. They wouldn't let us go home even at Christmas."

"Is this the first time you've been back?"

Rachel nodded. "The school may not even be there any more. It's been over fifteen years. The church has been growing, but they may be putting their money somewhere else."

"Turn here?"

"I think so."

They were on a road curving around Drayton Harbour. On the right they could see Semiahmoo Bay, and White Rock across it, gleaming in the afternoon sun that broke through the thin clouds. The tide was out, but the sand looked bubbly with water.

"It was along here," Rachel said. A strand of hair had come loose from her French twist, and she was wrapping it around and around her finger.

The road now was residential, with modest homes on acreages on either side, but there was also the inevitable redevelopment sign promising two-hundred-new-condos-coming-soon. If she stayed on this route, Vicky knew, she would wind up on the wide and tree-lined road that led past the gated communities and private golf courses onto the spit with Semiahmoo Resort at the end of it, where Conrad had taken her once, about five years ago now, and about this time of year, on Valentine's Day. She closed her eyes for a second. Don't remember: don't. It was Rachel she was here for, not herself.

"There!"

Rachel was pointing to a building on the right, its property on the water. It was a large house, three storeys high, with white siding and dark-red trim. It looked to be about forty years old. But the tile roof was new; the row of narrow vertical windows facing east was clearly a modern addition; and the wide veranda in front and steps leading up to it had the unweathered look of freshly cut lumber. The house appeared to have at least thirty rooms, but there was nothing institutional in its look. Vicky didn't know what she had been expecting, some grim and crumbling Bates Motel, perhaps, but this building, in spite of its size, looked welcoming, homey even. The grounds were well-kept, full of the ivies and grasses and laurels that stayed green and healthy all year. Two arbutus trees grew near the water, their red bark matching the trim of the house.

"You sure this is it?"

"Yes. It's ... changed a little, they've added that glassed-in part, but that's it. My room was up there." She pointed to a window on the third floor. The forefinger of her other hand was twirling, faster and faster, in the coil of hair along her neck, loosening the hairpins.

A van swerved by them, and the driver gave Vicky an angry look because her car was barely moving. Without asking Rachel, she turned into the driveway.

There was a sign, she could see now, above the front door: Pacific Chiropractic Clinic.

Rachel began to laugh. It sounded a little hysterical. "It's a chiropractic clinic! They've turned it into a chiropractic clinic!"

"So they have. Do you want to go in?"

"Is there any point?"

Vicky pulled into a parking space beside the steps.

"Well, now that we're here. I agree there's not much point, but you never know. Somebody may be able to tell us the history of the place." Vicky could see a faint beading of sweat on Rachel's forehead. "Are you okay? We don't have to go in if you don't want to."

"I'm okay. Let's go."

They went up the walk, opened the door. The lobby was painted so bright a white that Vicky had to squint. A glassed-in bulletin board on the facing wall listed the names of about ten chiropractors, and half a dozen people reading magazines were sitting in chairs along the same wall. Behind a chrome semi-circle of a desk sat a receptionist in a pale-blue lab coat, typing at a computer while a printer pulled long buff-coloured pages through itself. The woman, dark-skinned and large-featured, with an eye-catching mole above her right eyebrow, smiled professionally up at them and asked if they had an appointment.

"Well, actually," Vicky said, "I'm hoping you can tell me something about this building. About fifteen or twenty years ago it was a school, I believe, run by—" She turned to Rachel. "What was the name of the church?"

Rachel's eyes were flitting around the room, but she seemed to be looking less for something familiar than for a way to escape. "The Free Christian Alliance Church," she said faintly.

The receptionist's professional smile took on a twist of amusement, or distaste. Vicky couldn't blame her. "The school was called The Hammond Christian School for Girls," Vicky continued, "and we were hoping to find out what happened to it, if it moved somewhere else, maybe, and who the staff were. We have a photograph of the staff, and we were wondering if somebody here might be able to identify a man in the picture." She could see the receptionist begin to shake her head, so, perhaps to forestall it, Vicky turned quickly to Rachel and said, "Show her the picture."

Rachel fumbled in her purse, pulled it out. Vicky was relieved to see she had apparently left the accompanying card, with its insinuative message, at home.

The receptionist glanced at the photograph. "I'm sorry. That's all before my time. The clinic has been here for about five years, I know that. Before that, well, I think the place was empty, but there could have been a school here once."

An elderly woman using a cane with three small splayed legs at the base had gotten up from her chair and come over to the desk. She was trying to peer at the photograph in Rachel's hand. Rachel drew it back, uncertain.

"I couldn't help overhearing." The woman smiled reassuringly. "I remember the Hammond School. I used to drive past once in a while, and I'd look up here and wonder about the girls. I was a teacher, you see, and I'd be wondering what curriculum they were using. I knew one of the teachers, she was a real teacher, but the others, well, I don't think they had the proper training, not all of them, there was a bit of fuss about that. And that man" —she pointed at the circled face— "I do remember him. Now what was his name? Someone appropriate for a religious school, I remember thinking, something like Angelico, Angeletti—"

The picture was fluttering to the floor. Rachel was running

from the lobby, her hair a long blond swirl behind her. She jerked open the door and was outside before Vicky had realized what was happening.

The elderly woman bent down and picked up the photograph. Something crackled in her spine as she straightened. "I'm so sorry if I upset her," she said. "I thought you wanted to know about the school."

Vicky took the photograph from her. "We did. Thank you for your help. I'm sorry if my friend is a little ... distressed. You've been very helpful, really."

She walked to the door, concentrating so hard on avoiding the eyes of the seated patients that she almost collided with the large ficus by the door. "What are *you* looking at?" she muttered at it.

Rachel was leaning against the trunk of the car, facing the road. One hand was pressed against her stomach. She looked as though she might throw up.

"I'm sorry," she said. She swallowed. "That was so childish. To run away like, like some scared rabbit."

"Did you recognize that name?" Vicky tried to make the question casual, almost disinterested.

"Angeletti." Rachel was barely whispering. "Angeletti."

That was a yes, Vicky deduced. "We could probably find out more around here if we tried."

"No. Let's go home."

Rachel went to the passenger door, waited until Vicky unlocked it. Her face seemed to have sealed shut, emitting no expression. It was, Vicky thought with dismay, the same empty look that had been on Rachel's face the first time Vicky had ever seen her, walking down the street in White Rock, with Dennis shouting and pulling at her.

◆

Vicky was awake, suddenly. She sat up, her ears straining. It was raining, the drops rustling into the holly bush by her window. But there was something else. Voices? Then under her door she noticed a faint hem of light. She went over, listened. It was a woman's voice, soft, a murmur only.

Vicky opened the door, slowly. The light was coming from the living room, and the voice was Rachel's. Judging from the pauses and cut-off sentences, she must be on the phone. Vicky glanced at the illuminated clock on her bedside table: 1:00 a.m. She pulled her dressing gown from its hook on the back of the door, put it on, and went into the bathroom, not trying to be quiet. She put the light on, ran a glass of water, and then headed down the hall to the living room.

"I have to go." She could hear Rachel's quiet voice. "I think I've woken Vicky."

Vicky came around the corner, yawned, probably not convincingly, and said, "Hi. Couldn't sleep?"

Rachel was in her pyjamas, sitting on the couch, her hand still on the phone. There was the faint odour from her of perspiration, the acrid kind, of fear.

"I woke you. I'm sorry. I tried to be quiet."

"It's okay. I should leave the cordless phone with you overnight." The cat had come out from whatever mysterious place he found to sleep and was watching them, his eyes wary, from across the room.

"I won't need it. I don't know what was the matter with me. I phoned Dennis."

"*Dennis?*" Vicky sat down on the arm of the sofa, tried not to stare, not to say something angry and sarcastic. In *The Stalker Victim's Handbook,* calling the guy at one in the morning would top the list of "Never Do This."

"It was so stupid. But I had that dream again, that awful dream, and I just couldn't stand it, it was so terrifying. I was afraid to go back to sleep, so I got up and walked around, and then I thought, I *have* to ask Dennis why he sent that picture to me, what he knows." Rachel hugged herself, shivered.

"And what did he say?"

She smiled faintly. "A woman answered."

"Really?"

"When I asked for Dennis and she put him on, he kept raging at me about how I'd driven him to other women, and he pretended not to know anything about the pictures."

"Well, you couldn't expect him to admit it." Vicky stood up. "Shall I turn the heat on?"

"No, no. I'll go back to bed." But she didn't get up.

"Did it ... bother you, about the other woman?"

"Bother me? Gosh, no. I was relieved. If he finds someone else he'll leave me alone. He'll agree to a divorce."

"So, maybe your call found out something useful, after all."

Rachel shoved her hands between her thighs, hunched her shoulders a little. "I guess so. But it's not going to help me get through the night. The dream this time was the worst. The man, I suppose it was Angeletti, was ... was raping me, like before, his face covered up, but this time there were other people there, too. Holding my arms. And my legs. Holding me down. One of them might have been a woman. Their faces were all covered. It was so horrible." She squeezed shut her eyes.

"Let me turn the heat up, Rachel. We can talk for a while."

"No, really. I'll go back to bed." She got up, came out from behind the coffee table. The cat galloped into the hall, then back again, his hair bristling, encouraging something else out of the ordinary to happen.

"Then take a sleeping pill. I'll get you one."

Rachel shook her head. "No, I can't. Even if these are just nightmares I have to have them. They might be trying to help me understand."

"But if they're that awful, if they stop you from sleeping—"

"You're the one who told me to pay attention to my dreams."

Vicky laughed. "Sometimes, you know, I am full of it."

There was, she had to admit, something in Rachel's attitude she admired. Vicky had always found it too easy to drug away her own anxieties, her own bad dreams. Rachel was more courageous.

"I think I'll turn the heat up, anyway." Vicky rubbed at her arms. "If we're going to have bad dreams at least we can stop them from being about freezing to death."

◆

The next day there was another envelope.

She took it to the window to see if she could make out what the card, at least, looked like, but the paper was too thick, so, reluctantly, she left it on the table at the top of the stairs. She would just have to wait until Rachel got home.

She made herself put on a fresh sweater and her black bolero vest and the long, striped skirt she kept around for times she felt compelled to dress like-a-lady. Ajit was coming for tutoring, and she felt, perhaps because he dressed always in a suit and tie and looked newly barbered, a subtle disapproval from him of her lumpy sweatpants and sweatshirts. Besides, she'd just read an article about how the most successful car salesmen were those who mimicked the speech patterns and body language of their customers. Tutors were car salesmen without the cars.

Ajit arrived a few minutes late, unusual for him, and Vicky was dismayed to see that he appeared to have been crying.

"How's everything going?" She hung up his coat, wondering how much she should be asking him.

Behind her she heard Ajit blow his nose. "Oh, not well,

Mrs. Bauer. In the school, yes, it's okay, but with me, at home, not well."

Oh, dear. She turned, looked into his face with the beautiful large brown eyes, whose whites now were reddened and veiny. He was slightly-built, and only an inch or two taller than she, but his body suggested athleticism and muscularity more than did that of Travis, a hockey player.

"Come sit down," she said. "Tell me what's wrong."

He followed her to the dining room, slumped into a chair and dropped his arms onto the table as though offering them to be handcuffed.

"My parents," he said. "They want to arrange a marriage for me. With a girl in India."

"I see. And I gather this does not appeal to you."

He shook his head. "Of course not. Her family is rich, that is the only reason my parents want to do this. They think that if we are married her parents will send enough money to pay my way through university. If I want to be a doctor, my father says, then the money has to come from somewhere."

"I can see why this arrangement wouldn't suit you."

"Do you? I wish you could talk to my father."

"Well—it's not really my place to do that. Is there a school counsellor you could talk to, maybe?"

"Yes, I have told her about this. But she doesn't understand. She thinks it is because I object to the custom, to arranged marriages."

"And ... you don't?" Vicky rubbed at her ear, in case it had not been paying attention.

Ajit straightened, looked at her. "Well, no. I thought this was comprehended by you. It is because I cannot marry a girl. I am ... not made that way."

Vicky smiled. "Oh. Of course. Now I understand."

Ajit sighed. "If I do not marry her I cannot study to be a doctor. But if I do marry her I will be dishonest to my nature."

"To say nothing of being dishonest to her."

"Yes, of course. But she is unhappy at home. And there is some scandal, a man who rejected her, perhaps. She wants to come to Canada. For her, it may still be a good bargain."

Vicky frowned. "I think you know what you have to do."

"No. What do I have to do?"

Should she be a good counsellor, keep asking him the right questions to get him to work out the answer himself, or should she cut to the chase?

"I think if you marry her you'll be miserable. And you'll be cheating this poor girl out of a real marriage. If you're determined to be a doctor you can study hard and get scholarships and loans and work part-time. You're very bright; your English was the only thing holding you back, and now I bet it's better than that of many of your classmates."

He smiled, pleased. "Yes, it may be so. I like English. I speak it now at home. My mother doesn't like it, but my father is proud. He knows English is the language you need to get on."

"Your parents, do they know about ... your nature?"

"Oh, yes. It is no big deal to them. Two of my uncles are this way."

"Some parents aren't so open-minded."

"Mine are practical. They accept what is there."

"So they will accept whatever decision you make about this marriage?"

Ajit sighed. "Eventually, perhaps. But when it is something that can still be changed, they can be very ... you have a word.... Pigheaded! They can be very pigheaded."

There was a knock at the front door. Vicky glanced at her watch. It was too early for Rachel to be back, and, besides, she never forgot her key.

"Excuse me," she said to Ajit.

She went to the front window and leaned over the couch, trying to see who it was. She could just see part of a man's back and one hand; he seemed to be wearing a uniform and was holding a brown-wrapped package the shape and size of a book. She went to the door, put the chain on, opened it, peered through the crack.

Dennis.

She hoped her sudden fear did not show on the slice of her face Dennis could see through the crack. She wanted to slam shut the door, but she knew it would be better not to.

"You shouldn't be here, Dennis."

She looked down at his hands, waiting for them to clench into fists or to draw out some weapon from the package he now extended towards her.

"Yeah, yeah. Is she here?"

"No, she's not. Please go away."

"Well, I just wanted to give her this. Here, you give it to her." He turned the package sideways and inserted it through the crack in the door.

"I don't think she'll want it. You've been giving her enough things lately."

"*Take* it, for Christ's sake!"

He was shoving the package farther and farther inside, holding it now with only the tips of his fingers. His thumb seemed to be the circumference of her wrist. If she didn't take it, Vicky thought, he would drop it onto the floor. Gingerly, she put her hand on it, feeling the hard edges of a box under the wrappings, and as soon as she touched it Dennis let it go.

"It's a present," Dennis said. "For Valentine's Day. To say I'm sorry for having that woman there. Rachel knows it didn't mean anything. If she came home and was a real wife to me I wouldn't need to have other women."

"You can have all the other women you want. Rachel doesn't care. Just leave her alone."

"Give her that," Dennis said. He turned, his wide shoulders bumping the door in the confined space of the porch, and then he had cleared the steps and was striding down her walk, his bow-leggedness apparent even in the loose-fitting blue trousers that were probably part of his bus-driver's uniform.

She was surprised it had ended so easily. She waited until he reached the end of her walk, and then she closed the door, gently, wincing at the metallic crunch of the latch, as though the sound might draw him back.

The tape had come loose from one end of the brown wrapping paper, and she nudged the fold open, saw that the package was, indeed, a Valentine's gift, a box of Black Magic chocolates. She wondered if Rachel would eat any of them. She could imagine Dennis injecting cyanide into each choco-late. As she carried the box to the table by the back door, she took another look at it to make sure the cellophane was still intact.

She set the box underneath the letter that had come for Rachel, and returned to the dining-room table, where Ajit was sitting, staring at her.

"Who was that?" he asked.

"That," Vicky said, "was what happens when you make a bad marriage."

◆

Rachel was looking only at the letter, had probably not heard Vicky say that the box in the brown paper wrapping was also hers.

"You open it," she said to Vicky.

Vicky tore the letter open, her fingers as shaky and fumbly as Rachel's might have been. It was a card, as she had thought, and she was relieved to see on the cover the same picture of kittens as on the first three cards. She had been expecting another Munch, the white screaming face that, however much commercialized, still made her shudder. She opened the card, noted, even more relieved, its message-free interior, and only then looked at the picture.

The photograph was in black-and-white and was apparently another of Rachel, looking about seventeen, standing in front of what seemed to be the same small stucco house of the second photograph. She was wearing loose jeans and a V-necked pullover, and although she was smiling it might only have been because she was squinting into the sun. Whoever had taken the picture had been standing quite far back, probably across the street; the edge of a road or sidewalk showed at the bottom. Part of a large tree was visible to the right, and from the leafless branches it was clear it must have been late fall or winter.

She handed the picture to Rachel. "At least it's just you. Not as disturbing as the last one."

Rachel took it. "Maybe I'd rather it *had* been another like that. Something that might help me make sense of all this." She looked at the photograph carefully, tilting it to the light.

"It's from your parents' album?"

"I suppose so. Funny, I can't remember this one. Or who would have taken it. Dad, I suppose." She kept peering at it, frowning.

"Odd that it's in black-and-white when the last two were in colour. And it's a little larger than the others. It might have been taken with a different camera. And processed at a different place."

Rachel nodded. "Maybe it's not from my mother's album."

"Where would it be from, then?"

"Maybe someone else took it and kept it. A visitor."

"The Hardings, maybe?"

"I doubt it. My father more or less forbade them to set foot in our place after my mother died. Besides, how would Dennis get the picture if it belonged to someone else? No, it *must* have been in the album. It's only the early pictures I remember well. Because I looked at them so often when I was growing up, I suppose."

"So this makes, what, six now? One of the Hammond School and the others all of you, a little older in each one."

Rachel closed her eyes, leaned her head back against the wall. "How long can he keep doing this?"

"By the way," Vicky said. "That box. It's for you, too. But he delivered it in person."

Rachel looked blankly at the package, then at Vicky. "Dennis?" Her eyes flew back to the box.

"I peeked inside. To make sure it was nothing explosive. It's chocolates. For Valentine's Day. He said it was to say he was sorry for having that woman over last night."

"Oh, God." Rachel made no move to pick up the box.

"Should I get rid of it?"

"I—oh, well, leave it with me. Poor Dennis. He thinks if he—"

"What do you mean, 'Poor Dennis'? Don't you let him manipulate you. With one lousy box of chocolates, for heaven's sake!"

Rachel looked down, biting her lip. Vicky had to make herself laugh, say more jovially than she wanted to, "Sorry! Now *I'm* bullying you!"

"No, you're right, he *is* trying to manipulate me. But, well, is it wrong to feel a little sorry for him?"

"It's what he wants, to make you feel sorry for him, to forgive him—"

"But if I'm not going back to him, I can feel sorry for him, can't I?"

"I suppose so," Vicky said warily. "So long as you mean it. About never going back to him."

Rachel was silent for a moment. Then she reached out and ran her finger the length of the box, gently, a gesture Vicky would have, dismayed, seen as loving, except that

Rachel accompanied it by saying, "I think I'm about ready. To start divorce proceedings."

◆

When she was awakened later that night by a thudding in her basement, Vicky, after the initial start, was less alarmed than she might have been. She pulled on her robe, put on the light, and went to the top of the stairs.

"Rachel? You all right?"

There was no answer. Vicky felt the prickle of fear. She took two careful steps down the stairs, her bare feet bracing for a fast retreat.

"Rachel?"

"I'm okay. Sorry."

"That's all right. I thought I heard something fall."

Rachel's door opened. She came out, dishevelled, squinting at the overhead light. "You did. I had that dream again. And when I woke up I was so disoriented, I just started flailing around, looking for the light switch, and I knocked over the glass of orange juice on my bedside table and sent it flying."

"Oh, dear." Vicky came down to the bottom of the steps. "Did it break?"

"No, but it splashed all over my jacket. What a mess. I suppose I should wash it so I can wear it to work in the morning."

"No, no. Wash it later. You can wear one of my jackets. Take the green one, the Gore-Tex."

"Are you sure?" Rachel was rubbing her eyes with her fists, her face still scrunched up, like a child's.

"Of course."

Rachel put her hands down. "It was that same dream. Angeletti. And the others, wearing masks, holding me down. It was so horrible.... Maybe I will take a sleeping pill, after all."

The cat came cautiously down the stairs, his fur standing out a little on his neck. He sniffed at the door frame, as though the bad dream had left its scent there.

CHAPTER SIX

*T*HE COMFORTER UNDER Vicky's arm had started to unfold and was tangling around her legs. She had to stop to gather it up, and then she began to run again. The thin rain flicked at her face.

At the end of the block, almost directly under the streetlight, Vicky could see the body at the side of the road. She stumbled on, her sandals flapping on the pavement, her breath coming heavily through her mouth, puffs of misty vapour pushing out ahead of her. She was aware, incongruously, of the lights on in the houses around her: small caves of safety, of warmth, of life going on as normal. She almost lost her footing on the pavement, which was unevenly patched and pitted, worn with runnels of rain.

She looked behind her. At the end of her front walk she saw Lois, waving at the ambulance, which had just turned the corner. Birdy's two megawatt front porch lights flared on, and Vicky had a sudden image of her picking up her broom and opening the door, ready for anything.

She turned around, kept running, slower now, because she was only a few yards from the person lying at the side of the road. Please, please, she was praying. "Please." Saying the word out loud to the heavy, wet night.

But she could see that it was Rachel. It was her own green jacket she recognized first, then Rachel's brown canvas purse lying a few feet away, and then the blond hair. Rachel lay on her back, her legs pulled slightly up and to the left, her head turned in the same direction.

Vicky bent down, dropped the comforter. "Rachel? Rachel?"

Vicky couldn't look at her face. Rachel's left arm was flung out from the side of her body, and the palm, that tiny white hand, was facing up, open, and Vicky fixed her eyes on it, on that exposed white palm. She knelt down, reached for it, put her own hand gently into it. It was cold, clammy.

The ambulance was almost beside her now; she could see the strobing lights reflected in the ditch. They must have turned the siren off because everything seemed suddenly very quiet.

She withdrew her hand. Rachel would have winced at her uninvited contact. But the open palm looked so exposed, something intimate and sexual, that Vicky, from that terrible helplessness to do anything else for her, turned it over, towards the privacy of the earth.

Two men jumped out of the ambulance. One was carrying a red bag, the other a small oxygen tank and, under his arm, what to Vicky looked like a surfboard until she recognized it as the immobilizing support for carrying accident victims. A spine board, it was called, she remembered dully.

The men, Vicky knew, would do the things they had been taught, the things to preserve life, but she was sure that Rachel was dead. She stood up, turned to them.

"How long's she been here?" asked the first man. He was tall, broad-chested, wearing a blue uniform, and for one blank second Vicky thought he was Dennis.

"I don't know. I just got here."

"Looks like a hit and run," said the second man. "Did you see what happened?" He knelt down beside Rachel.

"No." She backed away, letting them do their job, letting them have Rachel. The one kneeling put his fingers to her neck, feeling for a pulse.

"Hello," he said loudly. "Can you hear me?"

When there was no answer, he put his cheek to her chest, listened, then inserted a small plastic tube into her mouth, breathed into it.

"You should call the police," Vicky said. "If it's a hit and run the police should be here."

"They're right behind us." The first man knelt down, too, laid the board beside Rachel. "Ready for C-spine control."

"Sandbags," said the other one. "Straps."

They were snapping a hard, plastic collar around Rachel's neck now, getting ready to lift her onto the spine board.

Vicky closed her eyes, backed away. She was finding it hard to breathe, the cool night air sticking in her hot throat. She walked to the ambulance, leaned her forehead against it. The strobing lights were visible even through her closed eyelids.

"No," she heard one of the paramedics say. "Shit."

A car door slammed beside her, and she jumped, took a step back, half-tripping over her floppy sandals. Two policemen were walking towards her, the flashing lights on their vehicle mixing with those of the ambulance. One of the men went over to the paramedics, holding a flashlight, the back end propped on his shoulder, the way she had seen it done in movies, masculine, professional, not the way she would have held it, in front of her, at stomach level. The other officer stopped beside Vicky. The lights were confusing his face, turning it white, red, black.

"You the one who found her?"

Vicky nodded. She kept watching the other policeman's flashlight, concentrating only on it, not on where its beam was trying to direct her eyes. "Find her?" She felt numb, her tongue large and clumsy in her mouth. "Oh, I guess, no, I didn't. The girl at my house, up the road, Lois, did. She was coming for a tutoring session. Then she ran to get me. I phoned 911."

The policeman had taken out a notepad, wrote something on it. "And your name is?"

"Vicky Bauer. B-A-U-E-R."

"Do you know this woman?"

"She lives in my house. She was walking home from the bus stop. Her name is Rachel. Rachel Mandaro."

"Mandaro?" The officer's pencil didn't write it down.

"M-A-N-D—"

"I know how to spell it. Is she Dennis Mandaro's wife?"

"Yes."

"The guy we had the restraining orders on?"

"Yes."

"But there's not one on him now, is there?"

"She thought if it didn't help her then, it wouldn't help her now."

They were carrying Rachel past her, hurrying, as though they needed to, as though the hospital might cure her, as though there were still hope. It was what they were required to do, Vicky knew. She turned her face again to the ambulance, closed her eyes.

"I'm sorry," said the policeman. "You can go home if you want. We can take your statement later. You want a ride?"

"That's all right. I can walk. I'd rather walk."

"Are you sure?" He reached down to his side, grasped something that Vicky, looking from the corner of her eye, was sure must be his gun, but it was only a phone. "We have to get some back-up, anyway. We thought this was just a car accident."

"And it's not. Not an accident."

She hadn't made it a question, so she shouldn't have expected an answer, and she didn't get one. "We'll come by to talk to you a little later, then, if that's all right."

"Yes, sure. I'm up there." She gestured vaguely up the street. "Where Lois was."

The ambulance vibrated a little, and she realized they were sliding the spine board and Rachel into it. She stepped back, quickly, turned, and began walking away, concentrating on each step. Most of the outside lights in the block had come on, and a man standing on his front step called to her, "What happened?"

"I don't know," she said, and kept walking. I don't know, she repeated to herself. I, step, don't, step, know. Behind her the ambulance turned on its siren. All she had to do was get back to her house, and it would be okay. She would close the door and turn on the stereo loud loud loud, and then maybe she would, just this once it couldn't hurt, just this once she needed it so badly, pour herself a drink.

It startled her to see her front door open, the outside light on, and startled her even more to see someone standing in her doorway. Lois. Oh, God. She still had to deal with poor Lois.

She started up the walk. Lois waved at her, as though Vicky might not have seen her or might be intending to go somewhere else and needed to be drawn inside.

As she went up the steps, the cat dashed in front of her feet and then leapt into the bushes. She should have been expecting it, this stupid game he liked to play in the dark, but it frightened her enough that she stumbled against the railing.

"What happened?" Lois was shivering so much the words came out wavery, barely recognizable.

"You're freezing," Vicky said, drawing her inside and closing the door. For some reason the girl had taken her coat off and had been standing there in just jeans and a thin cotton T-shirt.

"What happened?"

"The ambulance took her away."

"Was she ... dead?"

"I'm not sure." It wasn't, she supposed, a complete lie. "Look, I'll make you something warm to drink. Then maybe we should call your mother."

"I already did. I hope you don't mind."

"Of course not.

"She wants to come and get me. Is that okay? If I miss my session?"

Vicky had to stop herself from laughing wildly. "Of course it is. You've had such a terrible shock, Lois. But you did all the right things."

"It doesn't feel like I did. I ran away."

"No. You ran to get help. That was exactly the right thing to do."

Vicky went into the kitchen, made them each a hot chocolate. It was a good thing Lois was here, she thought, or she might have reached up into the cupboard over the fridge for the bottle she kept there because she needed to know that every day she was making a choice about it, that she was both stronger than it but weak enough to want it to be there, for the time she might really need it, the time she might not be able to stand it. It had been over a year now since she hadn't been able to stand it. It had been the day Conrad died. The day she became a widow.

She pressed her hands flat, hard, on the kitchen counter, took a deep breath, let it out slowly. It was Rachel she had to think about, not Conrad, not herself. The policeman would be coming to talk to her. She had to sound rational.

The microwave beeped, and she took out the hot chocolates, handed one to Lois, who was looking out the front window, waiting for her mother. Vicky had to stop herself from pulling the drapes, from explaining how visible they were from the street, easy targets. She was relieved to see, only a minute later, a blue Explorer pull up: Lois's mother.

"Mommy's here!" Lois's voice sounded like a five-year-old's. She set her cup down, grabbed her coat, and ran to the door.

It was only when she saw her getting into the car that it occurred to Vicky that the police would probably want to talk to Lois, too. Well, too late, she thought, reaching over to tug closed the drapes, to shut out the dangerous night; they would have to go to her house.

She realized one of her sandals was full of mud. She had no memory of it getting that way, but she knew where it must have happened. She kicked the shoes off quickly, then turned out the living-room lights and sat on the sofa and drank her hot chocolate.

Rachel was dead. How could Rachel be dead? She should be downstairs, and later come up and let herself be persuaded to have supper with Vicky, and they would talk about how work had gone for each of them today, and then they might decide which books Rachel would read next, all the M's to choose from, Alice Munro and Iris Murdoch and Toni Morrison and not Norman Mailer because no matter what he'd written he'd tried to kill one of his wives—

How could Dennis have done this? People had warned them, but still Vicky had not quite believed it possible. Dennis was a bully, and, yes, he was dangerous, but to kill her, to run her down on the road and then drive away ...

Denial. They'd both been in denial.

The doorbell. She jumped up, startling a lick of hot chocolate from the cup onto her hand.

The bell went again. "Mrs. Bauer?" said a loud voice. "It's Corporal Kent."

She opened the door. The man standing there was holding her comforter, and it took her a moment to understand how that could be possible.

"I assumed it was yours," he said, handing it to her.

"Oh. Yes." She took it from him, an awkward bundle. The cloth was cold, faintly damp, nothing of comfort left in it. "I don't know why I thought I should bring it."

"It was the right thing to do," he said. "Keep them warm. You know."

"She *is* dead, isn't she?"

The officer paused long enough for his silence to be her answer. "I'm afraid so."

She thought he was the policeman who had talked to her beside the ambulance, but she wasn't sure. He was wearing the standard uniform, a navy-blue windbreaker over a beige shirt and dark tie and the familiar navy-blue RCMP slacks with the yellow stripe down the side. And a gun, of course. She tried not to look at it. The man was in his late thirties or early forties, with a slight but muscular build, brown hair cropped close to the skull, and a ruddy, round face noticeable for its irregular nose which had clearly been broken at least once and repaired with a list to the left. People with symmetrical faces were most attractive to the opposite sex, Vicky had read once, probably at the same time she'd read about the desirability of slim-waisted women. It made her angry to have something like that stumble through her brain now.

He sat down in the armchair she indicated, although he only perched straight-backed on the edge and declined her offer of a coffee.

"I don't have much more to ask, really," he said. "I know how hard this must be for you."

"Yes." She sat down on the sofa opposite him, perching on the edge, too, mimicking his posture. She kept the comforter on her lap, pushed her folded hands into it, hard, feeling the pressure on her thighs. She was aware of her bare feet, the left one still flecked with dried mud, and she let a corner of the comforter drop to cover them.

"So—" He took out his notepad, flipped it open, ran his finger down to the bottom of the page. "Just tell me again what happened tonight."

Vicky took a deep breath, and then she told him what helplessly little she knew. Before he could ask for it, she went to her phone directory and wrote down Lois's address and phone number.

"Do you think it was Dennis?" she asked.

The corporal shifted uneasily, crossed his legs, then uncrossed them. "I can't comment on that. But tell me what you know about him."

So she told him, everything from how she had first met Dennis to the photos to the box of Valentine's chocolates he had shoved through the door yesterday. Today was Valentine's Day. Rachel had been killed on Valentine's Day. The first, sudden tears pressed at Vicky's eyes; she swallowed, blinked them away.

"Do you know what kind of car he drives?" If the officer had noticed her tears he gave no sign of it.

"A black Honda. Why? Do you think someone might have seen him tonight?"

"Your neighbour" —he gestured at Birdy's house— "came out and told us that when she turned her outside light on to set out some garbage she saw a black car sitting in the alley. It was behind her hedge, but she saw it clearly when it drove off as she started down her steps. That was about six-thirty. Is that someplace he's likely to have parked?"

"He was waiting for us there once before."

"When did Mrs. Mandaro normally get home from work?"

"By five-thirty or six. Today, she told me, she had to work late."

"So if her husband were watching for her at her usual time, he might have waited in the alley."

"I suppose so. It would have been a long wait."

"But he might have gotten a good view, without his wife spotting him, around Mrs. Birdsell's house and down the street where his wife would have come walking?"

"I imagine so. I don't think there's anything to obstruct it. You could go check."

The corporal nodded, turned a page in his notebook. "Could you give us the names of Mrs. Mandaro's next of kin?"

Next of kin. Me, Vicky wanted to say. My kin, my sister, my daughter.

"There's her father. Jacob Cornelius. He lives in Richmond. And she works for her uncle, John Harding. I don't know of anyone else."

"Do you have their addresses?"

"For the Hardings. The father's I can't remember. I suppose Rachel has it downstairs." Has. Had. In one second the present tense turns, turned, into the past.

"Would you show me where it is?"

"All right." Vicky didn't think he'd needed to ask her permission. Not that he had, exactly, but she appreciated the phrasing.

She led him through the kitchen, resisting some instinct to apologize for the dirty dishes on the counter, and down the steps to the landing. She stopped, stared at the little table. The letter. She had forgotten all about it.

The corporal had almost run into her, and now he was shifting his feet behind her.

She gestured at the table. "There was another letter for Rachel this morning."

"Letter?"

"I told you. Dennis was sending her photographs."

"She was sure they were from him?"

"Pretty sure. It was some control game he was playing with her. She phoned him late one night after the fifth picture arrived—the one that had the man's face circled—and he denied sending them, but who else could it have been? There was a woman at his place that night," she added, remembering. "That was probably why he brought Rachel the chocolates."

The corporal took a small baggy out of his jacket pocket, picked up the envelope carefully by one corner, and dropped it inside.

"I don't suppose we could open it now?" Vicky asked.

Corporal Kent glanced at her, unable to hide his surprise. "No," he said. "We need to check for fingerprints."

"Of course."

They went downstairs, to Rachel's room. It was hard for Vicky to open the door without knocking, harder still to step inside. She had never gone into Rachel's room before. It was surprisingly unchanged from the plain, white spare bedroom she remembered: the double bed with her blue striped quilt lying neatly on it; the two bedside tables with tissues and drinking glasses and books; the two chairs draped with clothes; the dresser with a small stack of freshly washed underwear on top, as well the small hot plate on its heat-proof pad, a mug of pencils and pens, a jar of peanuts, a transistor radio, some cosmetics, a hair dryer, a sewing kit, a dictionary, a Bible, and the pink photo album with the word "Memories" embossed on it.

Vicky gestured at it. "That's the album he sent. I imagine the pictures are inside."

Corporal Kent took a pencil from the mug and inserted it into the album at about the third page, lifted it slightly. Vicky glimpsed one of the photographs behind an acetate sheet. Just as Dennis would have wanted. The officer dropped the album carefully into a large baggy.

"Did she keep the envelopes and the cards?"

"I don't see them. If they're not in the album she probably threw them out."

"Well, let me know if you run across them." He sealed up the baggy. There was too much air in it, making it taut and puffy, but he didn't reseal it. "Is there an address book anywhere?"

Vicky looked at him blankly.

"Next of kin. Her father."

"Oh. Yes." She couldn't see anything on the dresser top, but when she opened the top drawer she found a lined writing pad, a calculator, several file folders, and, lying on top of them, surprising her, a small Rolodex. She flipped to the C's; there was Rachel's father's name and phone number, in her tiny, leftward-slanted printing. Vicky left it open at that spot and handed it to the corporal. She thought he might just extract the card, but he took the whole Rolodex.

"Well, that's all we need for now, I guess." He glanced around the room. "Did she have ... any visitors here?"

The way he had paused before "visitors" made Vicky think he probably meant "men."

"Not that I know of," she said. "The Hardings may have popped in a few times, but not to stay, just to drop something off, maybe, or to pick her up. She didn't have ... company. She didn't entertain guests."

The officer nodded. He didn't appear to have noticed the slightly sarcastic emphasis she had given to "entertain guests."

As they were leaving the room, Vicky's foot bumped the wooden chair sitting halfway in the closet. When she grasped the back to push it aside she realized she was clutching Rachel's jacket, the one Rachel had spilled orange juice on last night. She lifted it up, gently.

"That hers?"

Vicky nodded, swallowed the pain in her throat. "She spilled juice on it last night. I let her wear my jacket today."

"She was wearing your jacket when she was killed?"

The sharpness of his voice frightened her. "Maybe it was just an accident, after all," she said. "A hit and run. Not Dennis, just some drunk or a scared kid."

He didn't answer, just picked up a sleeve of the jacket, rubbed it between his fingers, let it drop. "Well," he said after a moment, "I'll let you know if we need to go through her room again. Until then don't touch or remove any of her things."

They went back up the stairs. The cat, spooked, streaked up beside them.

"Jesus!" The corporal grabbed the handrail.

"I'm sorry. I thought he was still outside."

They were at the back door now. "I'll go out here, if that's all right," said Corporal Kent. "I want to have another walk down the alley." He gestured awkwardly in that direction with the Rolodex. The file cards flopped onto his hand. Vicky doubted if he was still marking the one for Jacob Cornelius.

"Of course." Vicky flicked the outside light on. And then she said, regretting it immediately, "I can tell the Hardings, if you'd like. I know them a little bit."

She could feel the man's eyes on her, evaluating her offer. "All right. That would be real nice of you. As you can imagine, telling the relatives is one of the worst parts of this job."

"I expect so. I don't envy you having to tell Mr. Cornelius." She supposed she should warn Corporal Kent what was in store, but she wasn't sure, herself. What would the old man say? That Rachel had deserved it?

"Well. We'll keep in touch, then."

When he was gone Vicky went back into the living room, sat down on the sofa, leaned back and closed her eyes. Now that she was asking the tears to come they wouldn't. Maybe she still didn't quite believe it. Maybe she still expected Rachel to come up the back steps any minute now.

She sat there, her eyes closed, growing colder and more numb, and it was only when the cat jumped up on her that she started, sat up, and remembered she had promised to phone the Hardings.

A busy signal. She hung up, walked around the room, shivering, hugging herself, but reluctant to turn on the heat, as though she had to deny herself such easy comfort. Her phone rang; she let the machine take it.

"Hi! This is Birdy. So is it true? That bastard killed Rachel? I saw it, you know, I saw his black car, parked there waiting for her. Well. You call me. When you feel like it." She paused. "This must be hard for you, eh?"

"Yes," said Vicky out loud, but she didn't pick up the phone. She pushed "Play," listened to the message repeat, erase.

She called the Hardings again; the line was still busy. She picked up the cat, carried him around until his struggles to get down enlisted the use of claws, and then she phoned again. Busy. She heated herself a glass of milk, drank it, called again. Still busy. It had been almost three quarters of an hour since she'd first tried. Why hadn't she just let the police handle it? They wouldn't have phoned; they would have gone in person.

She could do that, too, she supposed. Staying in the house felt too oppressive, anyway, and she had felt her mind reaching for the bottle of gin in the cupboard above the refrigerator. *This is one of those times*, it whispered; *this is too much to bear without help; I will make it go away.*

She pulled on socks and runners without bothering to wash her dirty foot, and, not pausing to turn off any lights, ran out to her car.

It took only ten minutes to get to the Hardings' house in Chantrell Estates, a development of starter mansions on small acreages. She had been there twice before, once to pick up Rachel and once to drop her off there for dinner, so even though she had forgotten to check the address it was not hard to find.

She parked in the driveway behind the glossy blue Mercedes. The garage door was open, and in front of the Mercedes she could see Junior's red truck with a load of plywood and pipes parked beside the yellow Tracker she had seen Linda drive. A movement-sensor light went on when she got out of the car, and she had to raise her hand to shield her eyes as she walked to the door. A neighbour's dog started barking savagely, accompanied by a rattling sound, as though it was throwing itself against a chain-link fence. She shivered, walked faster.

When she pressed the doorbell, the chimes sounded somewhere deep in the house. There was a faint smell of cedar in the air from the two well-groomed trees to her right.

A light went on in the hallway. She smiled up at the peephole. Junior opened the door. He was wearing jeans with a hole in the knee and a pullover with a bleachy stain on the sleeve. She realized she had never seen him except in a suit.

"Vicky! Come in."

She stood on the threshold, not moving. Now that she was here, what should she do, say?

"I kept phoning, but the line was busy."

"Sorry. What's wrong?" Junior was reaching for her elbow, trying to draw her inside.

"Rachel's dead," she said. "A hit and run."

John Harding had been coming down the hall, smiling as he recognized Vicky, and it was his face she was looking at when she said the awful words. He went pale, the smile dropping from his lips.

"What?" he said.

"Rachel's dead."

"What are you talking about?" demanded Junior. His voice was angry. "How can she be dead? I just saw her a few hours ago."

"It just happened. Not far from my house. She must have been walking home from the bus stop."

Linda had come out from the kitchen, wiping her hands on a dishtowel, and was standing, beside the large vase of daffodils in the hallway, staring at Vicky.

"What's happened?" she whispered.

"She says Rachel's been killed. A hit and run." John Harding put his hand up against the wall, perhaps to support himself, perhaps to stop Linda from coming any further.

Linda's hand went to her mouth. Her eyes were wide, all dark pupil. "Oh, no. No."

"It can't be," Junior was saying. He sounded even more angry, his voice shaking.

"Are you sure?" Harding took his hand down from the wall, came towards her, stood beside Junior. He seemed to have trouble breathing.

"Yes. I'm sorry. A student coming for tutoring found her, probably right after it happened, and the ambulance came right away. There was nothing anyone could do."

"Dennis. That bastard," Junior said.

He slammed his fist against the door frame, then slumped against the wall, his mouth twisting. He must have leaned against the light switch, because suddenly the hallway went dark. Vicky could see the three of them, Junior and John Harding and Linda, only as unmoving silhouettes, dimly backlit by the light coming around the corner from the kitchen. The daffodils beside Linda had gone from yellow to grey, as though their light had been suddenly extinguished, too. From farther back in the house she could hear a TV, the comfortable evening sounds of a sitcom, a laugh track.

She felt suddenly enormously tired. "I'm so sorry," she said. "I guess if you want to know anything more the police can tell you."

She turned and started walking back to her car. She thought they might call her back, but none of them did. The neighbour's dog began its frenzied barking again. She backed the car out quickly, before she turned on her lights, not wanting to spotlight the three people she could imagine were still standing, rigid with grief and disbelief, in their darkened hallway.

But as she got closer to home she could feel her foot easing off the accelerator. There was nothing to rush home for. The house would be empty. Rachel would never be there again.

She stopped the car on Buena Vista just where, on a sunny day, the sudden ocean view would take one's breath away, and she put her head down on the steering wheel and cried.

She didn't know how long she stayed like that, but eventually a man with a flashlight came out of the house beside her and shone the beam through her window, so she had to sit up and drive away.

She was glad she had left all the lights on in the house. She came in through the back door, went up into the kitchen without glancing down the stairs. The cat yowled, twisting himself around her feet.

"Rachel's gone," she told him. "Get used to it."

The answering machine was flashing: three messages. Vicky sighed, sat down, pushed the play button. The first message was from Amanda, asking if Vicky wanted to go for lunch on the weekend. The second, a cold woman's voice Vicky did not recognize until it identified itself as belonging to Lois's mother, said, "We think it best that, in light of what's happened, Lois not continue her tutoring with you. I trust you understand. We'll be mailing a cheque to cover your services to date." *I trust you understand*: well, she did, actually.

The last message began. Vicky caught her breath, sat bolt upright. The voice was loud, lurching, repeatedly breaking off.

"Vicky. This is Dennis. Dennis, Rachel's Dennis. She can't be dead, she isn't dead, is she? The police came and they told me she was dead. Oh, Jesus. Oh, Jesus. It's not true, is it? Not Rachel. They said—they said she was hit by a car. They probably think I did it. But, oh, Jesus, how could I—how could I kill her, I love her. You know I do. I brought her those chocolates. She's not dead, is she? Is she?" He was crying now, sobs cutting into his words, and then there were no more words, only his crying, and after a few more seconds he hung up.

Vicky put the machine on pause, trying to remember how to save the message on it. She could try to take out the original tape, but she had no idea how to replace it, and the manual, of course, was long gone. Finally she found her pocket tape recorder and recorded Dennis onto it. The police would want his message. For when they arrested him. Because surely they would arrest him.

She listened to his message on the machine one more time before letting it erase. It was hard not to let herself believe him. Was he that good an actor, faking even his tears?

She stood up abruptly, walked away from the rewinding tape. Go to hell, she thought savagely. Maybe he hadn't intended to kill her when he hit her. Maybe he'd intended just another violent threat, like the fist in her hair, the shoulder jamming into her back, the foot kicking at the door. But he had shoved too hard this time, had pressed his rage onto the gas pedal and this time he had killed her.

It was deep into the night before she could get to sleep, and then she was awakened almost immediately by the dream. She sat up, the sheet damp with sweat, her breath ragged.

She had been lying down, on a hard bed in a white room. She was terrified, struggling. People were holding her arms. A man with his face covered was leaning over her, forcing her legs apart, raping her.

CHAPTER SEVEN

THE DOORBELL. She struggled awake, pushing at her bed-clothes as though they were making the startling sound. She looked at the clock. Eleven. Judging by the light it must be morning. The bell went again. Maybe it was Dennis, come to demand she hand over Rachel—

Her arm stopped abruptly on its way into the sleeve of her dressing gown. Rachel was dead. Vicky closed her eyes against the sudden flood of remembering, sank back onto the bed.

The doorbell went again. Maybe Dennis was coming for Vicky now; maybe she was the one he had wanted to kill all along; hadn't the corporal last night seemed interested that Rachel was wearing Vicky's jacket when she was hit—

She ran her hand over her face, hard, and then through her hair. She had to made herself think clearly. Someone was at the door. It was unlikely it was Dennis. Still, she picked up the cordless phone as she went down the hall. Just in case.

When she looked through the peephole, she groaned. Kristin. She had forgotten to cancel her tutoring sessions today. She pulled her dressing gown more tidily closed, affixed something less than a frown to her face and opened the door. Still, she could tell by Kristin's expression that she must have looked singularly unwelcoming.

"Oh!" Kristin glanced at her watch. "I thought I was scheduled for eleven o'clock."

"You are, you are. I'm sorry. I forgot to call you to cancel. But we can still have our session if you want. It's just that ...

something happened last night that has, well, made me rather disoriented."

"What happened?"

She would have to tell her, tell all her students, eventually. Only Dulci, whom she tutored at home, had never met Rachel.

"The woman who was staying here with me, Rachel, she was killed last night. A hit and run."

"What?" Kristin stared at her.

"I'm sorry. I know it must be a shock."

Kristin simply kept staring at her. Her face went white. The hand at her side fumbled for a hold of the handrail. She took a step back and would have fallen down the first stair if she hadn't been holding the rail.

"She's been *killed*? How can she have been *killed*?"

"She just ... It happened."

"How can she be *dead*? I just saw her a few days ago."

It was same baffled response Junior had made, Vicky thought, watching Kristin helplessly: I just *saw* her, how can she be *dead*?

"I'm sorry. I can't make it unhappen."

She had sounded more brusque than she intended, and to her dismay she saw tears forming in Kristin's eyes. The young woman nodded, looked down. The birthmark on her neck seemed to turn a darker purple.

Vicky reached over, rubbed her hand up and down Kristin's arm. "Why don't you go home? Call me tomorrow. We'll reschedule. And tell your parents I won't charge for that session."

Kristin nodded, didn't look up. They stood there awkwardly, and Vicky was just thinking she would have to ask her in when Kristin turned and headed down the steps. Vicky was closing the door when Kristin stopped, turned back, and said, "Where did it happen? The hit and run?"

"Down the street a ways," Vicky said, resisting the urge to look or gesture towards it. There was a ghoulishness about the young, she thought. "Well, take care now," she added lamely, and closed the door.

She was still holding the cordless phone, so, before she found reasons to forget, she sat down to call her other students to reschedule her sessions for the next few days. Ajit's father took a message for him; under other circumstances she might have wanted to talk to him about his son's matrimonial options, but now she would have had to feign interest. Dulci answered eagerly on the first ring, not disguising her disappointment that it was only her tutor. "I hope you feel better soon," she said dutifully, even though Vicky had not said why she was cancelling; but illness was, of course, the only excuse teachers were allowed, and Vicky didn't contradict her. There was no answer at Rob's house. Travis kept saying, happily, "No problem, no problem," and Vicky had to keep repeating that they needed to book new times.

Of course she did not need to call Lois; Vicky doubted if her mother would ever contact her again. But she wished she could talk to the girl. It seemed unwise, although understandable, of the mother to stop them seeing each other, as though together they shared some blame, as though apart they would find it easier to forget. She would call Lois again in a week or so, Vicky decided, in case her mother's solution wasn't working out.

She had intended to tell the students why she was cancelling, but she couldn't make herself do it. They would find out soon enough, she thought. Maybe it would be easier for all of them if some time went by first. Of course, they might read about it in the paper. She could imagine the reporters outside now, taking pictures of the yellow do-not-cross ribbon the police would have put up around the site and wondering if they could make the Sunday deadline. The young were no more ghoulish than the rest of us, she thought grimly.

She made one more call.

"Meet me for lunch at the pier," she said when Amanda answered. "I have need of your ear."

"I'll bring the other organs, too. Just in case."

◆

They stood at the end of the pier, looking out across Semiahmoo Bay at the spit of land across the border where Vicky and Rachel had been driving only three days ago. The sky was the pale grey of a settled low front and it was raining lightly, which, Vicky thought, was just as well, since it meant they were almost the only ones on the pier. A flock of yellow-billed loons circled in the water below, their sleek black heads and checkered backs disappearing periodically as they dived for food.

"So, have they arrested him?" Amanda pulled the collar of her jacket more tightly closed against an east wind blowing the rain at their faces.

"I don't think so. They may not have enough evidence."

"What about all his history with her? How can they not charge him?"

"Maybe that history isn't evidence. I think they believe he did it, but they don't have proof. The smoking gun, so to speak."

"So the bastard might actually get away with it."

"He left a message for me on my answering machine. He sounded ... Well, he sounded convincingly shocked and upset at the news."

Amanda stared at her. "Surely *you* don't think he's innocent?"

"No, I guess not. But there are loose ends. Those pictures he was sending her. What was that all about? Who was this Angeletti? Last night I had Rachel's dream, the one where she's being held down and he's raping her."

"Oh, Vicky. You better go see a counsellor. I mean, Conrad only died a year ago and now here's someone else you were living with getting killed. It's a lot to deal with."

"I'll be okay."

"You haven't ..." Amanda cleared her throat, looked uncomfortable. Finally she put her thumb and forefinger together, as though she were holding an invisible teacup, and made a gesture to her mouth.

"No," Vicky said stiffly. "I haven't."

"Don't get prickly. I just meant that, well, it would be understandable. If you did."

"We should get back. It's freezing."

They started down the pier. White Rock lay on the hill in front of them, grey and drowsy in the rain. Two seagulls circling overhead landed a few feet in front of them, eyeing them hopefully, barely hopping aside when the two women neared. To the west they could see the Amtrak train coming along the tracks on the beach, heading for Seattle. The tracks ran dangerously close to the seawall walk, and Vicky couldn't keep her eyes from moving to the east, to the big white rock for which the city had been named, to where a boy had been hit recently. She bent her head down, walked faster.

"Want to go to a movie or something tonight?" Amanda asked when they got to her car. "To take your mind off things?"

"Thanks, but I'd rather not. Besides, I should probably be at home. In case the police call or need to look at Rachel's room again or something."

"Okay. But, good grief, they can't expect you to sit at home waiting for them."

"Good grief." Vicky smiled. "Is that an oxymoron?"

"No. The therapy for grief is grief. So they say."

◆

It wasn't until the next day, Sunday, that the police contacted her. She'd had Rachel's nightmare again, the sinister man called Angeletti forcing her legs apart, someone else holding her arms; and when she'd at last woken up, shaking, she wanted only to stop it from happening again. She took two sleeping pills, which drugged her into an empty sleep until the phone rang the next morning.

"Could I come over?" Corporal Kent's voice asked. "In half an hour?"

"All right."

She drank two cups of coffee, fast, and got dressed, in the kind of schoolmarmish way, a white blouse and calf-length corduroy skirt, that she thought the police might expect. Then she sat on the couch waiting. The cat jumped up on her lap. She picked up the fine-toothed comb she kept under the couch and concentrated on combing him; he writhed in pleasure and discomfort. By the time the doorbell went, static had glued most of his shed hair to her skirt.

"Come in." On the street she could see the police car, white, with its modern multicoloured stripe down the sides and, on the rear fender, the logo, faintly comforting and faintly comic, of a Mountie on a galloping horse. The RCMP, she remembered, had licensed their image to Disney. Maybe they should be putting Mickey Mouse on the fender now.

The corporal handed her the newspaper he'd picked up from the stoop.

"Thank you," Vicky said. "Would you like a coffee?"

"That would be nice, actually, yes." He wasn't wearing his uniform today, Vicky noticed, just a green sweatshirt and slacks and a jacket whose cuffs and elbows had seen better days. She felt overdressed, wished she had put on jeans.

"Is there any more news?"

"We've arrested Mandaro."

"Really? That's a relief."

"I suppose. Although it would be nice to have an actual eyewitness. The woman he gave as his alibi said she wasn't with him. And she gave us ... other information as well."

She was hoping he would elaborate, but he didn't. He'd probably already told her more than he should have.

"Did you find any evidence on his car? That it might have hit someone?"

He coughed into his hand. "I can't give you the details. But with your neighbour's testimony, well, it's a pretty good case."

Vicky went into the kitchen, poured them each a coffee. The corporal came up beside her, added sugar to his cup, stirred briskly. Ping, ping, ping: the spoon hit the sides.

Ping. Vicky was dismayed to feel the tingle of sexual attraction.

She stepped back, ran some water in the sink as though the plate in it needed to be soaked. How could she feel something like that, for a man investigating Rachel's murder only two days ago?

"So," she said brusquely, twisting the tap off, hard. "Do you need anything more?"

Someone knocked at her back door. "Oh," said the corporal. "That'll be Constable Kulyk. He was in the alley taking some pictures. He'll be taking some of her room, too. We won't be long. I don't expect we'll find anything useful. She didn't seem to have settled in too much."

Settled in too much. No, she hadn't, Vicky thought. It had been a temporary arrangement: Rachel hadn't forgotten that, even if Vicky might have.

"Sure," she said. "Go ahead."

He let the other officer in, and they went down the stairs together. Vicky supposed she could come down, too; but what was the point? It would only be painful, watching those businesslike hands going through Rachel's small collection of necessities. The thought crossed her mind that the police could accuse her of having an illegal suite; the hot plate alone was probably a fire violation.

At least they'd arrested Dennis. There would be justice, of a sort, if only the dispassionate revenge of the state.

When the officers came back up, the constable went out through the back door; Corporal Kent came into the living room where Vicky was pretending to read a textbook. He was carrying an open cardboard box, which Vicky thought Rachel might have used for her dirty laundry and which the corporal had filled with papers.

"Find anything?" she asked.

"Not really." He set the box down on the dining-room table. "These are mostly empty files, a few letters, bills, nothing that I expect will be useful. But you never know."

"I meant to ask you," Vicky said. "About the envelope that came for her Friday. You know. The one that probably had another photograph in it."

As though he had been waiting for her question, the corporal reached into an inside jacket pocket and withdrew the envelope. Vicky assumed it must already have been dusted for prints. "Maybe you can tell me when it was taken," he said.

"I doubt it." Vicky pulled out the card. The familiar two Persian kittens were on the cover. She opened it. Her hands felt clumsy, too many fingers.

That there was no writing in the card she noticed only peripherally as her eyes scanned the photograph. It was of Rachel, sitting on Vicky's front step, looking towards the street and smiling. Through the front window another shape was visible. Herself.

"God," she said. She touched Rachel's small face, the way Rachel herself had done with the other pictures.

"Any idea when it was taken?"

Vicky shook her head. She couldn't take her eyes from Rachel's face, the way the wind had blown a strand of hair across her chin. And in the window, herself, blurred, not paying attention.

"If her husband took the picture, is it likely she would have been smiling like that?" asked the corporal.

"She doesn't seem to be smiling at the photographer. She's looking away to the west, and the angle of the picture is from the east, from across Birdy's front lawn. If someone was sitting in a car across the street from Birdy's, especially with a zoom lens, Rachel wouldn't even have noticed."

The corporal leaned over to look at the picture. She had to stop herself from stepping away from him. "How about when it was taken?"

"I don't know. It could be any time in the last two months. The sun is shining. In this climate that narrows down the possibilities."

"Any idea who she was looking at?"

"Probably nobody. She sometimes just liked to sit on the front step and watch the sunset. Maybe Dennis wanted to show her that she wasn't safe. I suppose he expected her to get this picture before he killed her. It would have been like saying, 'Okay, this is the present, I've caught up with you now.'" Vicky handed the photograph back, reluctantly. On an impulse, she asked, "Could I get all the pictures back, do you think? I mean, they have sentimental value. For the family. They were stolen, after all."

Corporal Kent looked at her. She realized the ambiguity in "they were stolen"; he might think she meant they had been stolen by the police. She was surprised when he said, "I suppose I could get the lab to make copies for you, at any rate."

For you. Not, *for the family.* She wondered if she had been that transparent.

"That would be very nice," she said, trying not to sound grateful. "By the way, have you checked out the fifth picture? The one with the man's face circled?"

"We're making preliminary inquiries. Digging up something from fifteen or twenty years ago and involving the Washington police: well, it's not that easy."

"But ... it *is* important, right?"

The corporal put the picture back into the envelope and slid it into his jacket. "We'll look into it," he said, a little stiffly.

"Well. I guess I'll be going."

He was opening the front door when she remembered the tape she had made. "Oh, wait. Corporal ..." She had forgotten his name.

He turned. "Kent." He shifted his feet slightly. "If you prefer you can call me Clark."

"Right. Clark Kent." She gave a silly little laugh, realizing he must be joking, even though his expression hadn't reflected it. "You keep your cape in the car?"

"It's no joke, I'm afraid. Blame my father."

"Oh. Well, it's quite ... charming, really. Especially for a policeman."

"I live with it."

Would it hurt him to smile? Vicky wondered if the man knew how.

"Anyway," she said, "Dennis called me the night Rachel died and left a message on my machine. He says the police had just been to see him. I made a copy of the tape. Not that he says anything important. But I thought I should save it." She handed it to him.

"Thanks." He took it, bounced it lightly in his hand. "Did your machine register the time of the call?"

"I'm afraid it doesn't do that. But the call would have come in sometime around nine. When I was out. At the Hardings. To tell them about Rachel."

"Around nine. I see. Well. I'll be in touch." He raised the tape to his forehead, an odd mock salute.

He had been gone only a few minutes when the phone

rang. As soon as she heard Rob's voice she realized she had forgotten to call him back to cancel his session this afternoon.

"Is it true?" he kept saying. "Is it true?"

"True?" She couldn't seem to understand what he was asking.

"Rachel. That she was killed. The woman who lived with you. I saw it on the news. What happened?"

"A hit and run." If he'd seen it on the news he probably already knew more than he needed to.

"Ah, God. The poor thing. That's just ..." He paused. She could hear the slight fumbly sound of him passing the receiver from one hand to the other. "That's such a tragedy. She was ... she was so pretty."

The deaths of unpretty people weren't tragedies, then, Vicky stopped herself from saying. Rob was young; he had been attracted to Rachel; what other feelings was he supposed to have?

"I'm sorry," she said, making her voice kind. "I know it's shocking. I tried to call you yesterday to cancel our session but you were out. Is it okay with you if we rebook? Maybe for Thursday? At two?"

"Thursday. Yeah, sure, okay, it doesn't matter."

"Well. I'll see you Thursday then."

"I just ... feel so bad," Rob said. "Like I wish there was something I could do."

"I know."

◆

She had the dream again that night. She got up, wandered around the house. It was as though Rachel had left her nightmare behind, had left it for Vicky to understand.

She wondered if the police would even bother investigating Angeletti and the Hammond Christian School for Girls. They had their guilty party. They could use more physical proof, but they didn't need more motive.

The cat was downstairs, meowing, scratching at Rachel's door.

"I know," Vicky said.

CHAPTER EIGHT

*I*T WAS SEVERAL DAYS before she heard from Corporal Kent again.

"I thought you might want to have those prints," he said.

It took her a few seconds to remember. "Yes, of course. The photos."

The cordless phone was snappy with static; she walked across the room trying to find a spot where it was happier.

"I thought I could ... Well, I was wondering if we might meet over lunch somewhere."

Vicky stared at the cat, as though he were the one who had said something startling. Was the man asking her on a *date*?

"Sure. That would be fine. Shall I meet you?"

"I can pick you up."

"All right. The neighbours will just think I'm being arrested."

"I can come in my own car if you prefer." His voice did not suggest he knew she had been kidding.

Maybe she hadn't been. Except for Birdy, Vicky had not had much success with the neighbours. The couple for whom she'd refused to babysit barely nodded to her now, and the people across the alley had only last month put up a small sign on their lawn with a certain ambiguity in the punctuation: "Keep out. Your cats." Vicky was not unsympathetic; her cat had an unseemly territorial nature.

When the corporal did arrive it was in an inconspicuous old-model Taurus, though he himself was in uniform.

"Sorry about this," he said, gesturing vaguely at his clothes and his gun as they walked out to the street. "I hope it won't upset the neighbours."

"That's fine," she said.

"I mean, I'm still on duty."

"Oh. So this isn't a date." *Stupid.* She gave a feeble laugh which she was sure he would not know how to interpret and opened the passenger door quickly, before he could come over and do it for her.

The car was not exactly clean inside. The dash was dusty, except for spots around the knobs and dials, and the floor had enough empty Styrofoam cups and wadded-up papers that she had a hard time finding a place for her feet.

He got in, started the motor. Not looking at her, he said, "Well, it could be. If you want. A date."

She had never felt so foolish. "I'm sorry. I was just making a joke."

He put the car in gear and pulled away, not answering. It was, she suspected, an annoying but effective habit: if he wasn't sure of what to say, he said nothing. It was something few women could get away with.

They were heading down Buena Vista to the beach before he asked if the Boathouse would be okay. Of course she agreed. The Boathouse had the best view of the bay and the Gulf Islands. Even on an overcast day like today it would be nicer than sitting at street level on Marine Drive listening to the trucks and boom cars going by a few feet from their table.

The leggy young waitress who handed them their menus said, "Clark! Great to see you. Dad was just asking about you a few days ago."

Clark. So it really was his first name. His father, Vicky thought, had had a sense of humour, all right. No wonder his son must have decided he was better off without one.

They ordered seafood dishes and side salads.

"Would you like a glass of wine?" Clark asked. His eyebrows, she couldn't help noticing, were thick and curly and not symmetrical. They overhung eyes of an unusually dark blue, the colour of sky at dusk just before it went black. "I can't join you, I'm afraid. On duty."

"Thank you, but nothing for me, either." It was on the tip of her tongue to tell him why, but she bit back the words. There was no point in making herself sound more unreliable than necessary just to disconcert him for a moment.

He reached into his jacket and drew out a small square envelope, handed it to her. She lifted the unsealed flap. The seven pictures, she could see, had all been reproduced in the same size. Like the originals, four were in black-and-white, and three were in colour. The one on top was of Rachel at fifteen, wearing a red dress, her face already shining with adult beauty, her eyes looking straight out at Vicky.

She closed the flap, set the envelope down. Why had she wanted them, and all their pain?

"Thanks," she said. "Her father will appreciate these."

"Possibly. Hard to know, when a man tells you his daughter is dead because she disobeyed God."

"Is that really what he said?"

"More or less."

Vicky sighed. "He's a charmer, isn't he?"

"Yeah."

"Did you find Dennis's prints on the pictures?"

"Well, it might be odd if he *hadn't* touched any of them."

He had only parried her question, but she supposed it was the only answer she would get.

The waitress brought their meals then. There was more than Vicky wanted, but she was hungry, and she had no intentions of eating sparsely. This wasn't a date, after all; she didn't have to impress Clark Kent with a delicate Scarlett O'Hara appetite.

He lifted a prawn to his mouth, then lowered his fork.

"By the way," he said. "I *can* tell you that we found Angeletti."

"Really?"

Clark lifted the prawn again, put it in his mouth, chewed, slowly. Vicky felt like jabbing him with her fork: the man's way with silence was distinctly irritating. She made herself take a mouthful, too, and wait.

"It was quite easy, really," Clark said at last. "The church that ran the girls' school still exists, although the school has been gone for some time. Angeletti worked there, all right. Then he moved to Florida. Unfortunately, he died there two years ago."

"Dead? Oh, shit." Vicky sat back, not caring if he saw her disappointment.

"So even if he did, well, rape Rachel all those years ago, there's nothing we can do about it now."

"But why would Dennis have sent her that picture?"

"He must have found something out about the school, and, from what you say, he expected it to upset his wife." Clark began eating rapidly now, as though he needed to make up for his earlier pauses.

"It gave her these dreadful nightmares. Now I'm getting them."

"You're getting her nightmares?"

Vicky laughed weakly, waved the subject away with her fork. "Yeah, well. It was hard not to become involved with Rachel's life."

"But you only knew her two months."

"She brought out my maternal instincts, maybe." She tried not to sound annoyed. Maybe he had suspicions, too, like Dennis, that her interest in Rachel was not platonic.

Clark took a large swallow from his coffee, emptying the cup. He glanced at his watch, then rubbed his palm along the side of his neck, wincing slightly. "I should go soon," he said. "You about ready?"

"Whenever." She had made the mistake of setting down her fork for a minute. She looked with some yearning at the rest of her prawns and salad.

"I don't want to rush you."

"That's fine, I'm ready." She reached for her coat.

The waitress hurried over. "No dessert?" she exclaimed.

"'Fraid not. Just the bill." Clark pulled out his wallet.

"Is this a business expense?" Vicky asked. "Or should I pay for my own?" She didn't care if he took it as a joke or not. The waitress turned her little giggle into a cough, then walked quickly away.

For the first time, Vicky saw him smile. At least she thought it was a smile, that twitch at the right side of his mouth, making his face even more asymmetrical. "I thought this was a date," he said.

"I thought you said it wasn't."

"I thought you didn't want it to be."

She had to return his smile, trying to pull up the side of her mouth wryly, the way he had. "Women pay their own way on dates these days."

"Well, then it's a business expense."

When they got back to her house, Clark cleared his throat, took his hands off the steering wheel. "Do you, uh, want to try a real date? A movie or something?" He didn't look at her.

"A real date." She hadn't been on a real date in a long time. What do you think, Conrad, her mind asked, but Conrad had been silent for a long time now. Amanda, what do you think? Go for it, Amanda said. But he's a *policeman*, Amanda. Oh, for heaven's sake, said Amanda.

"All right," Vicky said. "That sounds nice."

He nodded, as though they had agreed on some awkward necessity. "This Saturday, maybe?"

"Okay."

"I'll call you."

She got out of the car, walked to her front door. Behind her she could hear the Taurus start down the street. The motor needed a tune-up.

She was putting her key in the lock when she saw Birdy coming around the boxwood hedge separating their front yards; Birdy had trimmed the hedge so low she might as well just have stepped over it. Vicky's instinct was to turn the key, fast, and leap inside, pretending she hadn't seen her neighbour, but she knew she was too late to be convincing.

Birdy was carrying her old one-eyed tomcat. He lay so limply in her arms that Vicky had the alarming thought that he had died and that Birdy had come to ask her to bury him.

"So," said Birdy, "that cop want to arrest you, or to sleep with you?"

Vicky laughed. The tomcat, to her relief, pulled his ears back a little at the sound. "Maybe both."

"Well, he's kinda cute," Birdy said. "He can take me in for questioning any time."

"His name is Clark Kent. Can you imagine parents doing that to a kid?"

Birdy hooted. "Couldn't very well join the Mafia, could he?"

She bent down, grunting, and deposited the cat, with great gentleness, on the ground. He peered around with his one rheumy eye and then headed slowly back home.

Birdy straightened. "The cops called me yesterday. Said I might have to go to court and testify. About seeing the husband's car in the alley."

"You're sure it was his?"

"Well, not absolutely one hundred percent. But, a black car, with a clear view up the street, lurking there in the same place he'd been before? A man like that, not wanting to let his wife go? Sure it was him."

"But there's room for doubt."

Birdy gave her a squinty one-eyed look she must have learned from her cat. "Now *you* have doubts."

"I just wish the case were rock solid. So that if he did it there's no way he could get away with it."

"*If* he did it?"

Vicky shifted her feet uncomfortably. Of course Dennis was guilty. Why couldn't she put his stupid, lying, manipulative phone call out of her mind? Why did she think knowing more about the pictures would make any difference? Even if by some chance he wasn't the one who sent them he was obviously the one who killed her.

"You're right," she said. "I remember from my Philosophy class, Occam's razor saying that the simplest theory should be preferred to the complex."

"A razor said that?"

"Yeah, well. Those old philosophers." Vicky was never sure when Birdy was faking her ignorance. She turned the key in her lock. "See you later."

Birdy frowned, scratched at her eyebrow. "Don't cut yourself shaving."

Vicky had barely gotten inside when she saw a black Camaro pull up in front of her walk. A black car: what if Rachel's killer *had* mistaken Rachel for Vicky because of her jacket? What if he was coming back now to get the right person? What if it was Dennis out on bail and in a different car? What if she had another passionate enemy, maybe just someone she had cursed at in traffic, or some man she had rejected, or some student she had failed—

Student. She laughed. It was Rob. She had completely forgotten about his tutoring session at two. When she met him at the door she was smiling in relief.

The smile Rob returned seemed a bit forced. "Hi," he said. "I hope it's okay. To have a session today? I mean, so soon after, you know, Rachel."

Vicky quickly dropped her smile. She must have seemed callously jolly to the young man. Maybe she shouldn't have agreed to see him so soon, for his sake as well as for her own.

"No, no, it's okay. I guess I was just glad to see it was you driving that black car. It was likely a black car that killed Rachel, and I just had this lurch of fear—"

"But it was her husband, wasn't it?"

"Yes. He has a black car. I just, well, for a moment had this reaction."

"Maybe I better get my car painted." He gave her a somewhat forced smile. "Have they arrested him, the husband?"

Vicky nodded, led Rob inside to the dining-room table, where he set his book bag down, gently. "I was sitting right here when I first saw her," he said, putting his hand on the chair in front of him. "She came up from downstairs and asked if she could make herself a sandwich. I thought she was so beautiful. She was wearing a red cardigan and she had her hair pulled back with some kind of puffy red elastic. It's just so ... so sad."

"Yes, it is."

Rob was looking into the kitchen with such a sudden furrowing of pain on his face that Vicky looked away quickly, pulled her copy of Rob's history textbook towards her, and sat down. After a moment Rob sat down, too.

"Well," she said briskly. "How's it going? Your mid-term is next week, right?"

"Yeah. Short-answer and essay questions." He sighed. "My favourites."

"Is your instructor doing any review, or are you on your own?"

He flicked the zipper on his book bag. "I'm on my own, I guess."

She could have chosen a more cheerful phrase. "Well, let's see your notes for the last month. I can go over them with you." She reached for Rob's notebook, opened it, something she hadn't done before. There were only about four pages of writing. "Is this your second notebook?" she asked, without a great deal of hope.

"That's all I have. I don't take many notes. The guy just lectures from the textbook, so why bother?"

"You should *bother* because writing things down is a great way of learning them. Listening is passive. If you write down as much as you can of what you hear your learning increases by over fifty percent." She had pulled that figure out of the air, but she didn't suppose it mattered.

"It's harder to read my own writing than the text, so what's the point?"

"The point is that the act of writing things down reinforces them in your memory. Even if you never *do* read them over again—"

Rob stood up, abruptly, his knees jarring the table. "I'm not getting anything out of this. I might as well go home." He picked up his notebook, shoved it into his bag, turned and strode to the door.

Vicky stared at him, astonished. She'd said more critical things to him before, and they had slid easily off his back.

Before she could even get to her feet he was out the door. She could see him striding down the walk, almost but not quite running, the book bag bouncing on his shoulder. He started the Camaro with a roar and sped away, the rear wheel spitting a piece of gravel into Birdy's yard.

How could she have miscalculated so badly? Rob was her favourite student, and she had made him run out of her house. Maybe it had something to do with Rachel. He had barely known her, but he was young, and, for the young, death was not a familiar encounter. Or maybe she had been just one more person adding to the pressure of mid-terms.

She poured herself a glass of water, sipped it slowly at her kitchen window. It was starting to rain, an almost invisible mist in the air.

◆

It was Junior on the phone.

"I was just wondering if you wanted me or the folks to come over and pack up Rachel's things for you," he said. "I'm assuming that you don't really want to keep anything. And that it wouldn't be, you know, pleasant for you to have to do it."

"Oh." His offer had caught her off guard. She didn't know whether she should be relieved or offended by it. But Rachel's things *didn't* belong to her. They belonged, she supposed, unless a will surfaced, to Rachel's father. But what would he want with a few armsful of women's clothing, a box of hair curlers and a sewing kit and a mug of pencils? There was the Bible, of course. He would want the Bible.

"I'm sorry," Junior said, responding to her silence. "I didn't mean to sound insensitive. Of course you can keep every-thing—"

"No, no. I don't want it. And it's not mine, anyway. I appreciate your offer. I—yes, do come. Putting it off might only make it more painful."

As she stood at the kitchen window watching for his car, assuming he would park in her driveway off the alley, she told herself firmly that she had been right to tell him to come. Waiting to dispose of Rachel's effects would only make it harder; she could imagine herself becoming the kind of person who clung morbidly to souvenirs.

Junior was at her back door in less than twenty minutes. He looked a little flushed, his face and hair damp from the rain, as though he had run over instead of driven in his father's Mercedes, which stood making small pinging noises in the driveway.

"I didn't pack anything up," Vicky said. "In case the police wanted to have another look. But I guess that's unlikely. Still, maybe you should just check with them before you ... you know, dispose of things. Anyway, there shouldn't be more than a few small boxes and an armful or two of clothes."

"No problem," he said, patting the pockets of his floppy beige trenchcoat. "I brought some big garbage bags."

He must have seen her wince when he said "garbage bags," because he lifted his hands away quickly, rubbed them awkwardly together. They sounded dry, making the same crinkling noise the bags in his pockets had. He kept shifting his weight, as though standing on either leg for more than a few seconds was painful. Rachel had once said there was something a little Duddy Kravitz about him, and Vicky had assumed she meant his aggressively entrepreneurial nature; but maybe Rachel had been thinking less of Richler's book than of the movie, the twitchy performance of Richard Dreyfuss. She had only read up to the M's, after all.

"I appreciate this," Vicky made herself say. "It *would* have been hard for me to do alone."

"No problem. Besides, there was ... There were some things from the office I thought maybe she had at home."

"Just a pencil or two, that sort of thing. Oh, and a Rolodex. The police took that, and a few of her other things."

Junior cleared his throat. "They did, huh? Well, I wasn't implying that she was stealing office supplies—"

"I know."

Vicky led him down the basement stairs. She stopped in front of the door to Rachel's room. Rachel's room: but it wasn't any longer, was it, it was just her own spare bedroom and storage room again. She opened the door, gestured Junior inside.

"I'll get a box for the bathroom things," Vicky said. "And for anything that might break or spill. The clothes can go in the ... bags."

When she came back with the box, Junior had already emptied most of the dresser drawers into a big green bag, the heavy plastic kind used for garden clippings. She should be the one doing that, Vicky thought, watching him scoop up Rachel's underclothes, the pairs of socks Vicky had helped her pick out.

She cleared everything except the hot plate and the Bible from the top of the dresser, put them into the box. The hot plate was hers; and the Bible ... She felt a need to keep it, in case she might want it to pacify Jacob Cornelius. If Junior saw her slide it into the open top drawer he didn't say anything.

When he picked up the alarm clock and the books on the bedside table, Vicky said, "No, wait. The books are mine."

Junior didn't answer, just set them back down. *Under the Volcano. Sons and Lovers. A Jest of God.* Had Rachel had time to finish them all? There was a picture of Joanne Woodward on the cover of *A Jest of God*. From the movie *Rachel, Rachel.* Vicky hadn't remembered until now what the protagonist's name was. When Rachel had talked about the book she'd not mentioned it.

There were only the clothes hanging in the closet now, and Vicky left them for Junior as she cleaned out the bathroom. There was so little—that was all she could think of, how little there was, as she picked up the shampoo bottle, the hairbrush, the unopened soaps. The medicine cabinet had only a bottle of Aspirins, a water glass, toothbrush and toothpaste, dental floss, deodorant, a nail file, a small cosmetics bag. There would have been less to clear out of a hotel room.

She turned back to the bedroom, but stopped abruptly at the door.

Junior was standing in front of the closet, holding the last of Rachel's outfits, a white dress, and he was pressing it to his face. He heard Vicky at the door, and he turned but didn't lower the dress. Tears were running down his cheeks.

"I'm sorry," Vicky said.

"I miss her," Junior said, his first words since he'd entered the room. He lowered the dress. "I think I was falling in love with her." He laughed, a dull, raspy sound.

"She was easy to love," Vicky said.

"She was ten years older than I was, but, still. I could talk to her about things. She knew how hard it was for me, working for my father. I mean, sometimes I'm his son, sometimes I'm his employee, sometimes I'm just his whipping-boy. I could *talk* to Rachel about it. And about having to move back home again. About my ex-wife. Tina never wanted to be married to me. She just wanted me long enough to have a kid. To have somebody to pay her support."

"I didn't know you had a child."

"I hardly ever see him. I have to pay all this money, I had to give her the house, everything, and what I get is a kid who looks at me like I'm some stranger." He let the dress fall slowly through his fingers, into the open bag. "Life is so full of shit." He tied a knot into the top of the bag, hard, the plastic straining. "Well." He straightened, pulling his shoulders back, seeming to grow several inches taller. "There's no point dwelling on it. Is there anything else? I assume the bedding is yours?" His voice was suddenly brusque, businesslike, pushing her away from what he had just told her.

Vicky nodded. "I guess that's all. Did you find the things from the office you were looking for?"

Junior picked up the bag, hefted it in front of him. "It was nothing. Nothing important."

He started for the door, and Vicky had to back quickly out of the way. He was at the top of the stairs before she could even pick up her box and follow him. She set the box on the kitchen counter and locked the flaps, having to do it several times before she got the sequence right. It seemed important they be closed.

Junior had the trunk of the Mercedes open, waiting for

her. He was tapping his hand on the fender, shifting from one foot to the other, apparently suddenly consumed by urgency. He put the box into the trunk, slammed the lid, rubbed his hands together the way he had when he first came to the door. Vicky had to tell herself not to be annoyed, that it was just his way of handling things, not much different from what Rob had done earlier today, maybe, trying to outrun the memories, ashamed that someone had seen.

"Thanks, Vicky. I know this has been hard on you, too. You take care, now."

"I will."

She turned quickly and walked away, making it easier for him. By the time she got inside he was gone. She peeled herself an orange as she leaned over the kitchen sink and looked out at her forsythia bush, which was already starting to unwrap its frilly yellow blossoms. But she couldn't stop thinking about the big green bag and the box in Junior's trunk. She wondered what he would do with them, finally. It seemed equally likely that he would take them home and treasure them and that he would drop them off without a second thought at the Sally Ann.

She ran a bath, making the water as hot as she could stand, until the room was foggy with steam. She lay in the tub for a long time with her eyes closed. The grape ivy she had hung by the window had thrived on the light and humidity, and now it had nudged a tendril behind the shower curtain and seemed intent on anchoring itself on the grout at the lip of the tub. "You should give that plant a haircut," Rachel had said. Vicky coiled the soft end of the stem around her finger, let it uncurl against her neck.

At last she got up and got dressed and made herself a half-hearted stir-fry of left-over potatoes and peas and cauliflower. She put on an old Beatles tape, turned it up loud, but it only made her feel lonelier.

She should have kept something, something besides the Bible: the comb, the sewing kit, anything.

She *did* have something, she remembered. Something that maybe she should have given Junior, too, since it was on the pretence of giving it to the family that she had gotten it from Clark.

She took the envelope of photographs from her purse and spread them out, in order, on the dining-room table. The first one had come in the album and was of Rachel as a baby, on a cushion. The second had come in the first of the Persian kitten cards and was of Rachel about eight, in front of her parents' old house in Bellingham, Washington. The third was of her at about eleven, sitting on a piece of driftwood feeding two seagulls. The fourth was of Rachel about fifteen, in a red dress, beside a Christmas tree.

The fifth, the frightening fifth, arriving inside the Munch card, with the question *Don't you know what he did?*—it was of the staff of the Hammond Christian School for Girls. The circle around the face of the man in the back did not for some reason show up on the copy, but Vicky could still see it. Angeletti. A nice, ordinary face, with a nice, ordinary smile. Dead now, apparently. Did that mean, as Clark had implied, that whatever had happened back then no longer mattered? It must have mattered to Dennis. Or to whoever sent the pictures.

The sixth picture, arriving in a kittens card again, was the one Rachel hadn't remembered clearly, hadn't remembered being taken. She was about seventeen, standing again in front of her parents' stucco house in Bellingham. And then the last picture, the one that arrived on Valentine's Day, the one that Rachel never got to see: her sitting on Vicky's front step looking to the west and Vicky herself in the window, a dim grey shape. The picture gave her a chill even now. Her eyes went to the right edge of the picture, trying to imagine the camera, the eye behind it lining them up across Birdy's lawn, across the low boxwood hedge.

"It *was* you, Dennis, wasn't it? Why can't you admit it?"

The cat jumped onto the chair Rachel had usually sat in and lifted his head over the edge of the table, looking solemnly at the pictures.

"It was just Dennis, wasn't it?" she demanded of him.

He reached a paw up, batted a pencil onto the floor.

She sighed. "That's your answer to everything."

She just wouldn't let herself have the dream again. It was Rachel's dream, and Rachel was dead. Angeletti was dead. Their stories were finished. If she didn't have the dream tonight, she bargained with herself, she would send the pictures to Jacob Cornelius. And if she did have the dream ...

If she did, she would get Amanda to drive down to Washington State with her and see if she could find anyone who knew what had really happened to Rachel at the Hammond Christian School for Girls.

CHAPTER NINE

"S O—HOW ABOUT IT? I'll buy you lunch."

"Okay. I haven't been to the States in ages. Will I have to pack a gun?"

"They provide them at the border." Vicky put her foot under the cat and hoisted him away from the phone cord he had started to chew.

"I'm busy Saturday morning," Amanda said. "How about the afternoon?"

"I'm having my hair cut then. For my big date."

"You're getting your *hair* done? To go out with Superman? Like, why bother? Flying will just tousle you up."

"Ha, ha." Vicky was getting tired of the Superman jokes.

"I could still cut your hair, you know. I used to do a good job."

"You charge too much."

Amanda laughed. It was easy for them to banter about money since Amanda was working full-time now and Vicky had the money from Conrad's life insurance and car accident settlement. Not long ago neither of them could be sure of making it through the month.

"Well, how about Sunday?" Amanda asked. "You can dish me the dirt about Saturday."

"Sunday's fine."

"What movie are you going to?"

"He asked if I'd seen *The People vs. Larry Flynt*. It's showing at a film festival somewhere."

"Not exactly a romantic choice."

"Well, I suppose it will give us something to talk about after. I just have to hope his reason for wanting to go isn't that *Hustler* was his favourite magazine."

"Why don't you just rent the video?"

"It's a *date*. You go *out* on a date."

"All right, all right. Well, wear your jade earrings. If he gets obnoxious you can tell him they're kryptonite."

By the time Saturday arrived, Vicky was grim with dread. Why had she agreed to go out with the man? All they had in common was Rachel's death. That should make her avoid seeing him, not encourage it. She was almost glad when the woman who cut her hair that afternoon clipped the bangs too short, making them want to stick out straight, as though she had her hand on an electrostatic generator.

All the same, she was ready far too early, and, even though she had changed outfits twice, she still felt overdressed in her black leggings and loose tunic top. She kicked off her black pumps and put on her old crepe-soled loafers.

She phoned Rob again, but there was still no answer, not even a machine. She couldn't put out of her mind the way he had just walked out on her: something still needed to be settled between them. But perhaps he simply found their sessions no longer useful. Rob had been an unexpected bonus for her, anyway, as a college student, when her specialty was high school.

But with Lois gone, and now Rob, she was down to only Travis, Kristin, Ajit, and Dulci. Travis, her amiable jock, was sure to stay at least until the end of term, especially if she kept feeding him; and Ajit's father had signed a contract with her also until the end of term. But she had let Kristin and Dulci have a more casual arrangement, and she wasn't sure that either of them would stick with it through June. Kristin seemed to be losing interest daily in her studies, and Vicky wondered if she would even stay in school much longer.

She would have to put new ads up in the schools, Vicky

decided, pulling, annoyed, at the bra she had decided she'd better wear tonight. But it shouldn't be hard to get new clients. The stigma of having a tutor was gone. Amanda said it was her better students who had them, that it was "cool" now. Besides, with the panic of finals approaching, it would be a good time to scare up more business.

The doorbell. She glanced out her front window, saw Clark's silver Taurus on the street. The sun was making prismatic sparkles on the trunk, and Vicky realized they were reflecting from beads of water, the look of a car that had just gone through a carwash. Oh, dear, she thought. What have I done?

◆

Vicky waited until they were back in the car before she asked, casually, "Well, how did you like the movie?" At least he hadn't expected her to stay for the next feature, *Private Parts*. Larry Flynt and Howard Stern on the same night would have seriously challenged her gag reflex. The film festival was called, "Freedom of Speech: The Film," so she supposed Clark might be expecting from her a civil libertarianism she didn't exactly feel at the moment.

Clark turned onto Burrard, headed for the bridge. He took so long answering that Vicky thought he must not be intending to. Finally he said, "Well, it was hard not to appreciate it as entertainment. And I admit I enjoyed seeing Falwell treated like a reactionary hypocrite."

"But?" Vicky practically had to sit on her hands to keep them from gesturing her way into the conversation. She had vowed to elicit as much from him as she could before launching into any lectures. Maybe she could even restrain herself from mentioning her MA in film studies.

"But ..." He braked for the light at Broadway. A pop can rolled out from under Vicky's seat; she put her foot on it. The floor of the car, she'd noticed, seemed not only to have been tidied, but vacuumed.

He waited until the light changed before he continued. "I can't say I like seeing a scumbag like Flynt treated like some hero."

Vicky blinked.

"And, okay, I know as a movie it's allowed some liberties with the truth, but still." Clark shifted in his seat, repositioned his hands higher up on the wheel. "The movie gives us this guy Americans are supposed to be grateful to because, since he refused to give up, they live in a freer country today. But that's just not how it was. The real court case didn't extend any First Amendment protections, it just preserved what already existed. An earlier case against *The New York Times* set the precedent. All the Flynt case did was confirm that Falwell couldn't win on an 'emotional distress' libel claim. Big deal."

"I didn't know all that."

"And its take on free-speech issues is pretty one-sided. It makes this simple-minded point that pornography is harmless fun and that people who want to suppress it are more dangerous than those who produce it. Well, it's just not that simple."

They were on the Oak Street Bridge now, where the freeway began. The car seemed to develop a shimmy at higher speeds. Vicky realized she had flattened the pop can she had been rolling under her foot, and she eased it back under the seat.

"I agree," she said. "Opposition to *Hustler* came from a lot of good people, not just the religious right." Should she mention the F word? What the hell. Things were looking good so far. "Feminists like Steinem spoke out about how viciously misogynistic the magazine was. And racist. And homophobic."

"If it were up to me I'd pile all those damned magazines up and put a match to them."

Oh oh. "But," Vicky said carefully, "it's always the wrong magazines that get burned."

"Is it?" His voice took on an edge. "Maybe if you saw the kind of stuff we find in the apartments of guys who've just tortured or killed some poor kid you'd think differently."

"I imagine I would—"

"We find the worst. The absolute puking worst. We found it in Mandaro's house."

"Dennis?" She stared at him.

"Sorry." Clark ran his hand down the steering wheel, back again, as though he wanted to rub the words away. "I shouldn't have told you that."

Vicky wondered whether it was to spare her feelings or because he had said too much to a civilian. "Were the pictures ... of Rachel?"

He glanced at her, didn't answer for a moment. "No," he said. But maybe he was just giving her the answer he thought she wanted.

They rode in silence for a while, through the tunnel and on into the suburb of Delta. The traffic was heavy, dense clots of it that once meant a ferry had just come in from Vancouver Island but that now meant only that the lower mainland had too many cars.

"I had to go to this conference once," Clark said finally, flicking on the wipers as a misty rain began to fall. "This young civil-liberties lawyer talking to us cops, and he said, 'You'd be surprised at the raunchy stuff I've seen.' Raunchy! I mean, we all guffawed. Raunchy!"

"That's the problem, I suppose. The public has to keep believing it's just dirty pictures versus religious moralists."

"They don't *have* to. They *prefer* to. What nice intelligent person wants to support repression when they can support free speech?"

"We don't really have free speech in this country, anyway," Vicky said.

"Exactly."

Vicky wasn't sure how much farther she wanted to take the conversation. Maybe they should quit while they were still agreeing.

"How about a coffee?" she asked. "I've a coupon for a pair of cappuccinos at Starbucks." She checked her purse, as though she really needed to, as though she hadn't made sure to take the coupons before they left. In case, she had told herself. In case she didn't want to invite him in but was interested enough to want to extend the evening.

Clark glanced at his watch, pushed a button to illuminate the dial. "Okay," he said. "A quick one. I pull some early duty time tomorrow."

Vicky smiled. Maybe he had given himself a way out, too.

They went to the Starbucks in White Rock because it was the only one they were both sure they could find. Vicky wanted to say something glib about how if they got into a fight she could walk home from there, but she supposed Clark would just give her a neutral look and say he wouldn't advise it this late at night.

The place wasn't crowded but it was noisy and uncomfortable, and she had the feeling they were the oldest people the waiter had ever served. They sipped at their scalding coffees, probably faster than necessary.

"How did you come to know so much about the Flynt trial?" Vicky asked.

"I was down in the States when it happened. Studying law."

"Law? So how did you wind up here?"

Clark shrugged. "I guess I couldn't, finally, see myself as a lawyer. I'd been a cop too long. Besides, it had been more my wife's idea."

Oh, great. The wife. Well, she had better ask now while he gave her a chance. "You're divorced?"

He made her wait, looking into his cup. "She died. Cancer."

"Oh. I'm sorry."

"It was a long time ago. I've gotten used to it."

"My husband died, too. I'm still getting used to it."

He nodded, expressing no surprise. Vicky wondered if he had checked her out. She was sure there were things about her in police files.

"It gets easier," he said.

She shouldn't have mentioned Conrad. She could feel, suddenly, unexpectedly, her throat constricting, tears forming in her eyes. Clark, fortunately, was still looking into his coffee cup, his fingers turning the spoon beside it around and around.

"Do you want to go?" he asked.

How had he known? Maybe his work prepared him for those subtle changes in voice, in posture.

"Maybe we should."

They rode in silence, Vicky needing only at the last minute to direct him down the right street. They didn't go past the spot where Rachel was killed, and she wondered if he had made a point of avoiding it.

They sat in the car, Vicky's hand on the door handle. If she pulled it, the dome light would illuminate them both, and she had a sudden reluctance to cause that to happen.

"Well," she said. "Thanks for the movie."

"You're welcome."

She opened the door. The light seemed to disconcert him as much as her. "Goodnight, then."

"You want to do this again? Go out?" His voice had made it sound as though he were inviting her to a funeral. "It's all right. If you don't want to."

"No, it's— I mean, okay. Okay, why not?"

Did he smile? She guessed he meant it to be a smile. Asymmetrical, but a smile. She returned it, wondering if hers looked as ambiguous and somehow unenthusiastic as his.

When she got inside, she let herself drop onto the sofa. The evening hadn't gone badly, really, but there was a stiffness between them that hadn't seemed to ease. And the way she almost began to cry: what was that about? It had been a long time since she had felt like that, felt so suddenly overwhelmed by Conrad's loss. Maybe it had to do with Rachel, too. Too much death.

The cat jumped up on her chest, began kneading at her. "Your turn next," Vicky said. "You're no spring chicken."

She noticed the light on the answering machine blinking. She pushed rewind. Rob's voice.

"I'm sorry about the way I rushed out the other day. I just, I was upset about something else. My girlfriend and I had a big argument the day before and it was, I was, well, I hope you aren't mad at me. I'd still like to have some more sessions with you. Maybe after mid-terms. Let me know if that's okay."

Vicky smiled, relieved. Maybe Rob had been a small part of what she'd almost started crying about, too: another loss, another failure. She dialled his number, left a message with the man who answered for Rob to call her as soon as he wanted to meet.

◆

"So how was the date?" Amanda asked, as they waited in line at the border crossing.

"Okay, I guess. His take on the movie was better than I thought it would be, although we might have gotten into some arguments about censorship if we'd pursued it."

"Since he chose the movie, did you at least let him pay?"

"We went Dutch. Except for the coffees after. I got those."

"Tsk. You've undermined his manhood, my dear."

"I thought you paid for everything on *your* last date."

"I had no choice. I swear, the guy was so tight I could

have shoved a grain of sand up his ass and pulled out a pearl the next day."

Vicky laughed. "That doesn't sound like a bad investment."

"Huh. You didn't see his ass." Amanda stretched her arms up over her head, pressed her palms against the car roof. "So. You going to see your policeman again?"

"He asked if he could call. I'm not sure if he meant it."

Vicky pulled ahead to the booth, assured the customs officer they were travelling for pleasure, not business, stopping herself from adding, well, not that you could call this pleasure, exactly.... The man waved them on, his eyes already on the next car.

Vicky turned onto the I5, headed for Bellingham. Amanda pointed to a sign at the side of the road that said Drive With Car, someone having carefully removed the "e." They laughed, and Vicky said it reminded her of the huge sign they'd seen once near Chilliwack saying Prepare To Meet Thy Cod, someone having coloured perfectly over the loop in the "G." Amanda had said it must be a Newfie joke.

"Anyway. Give me details. What's Mr. Kent like?" Amanda kicked off her shoes, propped her feet up on the dash.

"Well, I wouldn't call him shy, but he's ... serious."

"So, did you at least have serious sex?"

"Oh, please."

Amanda sighed. "If you just want a *friend*, you've already got *me*."

"It might be nice to have a friend with a penis, even if I don't use it."

"A penis *and* a gun," Amanda sniffed. "What more could a girl want?"

"She could want you to keep your eyes on the map. Which exit do I take?"

Amanda picked up the map, which she had not so much refolded as wadded up around the Bellingham inset. "Hmm," she said. "To quote Yogi Berra, 'We're lost but we're making good time.'" She ran her finger along the I5. "Okay. Look for anything saying Lake Whatcom. A promising name."

Vicky had found the address for the church on, of all places, its Internet home page. It was a big organization, apparently, with over a hundred congregations. The one closest to the former school was on Lake Way Road, and although she'd thought about phoning first she had a vague feeling that it was better not to. Besides, since it was Sunday she might actually find someone around. As they turned onto Lake Way Road, a strong wind came up; she could feel it jostling the car. A grey seagull ahead of her was flapping its wings industriously and still moving backwards.

They found the church easily, just a few miles from the freeway. Free Christian Alliance Church, said the large wooden sign in attractive calligraphy on the tidy front lawn. The building wasn't in the mega-church category, but neither was it the little brown church in the vale. It looked to be fairly new, designed by an architect, with a concave roof that soared in one corner into a spire. It didn't quite escape the look of a skateboard ramp. On the ground floor the building seemed to house a windowless auditorium on one wing and on the other about a dozen smaller areas that might have been classrooms. The whole building was painted a vehement white, although it was the huge copper cross on the front door that drew the eye.

"Ah, gee," said Amanda. "Do I have to go in?"

"*Yes.*" Vicky gave her a fierce look.

Amanda opened her door. "You owe me."

They could hear the sound of an organ, but there were only three cars in the parking lot so it was unlikely a service was in progress. The wind wrapped their skirts around their legs as they walked. They had both worn skirts and long-sleeved, loose blouses, the kind of clothes they hoped would make them inconspicuous in a church. Amanda took her arm, and Vicky realized Amanda's nervousness might even exceed her own. Amanda's parents had been devout atheists, and it was possible they had told her stories about Christians as chilling as those Christians told of atheists. Vicky herself had been baptized in the United Church, mostly to appease the small rural community in which she was born, but beyond that she and her family had had few occasions to enter a church. "Missionaries," her mother had said angrily. "They came at us with those Bibles like soldiers with guns."

Vicky thought of the Bible lying downstairs in her house, Rachel's Bible, and then of Rachel's father, and how it hadn't been only First Nations people who had been fired upon with words from that book.

"I keep thinking something is going to jump out at me," Amanda said. "Something snarling, with lots of teeth."

Vicky smiled, trying not to show too many teeth. "They should put a Beware of God sign on the lawn," she said. "Dog. God. You know. Dyslexic humour."

Amanda gave her a look.

The cross on the front door wobbled slightly at the top, a loosening screw, as Vicky pulled the door open.

"Now I know how Dracula felt," Amanda muttered, keeping an eye on the cross.

Inside was a dimly lit lobby with a built-in desk on which sat something that might have been a guest book and piles of brochures with rubber bands around them. A stack of folding chairs leaned against one wall, and opposite them three large ministerial-looking leather armchairs faced a table the size of a trivet. The walls had framed pictures of religious art and of four stern-looking men who were likely church leaders. A bulletin board held notices of prayer groups and conferences, exhortations from charities and from letter-writing campaigners, and a photograph of a pale teenage girl taped onto a page that asked, in large black type, "Have you seen Sarah?"

The sound of the organ was coming from the auditorium wing. It was clearly someone practising, fumbling to a stop at the same place, then trying again. Vicky gestured in that direction, down a hallway to the right, and Amanda nodded. Overhead the wind was pulling at the roof, making the nails creak and moan. Something blew past the window—a bird, a piece of paper, a roof tile—it was hard to tell.

"Are we trespassing?" Amanda asked. "It feels like we're trespassing."

"No. Of course we're not," Vicky said, suppressing her own feeling that they were doing exactly that.

The lights flickered.

"Now I *am* scared," Amanda whispered.

"Prepare To Meet Thy Cod," Vicky whispered back.

Suddenly, from down another hallway, a woman appeared, holding an armful of daffodils, and came towards them.

"Oh oh," Amanda said. "We're gonna get it now."

"Shhh. She's smiling. Be nice."

The woman went to the desk in the lobby, dropped the flowers onto it. "Hello," she said, "Welcome. I'm Bitsy." Bitsy? "Aren't these lovely? They're the first from our greenhouse." She picked a daffodil up, smiled at it.

"They *are* lovely," Vicky said. At least the first thing she said didn't have to be a lie.

"Our service isn't for another two hours. Can I help you with anything?" The woman was in her sixties, her hair grey and stylishly done; she had a round, ruddy face and metal-framed glasses that took elaborate zigzags along the temples. The most surprising thing about her, however, was her lime-green jogging suit, which, except for the colour, was the kind of thing Vicky usually wore herself.

Vicky returned her smile, walked up to the desk. "I'm Vicky. And this is my friend Amanda. I was wondering if you could help me with some research I'm doing back in Canada about the Hammond Christian School for Girls. I understand it was run by your church?"

"That's right." The woman's smile went a little stiffer.

"I was sorry to see it was closed," Vicky said, feeling her own smile pull askew.

"We all were," said Bitsy, her face warming up again. "Why, we had girls there from all over North America. But the need seemed to diminish. Perhaps it was for the best."

Vicky pulled the photograph from her purse, handed it to the woman. "I was just wondering if you remembered any of the people from this picture. Mr. Angeletti, for instance—"

"Why, wherever did you get this?" Bitsy exclaimed.

"Someone sent it to me. I guess they heard I was researching the school's history."

"Why, isn't that the funniest thing!" Bitsy pointed at the photographs of the four clerical-looking men. "We had this same photograph—well, not this *one*, I guess, another copy of it—up on the wall there once. I wonder where it got to."

"What a coincidence," Vicky said. Her heart began to beat faster. "Did you know any of these people?" She gestured at the faces. "Of course it was a long time ago," she added with what she hoped was enough dubiousness to challenge the woman.

"Why, I knew them all!" Bitsy exclaimed. "That's Mary Oldham" —she pointed at the first woman on the left in the front row— "and that's Rebecca Butler, Rebecca Windham now, she has such a lovely set of twins, and there's Jane, oh, dear sweet Jane, God bless her, dead from a heart attack just two years ago. And Beth, I don't know what happened to her, and Ruth, oh my, Ruth, she had such a temper, and *that*" —she pointed at one of the two woman standing in the back, between Angeletti and the other man— "why, that's me! Oh, it *was* a long time ago. Twenty years! I'd hardly know myself. Bitsy Stuart, I was then."

Vicky was forcing herself to breathe.

Bitsy gently touched her own face in the photograph, the way Rachel had done. Amanda had come up now beside Vicky, was looking over her shoulder.

"Twenty years ago," Vicky said, encouragingly. "Was it really that long?"

"And more! But sometimes it seems like just yesterday!"

The overhead lights flickered again, then went out. They all three looked up, as though someone on the roof had called to them. Oddly, the room seemed no dimmer without the lights, although it was quieter, possibly because one of the lights had been buzzing.

"Oh, dear," said Bitsy. "The power. I do hope it comes back on before the service."

"I'm sure it will," Vicky said. She pointed again at the photograph, hoping she hadn't lost Bitsy. "Do you remember the two men?"

"Why, I guess *so*! Mark Angeletti, how could I forget him, such a serious, devoted man, and *this* man" —she pointed to the other figure— "why, I had better remember him! I married him, after all!" She gave the kind of girlish laugh a woman called Bitsy might be expected to give.

"Really? Well, you're certainly the right person to ask about all this."

"If you really want all the history, you should talk to my husband. Why, Philip was the one who set up the school!"

Vicky tried not to show her dismay at the prospect of being turned over to the man who stood so grimly in the back row. She could almost guarantee that Bitsy was the more useful and willing source.

"Your husband set it up!" Vicky exclaimed ingenuously. "I thought for some reason it was Mr. Angeletti."

"Oh, good heavens no. Dr. Angeletti had nothing to do with setting up the school."

"Doctor? A doctor of divinity?"

"Oh, no. A *doctor*. A medical doctor."

"But he taught at the school?"

"Oh, no. He was a member of the church. He would just come to deliver the babies."

Vicky simply stared at her. It was Amanda who finally had to ask, "Babies?"

"Why, of course. We promised the parents the girls would get the best of care, and that we had our very own doctor. There weren't many girls who had to go to the hospital. And with Beth being a nurse and all, why, we handled it all at the school."

"How many of the girls were pregnant?" It was Amanda, again, who had to ask. Vicky seemed unable to understand what she had heard. There was a thin, disorienting buzz in her ears, as though the defective light had come back on.

Bitsy looked puzzled. "Why, all of them, of course."

"So it wasn't just a home for unwed mothers," Amanda said, recovering. "It was a school, too?"

"Why, certainly! We made sure all the girls continued their schooling. The church oversaw it, of course, and we adapted the curriculum, but, oh, yes, we made sure the girls kept up with their studies. The babies were adopted into good loving homes, in the church, whenever possible, and when the girls went home they fit right back into their regular classes. We were very progressive."

Amanda nodded. "Indeed."

Bitsy lowered her voice slightly, glanced down the hall that led to the auditorium. Whoever had been practising the organ had stopped five minutes ago. "Now, I don't mind saying there were those in the church, and in the school, who thought the girls weren't being punished enough for what they'd done. Even Dr. Angeletti, God bless him, thought that. On principle he never allowed them painkillers, or anesthetic, the poor things, no matter how much they screamed. It broke my heart, frankly, hearing them, but it's in the Bible, after all. 'In sorrow shall you bring forth children.'"

Amanda smiled sickly. Vicky knew she had better not trust her to ask any more questions.

She made herself look at Bitsy, sigh, and say, "It *is* our punishment, I suppose, much as we'd wish it otherwise." She took a deep breath. "Do you think Dr. Angeletti might have, well, tried to make sure, that is, to help some of these girls, so that they wouldn't need to come back to the school? Maybe by performing another operation, as some doctors do after a birth...."

"Another operation?" Bitsy's face stiffened again, her eyes going wide.

"A tubal ligation, perhaps, to prevent them from getting into trouble again—"

Bitsy's face had gone pale. She gripped the edges of the desk. "Oh, no," she exclaimed. "He wouldn't have done that! Why, that's just, well, God wouldn't, well, I don't know what to say—" She glanced down the hall, less in apparent unease this time than in entreaty. "You have to speak to my husband."

The lights above suddenly came on again; the whole building seemed to give a shudder and begin to hum.

"There we are!" Vicky said. "And just in time." She glanced at her watch. "I'd love to meet your husband. But right now I've got to get to my appointment with Reverend Wright in Seattle. I'm sure you know how he doesn't like to be kept waiting!" Vicky gave a brisk little laugh, pulled the photograph from Bitsy's fingers, which made no effort to resist her.

"Why, no, but ... There's Philip now!" She gestured urgently at someone down the hall.

Vicky backed to the door, which Amanda was already holding open for her. "What a shame that we have to run. Thank you so much, Bitsy. I'll look forward to meeting your husband the next time."

She was out the door; Amanda let the wind slam it shut behind them, the huge cross shivering from the impact. The wind seemed stronger than ever, hurling a gust of dirt and sand at them.

"Reverend Wright?" Amanda said. "He related to Reverend Wrong?"

"Shut up and keep walking."

"If I look back will I turn into a pillar of the community?"

They reached the car; no one from the church seemed to be rushing after them.

"I can see the ghost of another dyslexic lawn sign," Amanda said. "Prepare To Meet Thy Doc."

"Shut up and get in."

Vicky had to try twice before she could get the car started.

"Well," Amanda said. "Wasn't that interesting?"

Vicky shook her head, turned back onto Lake Way Road. "I can't believe it. Rachel was there because she was *pregnant*? She had a *child* here? Could she really not have remembered?"

"It's pretty unlikely. But people *can* repress horrible memories, especially childhood ones. Or it's possible that she just didn't want you to know."

Vicky turned back onto the 15. "But she wouldn't have faked those nightmares, surely she wouldn't have, about somebody with his face covered raping her, others holding her down. And she knew it was Angeletti the moment she heard his name. She must have been on the verge of remembering. And what she would have remembered, apparently, was that the mask covering the man's face was a surgical mask, and that it wasn't a rape but a birth."

"It sounds so incredible. That she could make herself forget having had a *child*."

"But it makes sense, doesn't it? Do you have a better explanation?"

"Maybe it was just the birth she was repressing, not the

whole pregnancy," Amanda said. "That would make more sense. The birth must have been terrifying for her. Angeletti sounds like such a sadist. Too bad he's dead. I'd have liked to have punched him somewhere personal." Amanda leaned over, glanced at the speedometer. "Hey. Slow down, kid."

"Sorry." Vicky eased off the gas pedal. She must have been trying to press her foot down on Angeletti's neck. "Oh. Lunch. I promised you lunch. Where do you want to go?"

"How about the Semiahmoo Inn? You know, the one you can see from White Rock, out on the spit. Or is it too pricey?"

"We can go see. At least we shouldn't violate any dress codes."

Amanda pointed at the map. "Take the next exit."

"I know how to get there. I drove down most of the way with Rachel a couple of weeks ago. It's past where the school was."

She turned onto Drayton Harbour Road. They could see White Rock on the right, across the bay frothy with white-caps. The tide was in, and the wind was flicking a thin salty spray onto the windshield. Vicky turned on the wipers, which the wind seemed to want to rip free as they stuttered across the glass.

"There's the school." She pointed ahead to the right.

"Pacific Chiropractic Clinic," Amanda read, as they passed it. "I can see haunted, imploring faces in the attic windows."

"Don't even joke about it," Vicky said. A branch, possibly torn from one of the two arbutus trees on the clinic grounds, skittered in front of the car.

They turned onto a wide, tree-lined road, glimpsing golf courses and gated condominium communities through the woods, and then they were on the narrow spit, with only a few yards of low dunes separating them from the ocean on either side, that led to the resort. The wind was tossing so much water at them across the road that Vicky had to turn the wipers to a faster speed. The ocean was grey with roiling sand.

"'The unplumbed, salt, estranging sea,'" Amanda said. "I had a prof once who declared that was the only perfect line in English poetry."

"Mmm," Vicky said. Her mind wasn't on poetry.

At the resort, which turned out to be less elegant than they had feared, the only place they could find that served food was a bar called The Packers Lounge, named for the salmon-canning plant that had once occupied the site. Parts of the original building had been integrated into the new structure. The room was high-ceilinged, with dark mahogany and nautical artifacts, and it offered an impressive view of White Rock and the north shore mountains, buffed to a gleaming white today by the wind that had driven the yellow haze from the Washington refineries and Vancouver Island pulp mills farther on into the Fraser Valley. A few years ago Vicky had spent several weekends with Conrad going door to door collecting signatures on a petition protesting the sulphur-dioxide and nitrogen-oxide emissions, but of course nothing had changed. Except herself. She became more pessimistic, more cynical. Maybe, in a small way, Rachel had begun to undo that, had begun to make her feel some things could turn out right after all.

They both ordered the Seafood Sampler, and sipped coffee as they waited. Vicky could feel a headache starting in her temples, two small beating pulses that she knew was the adrenaline pulling back, saying, it's over now, you should rest. But it wasn't over. She had unearthed more questions about Rachel than she had answered.

"Why did you ask our friend Bitsy about a tubal ligation?" Amanda asked.

"I was just stumbling around trying to find an explanation for why Rachel would be infertile *now*, but not *then*. She had endometriosis, she'd had it since her early teens. It would have blocked and damaged her Fallopian tubes. But now I find out she *did* have a child."

"Well, the disease mightn't have been as bad then. And you can have endometriosis and still have children. Like my niece. In fact, there are still bloody doctors out there telling women that having a kid will cure them. Of course it won't."

Vicky looked out the window, at where her house was on the hillside across the water. "I wonder who the father was."

"No one at the church would ever tell you that."

Vicky kept looking out the window. In the water stood about a dozen old wooden pilings, remnants of the fish cannery, reminding her of Steveston.

"No one at the *church*," she said.

CHAPTER TEN

*I*T HAD BEEN a long hour. Vicky wondered why Kristin had even bothered to come. She had sat slumped lethargically at the table, answering Vicky in monosyllables if at all. Occasionally she would bat a pencil listlessly back and forth between her hands, but the cat would have done it with more apparent intelligence. Perhaps she had taken some drug. Or forgotten to.

Vicky glanced at the kitchen clock. Four-thirty. She wished she had kept her afternoon free, but the weekends were the best times for seeing students. And of course she could not have anticipated how distracting this morning in Bellingham would be. Maybe it was just as well that she was busy.

"The last couplet, at least," Vicky said. "If you can understand that you can usually get a good idea of what the rest of the sonnet is suggesting."

"I suppose."

Vicky waited, but Kristin offered nothing more.

"'For thy sweet love remembered such wealth brings/That then I scorn to change my state with kings.' That's pretty straightforward, isn't it?"

Kristin ran her finger along the fake wood grain in the Formica tabletop. "Not really."

Vicky sighed, tried not to lose her temper. Kristin's obtuseness today seemed entirely willful. "Being in love makes the poet feel happy, rich, as rich as a king. Right? You're a smart kid. You can see that. Try the next poem: 'This thou perceiv'st, which makes thy love more strong,/To love that well which thou must leave ere long.' Come on. Tell me what it means."

"Love and death. Everything's about love and death."

Finally. "Great! Love and death. Exactly. How does the poet connect them here?"

Kristin pulled herself up straighter, just a little, but it was the most she had moved in the last half hour. "I suppose he's saying that love doesn't last. We should love what we have because it will die soon."

"There you go! The rest of the sonnet builds—"

"Everything's about dying!" Kristin burst out. "What's the point of reading all this stuff about dying?"

"Questions about death are ones poets like to ask."

"Fine. Let them ask. But they shouldn't expect *me* to care."

Vicky pulled her lips into a thin line, an expression she supposed looked ambiguous. At their next session, she promised herself, she would have it out with Kristin. They were wasting each other's time, and Kristin was on the wide and welcoming road towards wasting her whole life.

The doorbell went. It would be Ajit, a few minutes early. Just as well.

"Next Sunday at the same time?" she asked Kristin.

"Whatever."

Whatever. It had become a word Vicky particularly loathed. One is not proud of oneself for having shrugged so much: it was something Vicky had read once, and she felt like repeating it now to Kristin. Who would probably shrug and say, "Whatever."

Kristin gathered up her books and slid her arms into the jacket she had shucked off on the back of her chair.

"Good luck on your quiz Wednesday." Don't forget to bring your brain, Vicky felt like adding.

"Can I go out the back door?"

"Sure. Why?"

"I don't feel like seeing anybody. Like, I just feel so, you know, ugly."

The cruelties of adolescence, giving women both lovely new bodies and the belief they were ugly. She was already softening the lecture she'd give Kristin next Sunday.

"You're not ugly," she said briskly. "You're beautiful." Besides, Ajit wouldn't care, she almost said. Especially if your family is rich.

Ashamed of the unkind thought, she was especially welcoming to Ajit. But even his enemies would have found it hard to resist his charm. Today he was wearing a white trenchcoat and a long black knit scarf that almost brushed the ground; he looked remarkably elegant.

"So," she said, leading him to the table. "Are you married yet?"

He laughed, unwound the scarf. "No, no. It does not happen that fast."

"But it *is* going to happen?"

Ajit sighed, dropped into the chair that Kristin had just vacated. "My father is talking to her father."

It didn't sound good. "It's up to you, you know. You're the one to make this decision."

He sighed again. One look at those large, dark, intelligent eyes, Vicky thought, and the poor woman wouldn't have a chance.

"I have seen in the paper that they have arrested that man," he said, changing the subject adroitly. "The one who hit the woman who was living here. Yes?"

"Yes. Her husband."

"Is he the one who came to the door that day?"

Vicky looked at him, puzzled.

"He handed you something ...?"

"Ah, yes." How could she have forgotten, Dennis shoving

the box of chocolates at her?

"A sad business," Ajit said, looking solemn. "My father said I should have brought you some flowers, to say we are sorry for your sadness, but my mother said it might not be appropriate."

She wasn't sure quite what to make of that, so she said vaguely, "That was thoughtful. Of both of them."

"Well. Today I have brought you my résumé. I am applying for summer jobs, and I am hoping you can make my English the best."

Vicky reached for the résumé, which covered six or seven pages. "First," she said, "keep it brief."

◆

She should have waited until the next day. It was already dark, and it would be after seven before she got there. But maybe if she'd waited until Monday she'd have decided against it. Besides, it might be better to arrive bearing a Bible on a Sunday.

The security booth at the entrance to the Hillcrest Retirement Village was, as it had been when she came here with Rachel, unattended, and the gates stood open. She was prepared for an interrogation at the front desk, and had intended to use the Bible as a persuasive entrée, but the lobby, too, was empty. Maybe everyone was at a church service somewhere, or still at supper. What would she do then? She had counted on surprising Jacob Cornelius, and confronting him alone.

The hallway leading to his room seemed more brightly lit than the last time she'd been here, and she had the urge to flick off the light switch as she passed it. She smelled meat cooking; maybe the residents *were* still at supper. But when she passed the dining room she could see, inside, only one woman in a pink uniform piling plates into a cart.

Two doors farther. She was here. Someone was singing inside the room, but it sounded recorded, probably coming from the TV. She took a deep breath, raised her hand to knock.

"Still so windy?" shouted someone into her ear.

Vicky's hand dropped to her heart, which had threatened to leave her body. "No, no. Much better."

The woman who had asked had come out of the room directly across the hall. She was leaning on a cane, without which her centre of gravity would have been so far forward because of her hunched back that she would surely have fallen on her face.

"Going to see Jacob?" she shouted.

Vicky nodded.

"Good luck," the woman bellowed, and shuffled back into her room. She pushed the door only part-way closed.

Good luck. She obviously knew her man.

Vicky knocked, loudly, three times. Someone inside said something. She took another deep breath, and turned the handle. Remember the man's daughter has just died, she told herself; no matter what he says you have to make allowances.

Jacob was sitting in one of the armchairs facing the TV, where a woman in a long white robe was singing "Amazing Grace." It took an effort for Vicky to pull her eyes from her to Jacob, who was wearing a navy suit and tie, although his feet were bare. He swivelled the chair to face her, pressing what must have been a mute button on his remote.

"You're the landlady." His hard blue eyes looked right into hers.

Vicky made herself smile. It felt as though her lips must be cracking open from the effort. "Yes," she said. "My name is Vicky, actually. I just wanted to tell you how sorry I was about Rachel."

"Huh. Lot of good that does."

Vicky held out the Bible to him. "This is hers," she said. "I thought you'd like to have it."

He looked at it for a moment before taking it. "I got my own," he said.

"Of course. But I thought this would mean more to you than to anyone else. That it could be a consolation, maybe, to think that she was ... at rest now." The pious phrases rolled with surprising ease from her tongue, the way they had when she'd spoken to Bitsy. But Jacob Cornelius was more suspicious than Bitsy; he would not be charmed, even with his own sentiments.

"At rest." He spat the words back at her. "She went her own godless way and she paid the price."

If Vicky hadn't already handed him the Bible she might have used it to beat his head in.

"She found her path difficult," she said, making her voice stay gentle. "Having that child when she was so young ..." Vicky shook her head regretfully, fixed her eyes on the white-robed woman on TV. But she could feel Jacob's gaze on her, the way his body stiffened, leaned forward.

"She tell you about that?"

"The police are interested, of course. They want to know where the child went, who adopted it—"

"I don't know. Some couple, they moved to Australia, I think."

"—and who the father was, that sort of thing."

"The father, eh? Well, I could tell them a thing or two about that, couldn't I?"

"Could you?"

A mistake: she had sounded too eager. She made herself look back at Jacob, try to resume a neutral expression. His left hand had begun to beat against his thigh, a cramped, epileptic rhythm. Alien hand, Vicky thought, remembering reading how in rare neurological cases a hand could disobey conscious thought and do weird and destructive things. In this case her sympathies were with the hand, which seemed to be trying to escape the body to which it was unfortunately attached. Jacob managed finally to stuff the hand down between the seat and the side of his chair.

"So what'd you come here for, anyway, landlady?"

"I wanted to bring you Rachel's Bible. Personally. I could have given it to Mr. Harding, but I thought—"

"That heathen! John Harding is as evil as they come. He tried to take my Rachel away from me."

"He was her uncle. I'm sure he just meant to be helpful—"

"Helpful!" Jacob laughed, a sound like a grating hinge. "That's one word for what he did. Yeah, that's one word for it."

Vicky stared at him. She could feel her abdominal muscles tighten.

Surely John Harding couldn't have been—

Surely not. Rachel was his *niece*. But she remembered the way he had reacted when she had mentioned the Hammond School, the way he claimed to know nothing about it, and her sense that he might be lying.

"Was he ... Was he the one—"

"The *one*. The *one*. Yes, yes, he's the *one*."

"You mean—"

"I mean you can get out of here and leave me alone. Do I look like somebody who wants your company, your stupid woman's company? My daughter's dead. I can't even tell myself she's in Heaven, that I'll see her there. You and John Harding, you'll both go to Hell. Maybe you'll meet Rachel there."

The hatred in the man made Vicky shudder. Maybe someday she would know how to have sympathy for Jacob Cornelius, who had lost his daughter twice, both in this life and the next. But right now all she wanted was to escape from this poisonous room. Besides, he had told her what she had wanted to know.

She turned, not speaking, and went out, closing the door quietly behind her. She heard the TV roar to life, a choir singing loud enough to make the door tremble, loud enough to wake the dead.

Even when she was outside she still seemed to hear the music, the voices shouting, discordant. She took deep gulps of air, which smelled of the ocean, briny.

She was so preoccupied with what Rachel's father had told her that she missed the turn-off for the tunnel and wound up crossing over the freeway instead of merging onto it. When she slowed down, a car behind her flashed its lights irritably at her. She pulled into a coffee-shop parking lot and sat there trying to make sense of what she had learned.

John Harding had gotten Rachel pregnant. When she was sixteen. Vicky could see Harding's face, his owlish eyes behind his thick-lensed glasses, his jaw gifted with, as Amanda would have put it, too many visits from the wattle fairy. It was hard to imagine him ever with such passions. Vicky had liked him, had thought him kind and decent and helpful to Rachel. *Helpful!* She heard Jacob's sneering voice. *That's one word for what he did.*

Maybe it wasn't true. Maybe she had misunderstood the man. There had been some ambiguity, deliberate, perhaps, in his remark. He would likely have had no scruples about misleading her.

Still, it made sense: Harding's evasiveness about the school, his sense of responsibility about Rachel, Rachel's need to repress what had happened.

It was almost ten by the time Vicky got home. She was just sliding her coat onto the hanger when the phone rang. She snatched up the cordless extension from the hall table.

"Hello?" There was no answer, just choppy static. "Hello?"

"Let it go."

"Pardon me?"

"Let it go." The voice was muffled, low-pitched.

"Are you sure you have the right number?"

"Let it go. It's none of your business."

The line went dead. Vicky set the phone down slowly.

Let it go. Was it a threat? The caller must have been referring to her snooping around about Rachel. She had been too surprised to pay attention to the voice itself. Did it belong to someone she knew? She tried to remember it, but already it was fading, only the words still vivid. Why hadn't she let the machine take the call? Then she would have had it on tape, something to give the police. But the man would probably not have left a message. If it was a man. It could have been a woman, lowering her voice.

She thought, suddenly, of the call return function on her phone. Quickly, she pressed it, listened to the mechanical voice give her the number of her last call, and dialled it. It would just be a phone booth, she told herself; only a moron would make such a call from home.

She was about to hang up when, on the tenth ring, someone answered.

"Yes?" A woman's voice.

"Oh. Hello. I ... was just wondering where this was. Someone just called me from there, you see, and I was hoping to speak to that person again...." Her palm was damp with sweat; she transferred the receiver to her other hand.

"This is Hillcrest Retirement Village. It's a pay phone in the lobby." The voice was abrupt, annoyed. "I've no idea who you were talking to. My office is down the hall."

"Oh. I'm sorry to have troubled you. Um, do the residents use this phone?"

The woman sighed, clearly impatient. "They can if they want. But they all have phones in their rooms."

"I see. Well, thank you, thank you very much."

Jacob Cornelius, Vicky thought. He might be sly enough not to use his own phone. Who else would be calling her from the Hillcrest Retirement Village, and at this hour?

"Well, I *won't* let it go," she told the cat. She went into the living room, turned on all the lights.

Before she could change her mind, she called the police station and asked for Clark, although she knew it was unlikely he would be there this late.

"He's actually away for a few days," the woman who took the call said. "Can someone else help you?"

"No, that's okay. You can tell him Vicky Bauer phoned."

After she had hung up she wished she hadn't left her name. What did she have to tell him, after all? As far as he was concerned, the case was closed. Dennis was guilty, and Dennis had been arrested. And one anonymous phone call, probably just from a nasty old man who couldn't harm her—well, what did it amount to?

She sighed, picked up the cat, set him on the shelf atop his scratching post. *Let it go*: well, she couldn't. She had to find out what had happened to Rachel all those years ago. Had John Harding really fathered her baby, or was Jacob Cornelius just trying to mislead her?

She would have to confront Harding. There was no other way. If she didn't, she might keep having Rachel's nightmares for the rest of her life.

◆

"Good. Now name the four main problematic factors involved in the world food supply."

Dulci wrinkled up her face. "How much land there is."

"How much *arable* land."

"Right—arable land. Current population. Rate of population growth. And ..."

Vicky glanced at her watch. Four-thirty. She had told herself that after her session with Dulci she would drop by Harding Refrigeration and hope she could corner John Harding. If he wasn't expecting her, her accusation might catch him all the more off guard. She would have to hope that Linda had already gone home or that they had hired a replacement for Rachel. If she ran into Linda or Junior, well, she had dropped the package of photographs into her purse so that if pressed she could use it as the excuse for her visit.

"And ... Oh, give me a hint!"

"Think about what is done with the land."

Dulci chewed at her pencil. Sixteen, Vicky thought, watching her: Rachel's age when she got pregnant. And like Dulci she had been beautiful, the beauty of vulnerability, of closeness still to childhood.

"Crops! Yield per acre!"

"Wonderful! You're a genius."

Mrs. Warner, a short, plump, dark-haired woman who looked to be, with a little added estrogen, a clone of her husband, popped her head around the corner from the living room as though she had been waiting to hear the word "genius" and beamed at them both.

"Do you want to stay for supper?" she asked Vicky.

"Oh, no, no thanks. I've got another commitment."

"You're always welcome, you know. I can't thank you enough for how you've gotten Dulci's grades up."

Dulci rolled her eyes. "It's got nothing to do with *me*, of course."

"Oh, I'm sorry, dear. Of course I meant you, too. You've been working *very* hard." Dulci's mother smiled apologetically, and her head disappeared again. Vicky had never seen parents as deferential to a teenager as the Warners. It was surprising that Dulci wasn't even more spoiled than she was.

"Well." Vicky turned back to her. "You've got this chapter

pretty well under your belt. So—how about this time next week? You'll have done the unit on cities by then?"

Dulci got up, stretched. Sixteen, Vicky thought, looking with envy at a stomach that actually seemed concave. "Guess so," said Dulci. "Unless I get hit by a car or something between now and then." She dropped her arms abruptly, looked at Vicky in dismay. "Sorry. I forgot about ... you know, about that friend of yours."

Vicky made herself smile. "It's all right."

"Well, at least they got the guy, right? The husband."

"They've arrested him," Vicky said, pulling on her coat. "It's pretty likely he did it."

And what if he didn't, she thought, as she got into her car; what if it was someone else, someone with a secret to protect? Someone she might be going to see right now? She was making what the movies called the stupid-woman move, walking brainlessly into obvious danger so the hero could intervene and save her.

Well, she wouldn't be brainless. Some of Harding's employees worked an evening shift, but if he was there alone she would talk to him some other time, somewhere public.

She had a sudden memory of a cartoon she'd seen, a cat lying dead outside Ye Olde Curiosity Shoppe. Was it just curiosity compelling her? That was a part of it, she had to admit. But a larger part was a sense that she owed it to Rachel to uncover the truth, the truth Rachel herself had only started to find and understand. She had to smile a little at herself at the pomposity of that answer. Still—that didn't make it wrong.

When she got to the plant, she was relieved to see several cars in the parking lot. Three workers in denim coveralls were manoeuvring a dolly with a huge freezer into one of the loading bays whose corrugated metal door was rolled up into the ceiling inside. The front office, she could see through its glass door, was empty; if Linda was still working here she must have gone home for the day. Vicky pulled the door open. The small bell that signalled her entrance made her wince.

Harding's office was straight in front of her. Her heart was beating so fast she put a hand to her chest, pressed, as though that would calm it.

"May I help you?"

The unexpected voice almost made her scream. A young woman stood up from behind the desk, smiling rather coldly and holding a file folder she must have just picked up.

"Oh." Vicky laughed clumsily. "You startled me. I thought Linda might still be here."

The woman's smile warmed up a little. "I'm from the temp service. Linda is ... Mr. Harding's wife? She'll be back tomorrow, I think."

"That's okay." Perfect, in fact. "It was Mr. Harding I wanted to see."

The secretary glanced at his door. "Is he expecting you?"

"He'll want to see me," Vicky said, and she stepped quickly to the door, tapped lightly on it, and pushed it open.

John Harding was sitting behind his desk, a large, black steel oval that might have been made from the same material as his refrigerators. He was leafing through a stapled sheaf of yellow purchase orders. The room was large and attractively decorated, with two expensively framed abstract paintings on the wall and a lush spider plant, healthier than any Vicky had ever raised, in a brass stand in the corner. The desktop was a messy contrast to the rest of the room, however, with the five stacked paper trays bulging with crumpled papers and file folders and computer print-outs. A necktie was wadded up in the top tray.

"Vicky!" Harding lowered the sheaf of papers.

Vicky closed the door behind her. She wondered how soundproof the room was, whether she should be glad the temp was just on the other side of the door.

"I'm sorry to bother you, Mr. Harding—"

"John." He pushed his glasses up higher on his nose, squinted at her.

"John." She forced a smile.

"Sit down."

She sat, stiffly, in the expensive swivel chair facing him. Suddenly she had no idea what to say, where to begin. Her fingers, without any apparent direction from her brain, fumbled in her purse, drew out the envelope of pictures, set them on the desk. What was she doing? It wasn't the pictures she'd come here to ask him about.

"These were the photographs I mentioned to you. The ones someone had been sending to Rachel."

"Oh. Yes."

He reached for them, took them from the envelope and fanned them out on his desk.

"The police will want them back," Vicky lied. She didn't want him to think he could keep them.

"Has Dennis said anything about why he was sending them to her?" Harding picked up one of the pictures, studied it, then set it down and picked up another.

"Actually, I wonder if it really *was* Dennis sending them." She licked her lips. Her tongue brought no moisture with it at all. She leaned forward a little, clamped her fingers onto the edge of his desk. "I went to see Rachel's father yesterday."

Harding made a face, as though he'd smelled something malodorous. "That's always fun."

"He didn't help explain the pictures, but, well, he did say something interesting." She made herself look at his face. She would have to read as much as she could in that moment of surprise.

"Yes?"

"He said you were the father of Rachel's baby."

John Harding's face went white. The picture he was holding

· 174 ·

fluttered to the desk.

"What?" His voice was barely a whisper.

"Is it true?" Vicky kept looking at him, trying to keep her gaze calm and level.

Harding swallowed; Vicky could see his Adam's apple move up, then, slowly, down. "I can't believe she told him that."

"Is it true?"

"I can't believe she told him."

Vicky let her fingers unclamp from the desk. Her knuckles felt bruised.

He had admitted it. Just like that. She should feel exultant, to have compelled the secret from him after all these years, but she just felt empty, sad, the truth something she might not have wanted to hear after all.

"Maybe she didn't tell him," she said. "Maybe he guessed."

"I suppose you must think I'm some ... some dirty old man."

"I suppose I must."

"Rachel was so ... so ... I'm not saying she seduced me, I'm not trying to say it wasn't my fault, but she was, she was, just so beautiful." Tears were forming in his eyes. Behind his glasses his pupils looked huge and shimmery.

"She was your niece. How could you do that to your own niece?" Vicky had to look away from those watery, amphibious eyes.

"I know. There's no excuse. None. I knew her when she was a child, for god's sake. Like a blood relative."

"What do you mean, *like* a blood relative?" Had she missed something?

"Well, she wasn't *my* niece. Good Lord. It's bad enough, you don't have to make it even more sordid. She was Anne's niece. My wife Anne was her aunt."

Anne? Vicky *had* missed something. "So ... Linda is your second wife?"

Harding's glasses had fogged up, and he took them off, ran the back of his hand quickly across his eyes, which, without the glasses, looked surprisingly normal. "Yes, yes. I thought you knew. Anne died a long time ago, when Junior was just a baby. Linda loved him and raised him like her own."

"Oh. I didn't know." It did make it a bit less sordid. But not much. "I assume Linda doesn't know anything about your affair?"

He shook his head. His skin had gone a jaundiced yellow. "I know I can't stop you from telling her. I can only ask you not to. Please. I'll do anything you want—"

Vicky gave a harsh, incredulous laugh. "You think I came here to *blackmail* you?"

"No, no, of course not—"

The idea made her a little nauseous. She had found out the truth, but what good was she doing by digging up the past, by hurting more people? It was ridiculous to think this man sitting crying in front of her could have had anything to do with Rachel's death. Dennis had killed her, of course he had.

She stood up, the urgency to leave like a hand pushing at her back.

A tap at the door. Vicky mustered a smile and turned to face the secretary. But it was Junior, not the secretary, who opened the door.

"Vicky!" he exclaimed. "I didn't know you were here."

Had he heard any of their conversation? If he had, his amiable smile was covering it well. Unlike his father, he still looked at the end of his working day as though he were just beginning it. If he'd been a woman, people would probably have called him perky.

"Yes, well ..."

Junior held up a clipboard and showed his father the paper attached to it. "The Seattle order just came in. Want me to sign for it?"

"Give it to me," Harding said. His voice sounded croaky. He cleared his throat. Junior handed the clipboard to him, a look of annoyance flitting across his face. Harding skimmed the page, scribbled a signature at the bottom, handed the clipboard back to Junior without looking up. He fumbled with the pen, set it down, picked up one of the photographs, set it down.

"What're those?" Junior asked, coming around the side of the desk.

"Vicky brought them. They're those photographs Dennis was sending Rachel."

"Let me see." Junior gathered them up, came back around to stand beside Vicky, as though she would want to look at them with him.

"This is her as a kid, right?" He handed her the top one, the second in the sequence.

"Yes," Vicky said. "She's about eight, I guess, and it's taken in front of her parents' house in Bellingham."

"She was so cute," Junior said, a sigh, a catch, in his voice. He looked at the next picture, the one of Rachel as a baby, and made no comment as he handed it to Vicky. "Where's this?" he asked. It was the one of Rachel about eleven, sitting on a piece of driftwood feeding two seagulls.

"A beach around here, I suppose. She said her mother took the picture."

"Aunt Joyce." Junior nodded. "I can't remember her at all."

"How old were you when she died?"

"Let's see. Rachel was twelve, so I'd have been four or five. She died about the same time my mother did, didn't she, Dad?"

John Harding had put his glasses back on and seemed to be studying the top page of the sheaf of purchase orders. "What? Yes, I guess so."

Junior handed her the picture, looked at the next one, the one of Rachel at about fifteen sitting beside the Christmas tree.

"Now this is how I really remember her! Every time I'd see her I'd think she was so gorgeous. Once she came over with all that long blond hair piled up on her head somehow and I asked her if I could take her to school the next day for show-and-tell."

Vicky smiled; she was afraid it must look like a sneer on her tense face. She wanted to snatch the remaining photos from Junior's hands and run.

But the next photograph was the one taken at the Hammond School. Vicky glanced at Junior's face. What would he know of it; what could she get him to admit?

"This is the staff at that religious school she went to?" he asked.

So he knew about the school, at least, if perhaps not its real purpose, neither of which things Harding had admitted to knowing the first time she had mentioned the school and photo to him.

"Yes," Vicky said. "On the original a face was lightly circled." She pointed at Angeletti. "It didn't show up in the copy."

"The police have any idea who he is?"

Vicky glanced at Harding. He was staring at the purchase order, a sheen of perspiration gleaming on his forehead. She could expose him now with a few casual words.

"I expect they do," she said. Harding didn't move. "But I don't suppose they care a whole lot about something that happened that long ago. It's Dennis they're interested in."

Harding lowered the sheaf of papers, picked up his pen, underlined something at the top of the page.

Junior had gone on to the next photograph, the one of Rachel about seventeen, standing in front of the stucco house in Bellingham. He turned it to catch more light. "What did Rachel say about this one?"

"I don't think she could remember it."

"There's something different about her."

"In what way?"

"I'm not sure. The house is their Bellingham house, I guess, but Rachel looks ... I don't know. I can't remember her hair ever being that short, for one thing. And she looks ... plump."

"Plump?" Vicky had to stop herself from prompting, *plump as in pregnant?*

Junior handed the picture to his father. "What do you think, Dad?"

Harding looked at the picture for several moments, turning it, as Junior had, to catch a different light. "You're right," he said. "She looks different somehow."

Junior rummaged through an untidy mug of pens, pencils and highlighters on the desk and pulled out a small magnifying glass. He squinted at the picture for several moments through the glass. His right foot began tapping lightly on the floor. Vicky felt like stepping on it, if only to stop herself from looking at it instead of his face.

"You know what? This isn't Rachel."

"What?" Vicky stared at him. Had he seen the obvious and not wanted to admit it?

Junior handed the glass and picture to his father, who studied it again for several minutes. If Junior's foot didn't stop tapping, Vicky thought, she was going to staple it to the floor.

"I think you're right," Harding said. "There's a resemblance, but ..." He put down the glass.

"Surely Rachel would have known if it was someone else!" Vicky exclaimed.

"If somebody gave me a picture of a teenage boy resembling me standing in front of my house and said it was me I'd probably assume it was," Junior said. "People aren't great at recognizing themselves in photographs. We look a lot different in them than in mirrors."

"I suppose that's true," Vicky admitted. If they were going to believe, or pretend to believe, it wasn't Rachel, how could she contradict them? They had known Rachel at that age; Vicky hadn't.

She picked up the magnifying glass, and Harding handed her the photograph. The young woman's enlarged, grainy face smiled up at her, the eyes half-closed as if squinting into the sun. Vicky scanned the body, dressed in loose jeans and a V-necked pullover, looking for a thickening at the waist. The woman seemed, as Junior had said, plumper all over, but that was common in pregnancy, wasn't it? And even if she weren't pregnant here, a weight fluctuation would not be unusual at that age. Vicky moved the glass back to the face, the uneven, self-conscious smile, the head tilted a little to the right.

She drew her breath in, sharply.

They were right. It wasn't Rachel. But Vicky could see now who it was.

CHAPTER ELEVEN

*S*HE WAS IN THE MIDDLE of her session with Travis when the phone rang. She let the machine take it, but when she heard who it was she leapt up, interrupting Travis in mid-sentence, and, dropping apologies behind her, ran over to get it.

"Hello," she said. "Don't believe the machine. I'm here."

"Oh, hi," said Clark. "I just got your message. I'm still up in Kamloops. Is it something important?"

What should she say? In light of what had happened since, she could barely remember the phone call about which she had wanted to speak to him. It seemed trivial now, not something threatening.

"Oh, I just had a strange call on Sunday, and I thought maybe I should report it. I'm sure it's nothing. Just some voice saying, let it go, it's none of my business, something like that."

"Let what go?"

So *now* what should she say? She could hardly fill him in on everything she had found out, not with Travis here. "I'm not sure. I assumed it had something to do with Rachel. I called the number back, and it was a pay phone in Rachel's father's retirement home. It was probably him. You've met him; you know what he's like."

"Yeah. Still." He said something she couldn't hear, then, "Sorry. I'm calling from the station here. It's a little busy."

"I shouldn't have bothered you with this—"

"Yes, you should. Look, I'll have a car cruise by there a few times tonight. To check. You know."

"It's all right," she said. "Really."

"Just be careful." He paused. The sound of other voices, laughter, doors slamming, a telephone ringing, came through the receiver. "Do you want to, uh, go out again this weekend? Supper or something? Or another movie?"

"Oh. Okay." She felt as though she had just said "duhhh."

She heard a voice in the background say, "Kent! Get off the damned phone!" and then Clark's voice replying, "Yeah, yeah." To her, he said, "Well, I'll call you when I get back. And you call the station if you get any more crank calls. Or anything."

"All right," she said meekly. Frightened woman calmed by strong male protector. She scowled at the phone as she put it down.

Travis had been working at the outline map of South America she had left for him, but she was disappointed to see that, except for labelling the Amazon correctly, he had few of the countries identified or in the right place. There was "Chilly" in Brazil, and "Brasill" in Argentina; Ecuador might be right, although all she could read of the word were the first and last letters.

He pushed it over to her apologetically. "Sorry," he said. "I had to miss so many classes last week because of the tournament in Seattle."

"You shouldn't let your schoolwork suffer." She told him this, with varying degrees of vehemence, practically every session.

He looked down at his hands. "I know," he said. He didn't sound convinced. "Maybe it's my dad you should talk to. He says, what do I need school for, I've got a good chance to get picked to play in the majors."

"And if you aren't? The odds are, what, a thousand to one? And even if you make it, you know how short a career that can be."

"I'll have made my millions by then. Dad says." He smiled.

Vicky shook her head. "You're right. It's your dad I should have the talk with."

"I *am* a good player, you know. You should come watch me sometime."

"I'm a hockey illiterate, I'm afraid. A disgrace to my country. I went to only one game with my husband, and he got quite cranky at how I couldn't understand the rules and at how I laughed at the vocabulary—the crease, the slot. Icing, I thought: well, that sounds like a good thing."

Travis laughed. "You need a tutor. You can hire me."

"Sounds fair." She passed him the flaxseed muffins, although she shouldn't have, because he had done so poorly on his map exercise.

When he had gone, she ate the one muffin left, standing at the kitchen sink and looking out at her forsythia bush. But she was barely aware of what she was eating or seeing, because she was thinking of the photograph of the woman who wasn't Rachel. She took it out, looked at it again. Rachel's face, almost, not quite, tricking the eye, a lie, the truth. *Ceci n'est pas une pipe,* Magritte had inscribed on his painting of a pipe.

She set the photograph face down on the table and waited.

Kristin was late, as usual. She slouched up to the kitchen table, dropped her book bag and herself down with a dispirited thud. She was wearing jeans and sneakers with one lace undone and a T-shirt under an unbuttoned plaid cotton flannel shirt which she seemed too tired to take off, even though, from the way it drooped off one shoulder, it seemed willing enough to go. Vicky had never seen her look so listless.

She sat down opposite Kristin, circled her fingers around her coffee cup.

"Tell me," she said, "did your parents ever live in Australia?"

Kristin looked up, surprised. "Yeah. Why?"

Vicky smiled. "Oh, I was just wondering if Jacob Cornelius had been making that part up."

Kristin stared at her. Her face went a pasty white, the blood seeming to drain into the birthmark on her neck. She took in a small gasp of air. Her hand went up to her throat, fell back to her lap.

"What do you mean?"

Vicky turned over the photograph on the table. "Now that I know, I can't believe I didn't recognize you right away. I suppose it's because the photograph was taken from a ways back. Still, your birthmark is visible, once I know to look for it. When I first saw it I suppose I dismissed it as a shadow, maybe a smudge on the negative. But you do look remarkably like her, at least in this picture. You've changed a little since." The change, Vicky didn't say, was mostly due to a further weight gain. "Even Rachel was fooled. Did you want her to be?"

Vicky made herself sit still, and wait. When at last Kristin did speak, her voice was so low it was inaudible.

"Pardon me?" Vicky said, more aggressively than she had intended.

Kristin winced. "I'm not really sure." Her voice seemed to strain to become only marginally louder than before. She picked up the picture. "I think I wanted her to recognize me."

"How did you find out about ... your mother? I thought the Hammond School people were pretty secretive about their records."

"I ... found some old documents. In my dad's safe deposit box. He must have forgotten they were there. He asked me to pick up his savings-bond certificates, and I found all the other stuff. About the adoption."

"But how did you track her down? Rachel. Your mother." Vicky couldn't take her eyes from Kristin's face, the face in which she now could see so much of Rachel. How could she not have noticed the resemblance before? It was like the photograph, she supposed—she'd seen only what she'd expected to see. And did she notice in Kristin a resemblance to John Harding, too? She thought she saw the faint outline of contact lenses in Kristin's eyes and wondered if she had inherited his poor vision.

"Through her father."

"Through ... Jacob Cornelius? You went to see him?"

Kristin nodded. She was leaning forward now, her face growing animated, eager. "It wasn't hard to find him. I pretended to be from the church—my parents belong so I knew what kinds of things to say, how to act like a Junior Christian —that's what they call teenagers. He was happy to talk to me, to tell me about his life. When he said he wished his own daughter had been more like me it was easy to get him to tell me about her."

"How often did you go to see him?"

Kristin shrugged. "Half a dozen times or so."

"And the pictures? I assume you're the one who sent them. How did you get them?"

"I just slid his album into my book bag when he wasn't looking. And returned it the next time I went. He probably didn't even notice."

Vicky didn't bother to contradict her. "So tell me why. Why this elaborate scheme? You must have known how upsetting it would be for Rachel to receive those photographs. If you wanted to meet her there'd have been easier ways, for God's sake."

Kristin picked at a cuticle on her thumb. Scarfskin, it was called, Vicky remembered irrelevantly, watching Kristin's fingers. If she didn't stop soon she'd be making herself bleed.

"Someone had written 'No Contact' on my birth certificate. I didn't know what that meant. And when Mr. Cornelius told me about Rachel going to the Hammond School and having the baby, he said that afterwards she was sort of strange, she pretended not to remember anything about what happened."

"I'm not sure she was pretending. I think she really repressed those memories."

"Whatever," Kristin said. Vicky gritted her teeth at the

word. "Anyway, Mr. Cornelius said the doctor there was pretty hard on the girls—"

"He probably also said they deserved it."

"Well, yeah, sorta. Because they'd sinned and everything. You know. Anyway, so I thought that leading Rachel up to that, and then maybe having her see the doctor's face and asking her a question like I did on the card would jolt her, like, into admitting what happened. Into remembering."

"In a cruel way, it more or less did," Vicky said. "She was having nightmares about Angeletti, starting to remember. And what were your plans then?"

Kristin's face seemed to tremble, its excitement at telling her story suddenly gone. "I would have told her," she said, her voice breaking. "I would have told her who I was."

Vicky sighed. She knew she should be angry with Kristin for what she had put Rachel through, but it was hard to work up much annoyance as she looked at Kristin's face. The young woman had just lost the mother she had worked so hard to find.

The mother. But there was also the father.

"Did Mr. Cornelius tell you who the father of Rachel's baby was?" Rachel's baby: Kristin. It was still hard for Vicky to think of them as the same person.

Kristin shook her head. "He was vague about it, and I couldn't ask him more directly without it sounding suspicious. Maybe he didn't know."

"Probably not," Vicky said. Thank God Kristin didn't think to ask if *she* knew anything. She didn't want to be the one to make that decision.

They were silent for a moment, then Kristin said, her voice not exactly rich with sincerity, "I know I used you. I'm sorry. But when I found out that the woman Rachel had just moved in with did tutoring it just seemed perfect."

"Perfect," Vicky said sourly. She picked up the picture of Kristin. It was still hard not to see Rachel in it. "Is the house the one in Bellingham, or did you just find one that looked like it?"

"It's the same house. It didn't seem to have changed at all from how it looked in the other photographs. We just waited until the people living there were at work, and then I ran up the front walk. It didn't seem like the kind of neighbourhood where the neighbours cared much what was going on, anyway."

"'We.' Who was with you?"

"A friend. I said I wanted a picture of the house because my grandfather used to live there. It was true, after all."

Kristin stood up, took off the flannel shirt and dropped it on the floor. She looked flushed now, as if she were coming down with a fever. She put one knee on the chair seat and clutched the back with her right hand.

"What about the picture of the staff at the school? How did you get it?"

Kristin didn't answer. She began picking again at her cuticle.

"Did you steal it from the church in Blaine?"

"Yes."

But there was something too quick in her admission, something that made Vicky wish she hadn't supplied the answer, that made her think the reason Kristin had initially paused was not just because she was reluctant to admit a theft.

"And how did you know which of the two men in the photo was the doctor? How did you know which face to circle?"

"He was the one who looked more like a doctor."

Was that true; had she just made a lucky guess?

Kristin sat back down, picked up her shirt from the floor, folded and refolded the sleeves on top of each other on her lap.

"Well," Vicky said. "I don't know how you could think such a complicated and frightening scheme was necessary. Have you any idea how upsetting it was for Rachel, especially with what she was going through with Dennis, to keep getting those pictures?"

"I know," Kristin said meekly. "I can see now that it was all pretty stupid. But I ... was so desperate. If I just walked up to her and said, hi, I'm your daughter, she'd freak out. I thought, this way maybe she could ... be ready, could be expecting it. I thought maybe the picture of me in front of her old house ..." Her voice trailed away.

"That one worked too well. She thought it was herself."

Kristin began to cry.

Oh, dear. Vicky was not good at this. But she knelt down beside Kristin, put an arm tentatively around her shoulders. She remembered Rachel cringing from the most casual touch. Kristin leaned into her arm as though it was what she had been wanting all her life.

"It's okay," Vicky said, wondering if she could reach the box of tissues on the bookcase without getting up. "Remember, your real parents are the ones who raised you. You didn't even know Rachel."

Kristin ran her hand across her eyes, her nose. "But *you* knew her. Tell me about her."

"I didn't know her very well or very long, either," Vicky said. She eased away, jerked some tissues from the box and stuffed them into Kristin's hand, which had fallen limply to her lap. "She was a nice person. She was very quiet, a little shy. She'd had a hard life, with her father and then with Dennis, but it didn't make her bitter. I think you'd have liked each other." She had no idea, actually, what they'd have thought of each other. She tried, and failed, to imagine what she herself would feel like if confronted by the grown daughter she might have made herself forget she'd ever had.

But her words seemed to be what Kristin wanted to hear. She wiped her eyes and blew her nose, and nodded when Vicky offered her a glass of milk. They sat, not speaking, as Kristin drank it. The cat jumped up onto the empty chair beside Kristin and tried to stick his head into the glass, and it made them laugh.

"I better go," Kristin said. She stood up, put on her flannel shirt. "Will you ... I mean, do you have to tell the police it was me who sent the pictures?"

"I suppose I do." Vicky hadn't thought about it.

"So my *parents* will find out!"

"Maybe you should tell them first, then."

Kristin sighed. But the prospect of admitting everything to her parents did not seem to fill her with as much dread as Vicky might have thought. Maybe she was relieved to have been exposed, to be able to confess. "I was wondering ..."

"Yes?"

"If I could, like, still go on with the tutoring. I mean, I need it, right?"

Vicky smiled, surprised. "Of course you can. But don't feel you have to. If it's too uncomfortable. I can recommend someone else."

"No," she said. "I'd like to come back."

"All right, then."

When Kristin had gone, Vicky drank a big glass of water, then put on a Janis Joplin CD, lay down on the living-room floor, and closed her eyes. So now she had the answers, or most of them. But what good were they, without Rachel to tell them to? Goddamn Dennis. If it was Dennis.

Why couldn't she get over her unease about his guilt? Okay, so he hadn't sent the photographs. But that didn't mean he hadn't killed Rachel. Vicky still didn't doubt for a minute that he was capable of it. So was it merely a coincidence that Rachel was killed just as her past was coming to light? And Kristin: she couldn't help thinking there were things that Kristin hadn't told her, things that were not quite lies but not quite the truth.

From the speaker behind Vicky's head Janis was urging her to get it while she could. Vicky sighed, got up, went into the study and played Tetris on her computer until her fingers went numb. Then she called Amanda.

"Let's go to a movie tonight," she said. "Something with a train and snow in it."

"Huh?"

"You know. Fellini. 'Only two things always look good in a film: a train and snow.'"

"Vicky. I am *not* going to go see *Dr. Zhivago* again."

CHAPTER TWELVE

*I*T WAS THE LAST place she would have expected to wind up on Saturday night with Clark. A poetry reading. She had actually laughed when he suggested it, thinking he must be joking, but then she remembered to whom she was talking. It turned out that one of the readers was the teenage daughter of a constable he worked with, and Clark had said he would try to make it because the man was afraid nobody else would show up. Vicky thought Clark might have been a little disappointed when she agreed to go, but she was hardly going to let herself be the Philistine here. She had written poetry herself, once.

The reading was at a local health-food restaurant, and there were enough people there to fill all the tables and the rows of chairs along the walls.

"I thought you said nobody would be here," Vicky said, squeezing her chair a little closer to the table to let people by.

"I thought so, too," Clark said, nodding at a middle-aged couple across the room who were probably the poet's parents. They were dressed as though they might be going to the opera after, the man in a dinner jacket and the woman in long white satin with pearls. Everyone else was as scruffy as possible, and Vicky wished she were a bit more scruffy herself. She was wearing a fairly simple black dress, but, well, it was a *dress*. Clark, in his navy sports jacket and slacks, looked, Vicky admitted to herself with some unease, quite handsome. The yellow lights reduced the natural ruddiness of his face to a romantically unhealthy pallor.

The MC, who had doffed the apron he had worn when he'd waited on them earlier in the evening, tapped the mike, and then read off about twenty names from a crumpled page.

"Anyone else?" he asked.

A girl standing near the door put up her hand. "Lindsay," she said. The man wrote it down.

"Oh, God," Vicky whispered. "It's one of those open-mike things. We'll be here all night."

Clark swallowed, looked even more sallow in the dim light. "I thought it was just going to be Bill's daughter."

The first youth got up to read. He had long blond hair tied in a ponytail, and he was wearing new jeans with the knees torn out. "So, hi," he said. "I just have this one poem, and I'm dedicating it to my girlfriend, Ally, and to all the guys from the snake pit, and to Mr. Hellman, who said I had talent, and to my mom, and to the two Michaels, who said I wouldn't have the guts to get up here, and I guess I'm showing them, right?"

The poem was, of course, anti-climatic.

The next reader was an anorexic girl who was probably in her late teens but who looked ten. She read, in a terrified voice that ran the words together to make them incomprehensible, five short rhymed poems that might have been about a pet dog.

The room was becoming close, the air so dry and stale that Vicky felt she had to breathe it twice to extract enough oxygen. Someone propped open the door, but all that seemed to be sucked in was traffic noise.

The boy reading next swaggered to the mike, said he had a poem in three parts and that he didn't believe in this five-minute time-limit censorship bullshit when what he had to say was important. He read a long meandering rant about what a pile of shit life was, although Vicky could see the promise in the piece if only he would part with most of it.

There was no smoking allowed in the restaurant, but Vicky caught the nostalgic whiff of marijuana. She glanced at Clark, to see if he noticed it, but if he did he was pretending he didn't.

The daughter of Clark's colleague was, unfortunately, among the last to read, and the audience, diminished by half during the brief break, was too dazed and hot to be much above comatose. Which was a shame, because her work was among the best of the evening: short, haiku-like pieces that showed the rewards of rewriting. Her parents applauded with feverish enthusiasm. Her father had taken off his suit jacket and tie and undone his shirt halfway to his waist; wherever the shirt touched him it was transparent with sweat.

"We can go now," Clark said.

"There are still three or four more readers."

"I don't think I can stay conscious that long," Clark said.

"Okay. Let's make a break for it before the next person starts."

They slithered their coats from their chair backs and, hunching over in a vain attempt to be inconspicuous, stumbled to the door. Vicky tripped over the legs of someone reclining full-length on the floor and would have fallen on her face if Clark hadn't grabbed her arm. The body she'd staggered over didn't stir. Damn this dress, she thought: she wasn't used to having her stride limited by the circumference of a hemline.

"Sorry. Sorry. Sorry," she whispered to anyone who could possibly care.

The air outside smelled wonderful. She gulped it in.

Clark stood beside her, wincing, pressing his hands into the small of his back. "I have trouble sitting still that long," he said. He moved his right hand to his left shoulder, rubbed at it.

And Vicky thought: Oh oh. Because what she felt, seeing him knead at the tight muscle under his polo shirt, was the unmistakable flare of sexual desire. She wanted to put her own hand there. She had felt nothing like this the last time she'd seen him; why now? Maybe it was the poetry.

"They should have had only half as many readers," she said.

"I had no idea it was going to be like this."

"But it was interesting. It's nice these kids have someplace to read, to get encouragement."

"Yeah. I suppose it's good for me, too, to go to things where I don't always see people at their worst. A woman on the force quit last month because, she said, that was what she couldn't stand about the job, always seeing people at their worst, when they're lying or cheating or beating somebody up."

"My husband used to call that the *Schweinhund* in us." Why had she mentioned Conrad? To make herself stop wanting to put her hands on Clark's shoulders?

"*Schweinhund*, eh?" Clark did a good job on the *Sch*. "Means, what, 'pig dog'?"

"It loses something in the translation."

They began walking back to Vicky's house, which was only five blocks away. A misty rain was falling. Still, she was glad they'd walked; at the very least it had given her an excuse to wear her runners and not the pumps she kept around for what Amanda called emergency gender identity.

"I read an article," Vicky said, trying to keep the conversation going, "about how the human brain is still evolving and how the more rational part, the cortex, is expanding and may eventually gain control over the more emotional part in the temporal region. That would get rid of a lot of the *Schweinhund*."

"A world full of Mr. Spocks. There might be less crime."

"But less poetry, too. I liked your friend's daughter's work, by the way. I thought it was the best there."

"Well. I'll have to tell Bill," Clark said. "A bona fide English teacher said she was the best."

"I'm not exactly an English teacher. My major is Social Studies. And my master's is in Film Studies."

"You have a master's degree?"

"Well, it's not as though I'm using it."

They crossed Johnston Road, headed down Pacific. Vicky's legs were starting to resent the cool air.

"You know that guy who read the poem about the rats?" Clark asked. "He's been arrested a couple of times on drug charges."

"If he's a writer maybe he needs the inspiration."

Clark glanced at her, didn't answer.

"It was a joke," she added lamely.

"I know. I'm not quite that thick."

"Sorry," she said, stung. "I wasn't implying you were thick. But you're ... serious."

"You're not the first person to suggest I have no sense of humour."

"That's not what I meant." But of course it was exactly what she meant. They were opposite the police station now, and she tried to find something she could say about it to change the subject, but her mind was blank. Shit, shit, shit.

Clark bent over, and, as Vicky gaped at him, he did a perfect cartwheel on the sidewalk.

A car going past honked, and a young woman rolled down the passenger window and laughed and blew him a kiss.

Vicky couldn't stop staring. The man had just done a cartwheel in the middle of the sidewalk, right in front of the police station where people he worked with could have seen him.

Clark picked up a pen that had fallen from his pocket, smoothed down his jacket, and walked on. Vicky had to trot to catch up. So he had a sense of humour after all. A weird one, but still. She could hear Amanda exclaiming: a penis, a gun, *and* a sense of humour—why, the man is perfect!

"So," she said. "Did you learn that at the police academy or at law school?"

"I learned it from my dad. His sense of the absurd extended beyond giving his son a comic-book name."

"Oh. Well, it's a great skill. You could use it to disarm your enemies. In several senses."

Vicky couldn't get rid of the image of his body suddenly going end over end. She glanced at him striding somberly along beside her now, and it was hard to believe she hadn't imagined it. She felt an almost overwhelming desire to touch him. Maybe she should just throw him down on the lawn of the police station and make crude and sweaty love to him. Take that, she would say afterwards, as they got up and straightened their clothes and waved at the faces in the windows.

Well, maybe that was less a lust fantasy than one about getting warm, she thought, pulling her coat closer around herself. Her knees had gone numb, and the unaccustomed nylons on her legs felt like wet, freezing gauze. Why hadn't she brought an umbrella? She was as bad as her students.

"Getting colder." Clark glanced at her, picked up his pace a little, and Vicky had to lengthen her stride to keep up. Her dress rode higher onto her thighs. If she walked much faster it would be shimmying up around her waist.

"Only another block," she said. A cold northeast wind was blowing a heavier rain into their faces, and it reminded her of Alberta. There would still be snow there, she told herself; stop complaining.

They came in through the alley, sending the dog at the end of the block into a frenzy. Birdy must have heard them or the dog, because her outside light suddenly went on, making them both freeze and shield their eyes from what seemed like a nuclear detonation.

"Good Lord," Clark said.

Vicky squinted at him, the light making him glaringly

black and white. "She's caused brownouts as far down the coast as San Francisco," she said.

It was Birdy's lights that had identified the car that killed Rachel, but she didn't mention that, and she hoped Clark wouldn't, either. She had intended telling him, when they got home, about Kristin and the photographs, but she was altering those plans now. She wasn't sure what they would talk about when they got inside, but she didn't want it to be about the case. She could tell him about Kristin later. Besides, she rationalized, it would give Kristin more time to talk to her parents. Vicky would have to tell Clark who Kristin's father was, too, she supposed, although she didn't enjoy the thought of complicating John Harding's life even more. Maybe the police wouldn't care about any of this, anyway; it had nothing to do with Dennis.

Still squinting against the light, Vicky felt her way along her back fence, almost stumbling into Clark's car because she had forgotten it was there, and then she led the way up her back steps. She glanced back at the alley. There was something ... Some unfinished thought, something about the car, something that might be important, had fluttered into her mind as they'd turned into her driveway. She frowned. It was gone now.

She opened the door. The cat slithered out between Clark's legs.

"What was that?" he said, staring after the cat, which had already vanished. "A pet snake?"

Vicky laughed. "Just the cat. He has retractable legs."

They went into the living room, and Vicky turned the heat up. When she looked at Clark, she realized she must look as wet and cold as he did. He rubbed his hands together, blew into them.

"A hot shower now would be nice," he said.

So what should she say? He had given her an opening. We can take one together, she could say. The thought of it, their two bodies under the hot beat of the water, made her a little dizzy. She simply stood there, shivering, looking at him.

He helped her take off her coat, hung it on a chair back. He was close to her, inches away. She reached up, brushed her hand across his face. He closed his eyes.

"You're so wet," she said.

"So are you." He combed his hand through her hair. It came away dripping.

She put her hands on his chest, ran them underneath his jacket to his back, where his shirt was warm and dry. "Do you want to ..." To what? She thought, a quick flash, of Conrad, but there was no resistance there. Everything in her had become simple.

He kissed her, lightly, slid his arms around her waist, up her back. She shivered, not with cold now but with desire. Water had run into her eyes, and she felt as though she might be crying.

Clark stepped back. His hands slid down her arms, fastened onto her wrists. "I should go," he said quietly.

Couldn't he tell she wanted him? She loosened her wrists from his grip, then took his hands in hers, looked into his dark blue eyes.

"You don't have to," she said.

"I know. I just ... don't want to rush anything."

Well. That was usually her line. Suddenly she felt ridiculous, some oversexed and aging woman throwing herself at an uninterested man. That he was right, that it *would* have been rushing things, didn't make her feel less foolish. She looked away, let go of his hands and picked up her coat, concentrating on straightening the collar, smoothing down the sleeves.

"Can I call you again?" Clark asked, behind her.

She made herself give him a smile that she hoped was less sickly than it felt. "Sure."

"Well. Thanks for tonight."

"It was interesting. Especially the cartwheel."

He shrugged. "I'm lucky I didn't break anything."

Just my heart, she wanted to say, but stopped herself in time.

At the door, he stood running his fingers along a chip in the jamb, looking at it intently, as though he would have to give her an estimate for its repair.

"Amygdala," he said.

"What?"

"The centre of our emotional systems in our brain. I was trying to think of it before. It's, you know, the part you said might be shrinking."

"Amygdala. Right."

Then the cat crept through the open door and brushed his wet fur against Vicky's legs and made her jump, so she was able to say goodbye with a laugh that was reasonably genuine. She waited until Clark had time to get to his car, then turned off her outside light.

"I bin spurned," she told the cat.

But already she was starting to feel less embarrassed. Of course Clark was right; it would have been absurd for them to leap into bed like randy teenagers. And he'd asked if he could call her again. Maybe it would all be okay. Her amygdala could handle it.

She had a shower, and then watched something altogether too grim about species extinction on PBS. She forgot to check her answering machine, so she was able to go to bed and sleep without worrying about the message Kristin had left her.

◆

"... And so I told my mom, and she was pretty freaked out at what I'd done, but she said I had to Make Right the lie—that's another church thing, where if you lie to or about someone in the church you have to confess to the person—and that I had to Make Right for Mr. Cornelius. So I went and told him everything, how I'd lied and how I was his granddaughter, right, and he was really angry, and he said some pretty awful things, I was all like crying and everything, but then as I was leaving I decided to ask him point blank who my father was. And he said *you* know who he is! Oh, Mrs. Bauer, you've got to tell me. Mr. Cornelius just kept saying it's better I hear it from you. So, please, you've *got* to tell me. Call me back as soon as you get this, okay?"

Vicky played the tape again, although there was no need to. She had heard it all too well the first time. Damn the man. She could imagine his voice jeering at her, *This is what your snooping gets you, landlady.* She wondered what the "pretty awful things" were that he said to Kristin. Terms like "spawn of Satan" were probably in his everyday vocabulary. A normal man might actually have been pleased to discover a granddaughter in his old age. She sighed. Maybe it *would* be better if she were the one to tell Kristin.

She made herself a coffee, a strong one, went back and sat by the phone. What should she say to Kristin? How on earth had she gotten herself so tangled up in this?

The phone rang. Relieved at the excuse to postpone her own call, she picked it up. It was Kristin.

"Did you get my message? You've *got* to tell me who he is! Please! I mean I just lost my real mother, if there's any chance I can meet my real dad— You've no idea how much it would mean to me. I'll come over, okay? Please!"

Vicky felt her face pinching with dismay as she listened. "Well, it's not a good time for me. I was just going out to do some grocery shopping—"

"I can meet you! Are you going to the Safeway on 24th?"

"I suppose so."

"I'll meet you there! If I walk fast I can be there in twenty minutes."

"It's not exactly a good place to talk—" Damn. Now she had agreed that they would be talking, somewhere or other.

"It's okay, it doesn't matter. I'll see you there. I'll leave right away."

"I'm not—"

But Kristin had already hung up. Good grief. Now she was going to have to tell or not tell someone who her real father was as she stood picking out a lettuce head.

She slid her grocery list from under the magnet on the fridge and went out to the car. The rain, though warmer than yesterday's, made her think of Clark, of the way she had wanted him, in some primitive, Sheena-the-jungle-girl way. She felt ridiculous. She slammed the car door, hard, and wished she had just stayed in bed.

When she parked in the Safeway lot and got out of the car, she was surprised to recognize the man pushing a huge cart of groceries past her.

"Junior," she said, feeling a surge of guilt, as though he must be here because he knew she was going to meet his half-sister.

Junior stopped, startled. "Vicky! Hi."

"You doing the cooking this month?" She gestured at the laden cart.

"I guess I am. I'm moving out. I've got a nice place of my own."

"Really? Well, that's great. I mean, I assume it's great."

Junior smiled. "Yeah, it is. It's silly for me to be living with my folks at my age."

"Still, it's a waste, that huge house for only the two of them."

Junior shrugged. "It's just to impress people," he said, his voice souring. "Dad likes to impress. When I was a kid I always felt I had to be invisible unless I was cute enough to be shown off to clients. As though they cared what kind of house or family their refrigerator repairman had."

Vicky looked down at her feet, not sure of what to say. "Well, it's a good business now," she ventured. "He must have impressed a lot of people."

"Oh, yeah. He's made his fortune in Freon."

"Freon." Vicky made a face. "At least he does care about the environmental impact it's had, doesn't he? It seemed to me he did." She remembered the conversation she'd had with him on her back stairs once. And the way he had gently brushed the spider off his arm.

"He's a realist. Being concerned about the environment is being realistic, that's all. Just another kind of self-interest. Besides, if you can say you've stopped using CFCs because you care, instead of because it's the law, it looks better, doesn't it? Better PR."

"That's ... an interesting way of seeing it." She wondered if it really *was* Harding's point of view; the way the man had brushed a spider off his arm once was, after all, a flimsy basis for a character evaluation. Or maybe it was Junior who held those views. Maybe both of them did.

Junior gave an apologetic little laugh; Vicky could tell he wished he hadn't said what he had. "I didn't mean for that to sound so cynical. I shouldn't complain about Dad. I should be glad to have a job I like, most of the time, anyway, and I suppose someday I'll own the company." He flexed his fingers on the shopping cart handle. "Well, I better go before the ice cream melts."

"Nice seeing you, Junior."

He had started to push the cart away, but he paused, turned back to Vicky. "Actually," he said, "I'm making another change. I'm going to start using my real name, dumb as it is. I want people to start calling me Vance."

Vicky smiled. "Vance. Okay. You'll have to give people a while to get used to it."

"I know. It'll be a change for me, too."

He had been glancing back at the store and now waved at someone there. Vicky turned to look. Linda was coming towards them carrying more bags of groceries.

"I gave Mom a ride," Vance said, sounding a little embarrassed. He wheeled his cart off towards his truck in the next aisle before Linda could join them.

Linda was wearing a calf-length coat that looked too warm and heavy for the west coast. Her face looked smaller than Vicky remembered it, probably because her hair, which was usually styled in puffy waves, was pulled back and tied at her neck above what Vicky hoped was a fake fur collar.

"Hi," she said. "I was just helping Junior get groceries."

Junior, not Vance. Vicky had to stop herself from making an amused comment. "He's getting his own place, I hear."

"Yes. I'll miss cooking for him."

"Are you still working at the plant? Or have they hired someone to replace Rachel?"

Linda winced slightly, looked away. Two teenage boys on skateboards thundered past them, narrowly missing a van backing out. Linda waited until the youths had reached the end of the lane and jumped off their boards before she answered. "I'm there off and on. They've hired a new girl, but I seem to have to keep coming in to help her. It's hard to find someone as ... as good as Rachel. Whatever else you can say about her, she was so well-organized, so careful to do everything right."

"I can imagine." *Whatever else you can say about her*: what did that mean?

"Sometimes the men come into the office and I can tell by this little startled look on their faces that they're still expecting to see her there." Linda was still looking away, after the skateboarders who were carrying their boards now into the Safeway. She blinked quickly several times.

"It must be hard," Vicky said.

"Yes."

Vance had pulled his pick-up alongside them and sat drumming the fingers of both hands on the wheel. He might have been drumming his toes on the gas pedal, too, because the pick-up made small surges of sound. Linda opened the door, dropped her bags inside.

"Junior's always in a hurry," she said.

Vicky watched them drive off. If only they knew what she was really doing here. She had an urge to run back to her own car, jump in and speed away after them.

She sighed, turned back to the store. Given the early hour, it was not particularly crowded. She wasn't sure whether that would be a good thing or not; a crush of people might give her an excuse to avoid Kristin or at least put off their conversation.

But Kristin was waiting for her just inside the doors. She looked as though she must have run the entire way. Her face was flushed and prickled with sweat; her hair on the right side had come loose from the rubber band at the back and was sticking out in a knotty lump; the cardigan she had probably started out wearing was now tied unevenly around her waist by the sleeves.

"Mrs. Bauer!"

Vicky doubted if anyone in her whole life had greeted her with more enthusiasm.

"Hi," she said, suppressing the panic that made her want to turn and push her way out the one-way door humming closed behind her. She still didn't know what she was going to say.

"You've *got* to tell me." Kristin was wasting no time. She took Vicky's arm and pulled her towards the bottle recycling desk.

"I need to get a buggy," Vicky protested as Kristin dragged her past the rows of carts chained to each other.

"Just tell me," Kristin said. "It won't take long."

"If Mr. Cornelius had wanted you to know, he'd have told you himself, don't you think?" As though what he wanted should matter to either of them.

"He said he'd tell me if you wouldn't. But he said I'd be sorry if he had to talk about it, about that dirty sin. That's what he called it, a dirty sin."

Vicky groaned, leaned against the photo drop-off counter. The bastard had trapped her. But why did she feel she had to protect John Harding? Rachel had suffered unbelievably for her "dirty sin." It was time Harding faced the consequences, too.

"If I tell you," she said, "you have to promise not to go rushing over there and making a scene. All right?"

"All right." Kristin's face was so close to hers that Vicky could feel her excited breath on her cheeks.

"The man is married, to a nice woman who doesn't deserve to be hurt. Do you understand?"

Kristin nodded, shifted her feet impatiently. "Who is he?" she whispered.

"May I help you?"

They both jumped, guiltily, stared at the woman behind the photo desk.

"No thanks," Vicky murmured, moving away to the produce section. Kristin was hanging onto her arm as though Vicky were trying to escape.

"Okay." Vicky took a deep breath, propped her hands onto the edge of the bin of bananas. "His name is John Harding. He was married to your mother's aunt. She died and he's been remarried, happily, I think, for a long time. He runs a business called Harding Refrigeration. Your mother was working for him as a receptionist when she was killed."

"Oh, wow. Harding. Okay. Got it. John Harding. He was married to my mother's *aunt*?"

"Apparently."

Kristin had picked up a small bunch of bananas, and she broke one off and began peeling it. She took a large bite, chewed energetically.

"Kristin. You haven't paid for that."

Kristin looked down at the banana in her hand as though it had suddenly grown there. She began laughing, a bit of chewed banana spraying out. She covered her mouth with her left hand, swallowed. "I was so excited I forgot where I was." She smoothed the drooping ends of the skin up over what was left of the banana and set it back in the bin.

Vicky sighed, picked it up, and the bunch it had come from. "Bananas were on my list, anyway."

"Sorry," Kristin said. "Oh, God, I'm just so excited."

"Remember what you promised me. About not rushing over there and making a scene."

"Okay, okay. You know him, don't you? Is he a nice man?"

Vicky thought for a moment, looking at the bananas. "I've only met him a few times," she said carefully. "He seems nice."

Kristin laughed again, breathlessly. "Thank you," she said. "Thank you, Mrs. Bauer." She made a move towards Vicky, as though she might want to give her a hug. Vicky's posture probably discouraged it, because Kristin stepped back, stumbling into an elderly man with a shopping basket on his arm.

"Oh, sorry," she said, backing away farther, and then she turned and ran. She hit her elbow on the skateboard under the arm of one of the boys Vicky had seen outside, but she didn't even pause.

"Whoa!" said the boy.

Kristin had already reached the doors. They had barely begun to lumber open when she pushed herself through them.

At least Vicky had got her to surrender the banana. She couldn't imagine anyone looking more like a fleeing shoplifter.

She stood for a while looking at the doors Kristin had gone through and feeling depressed, exactly why she couldn't have said, and then she went over to the chain gang of carts and paroled one with a quarter.

CHAPTER THIRTEEN

*T*HE FIRST TWO CALLS the next morning were welcome ones. The first was from a parent wanting a tutor for her daughter over the summer. The second was from Lois's mother, who, in a cool and cautious voice, said that Lois seemed to want to renew the sessions and, since she had gotten only an A- on her last test, "a continued association might be beneficial."

"Whatever you'd like," Vicky said, trying to match the woman's careful, professional tone.

The third call came just as Vicky was popping the bread into the toaster.

It was John Harding. "What the hell did you think you were doing?" His voice was shaking with anger.

Vicky shrank back into the corner of the sofa. "I'm sorry," she said. She wouldn't bother to pretend ignorance of what he was talking about.

"This girl— She came to the house! Thank God Linda wasn't home—"

Damn Kristin. "I told her not to do that," Vicky said meekly. "I didn't know she'd—"

Harding was saying something about how they needed the truck back by noon, and it took Vicky a moment to realize he wasn't talking to her. "Look, I can't talk now," he said curtly, to her this time, she assumed. "I'm at work. I have to see some people in White Rock at eleven, so meet me before that. Ten o'clock, that coffee shop by the theatre."

He had more or less ordered her to appear, but she swallowed her indignation and said evenly, "All right." He might have hung up even before he heard her answer.

Vicky pressed a cushion over her face and screamed into it.

She wasn't sure whether to dress up or dress down for her meeting with Harding, to go for the pity look or the power look, so she decided on something neutral, the beige tunic top and black leggings.

She didn't realize until she was almost there that the coffee shop he was referring to had to be the Starbucks she and Clark had gone to after their movie. Well, she would have to try not to think about that. She would have to try to just sit there calmly and let John Harding tell her how furious he was.

She was a little early, but Harding was already there, at one of the small round tables farthest from the door. He was staring fixedly into his coffee cup where his hand seemed to be needlessly stirring a spoon. He looked awful. The hair on both sides of his head looked as though he had grabbed it in his fists and tugged it into two limp, tangled sails. He was unshaven, and his sweater was buttoned up wrong, a little tab of cloth with its extra button poking up into his neck. His glasses were sitting on the table, and he looked at her with eyes unacquainted with recent sleep.

Vicky gave him a tense little smile, bought her coffee, then sat down opposite him in the chair that she remembered had probably been intended for more petite buttocks. She and Harding were, fortunately, the only customers.

"Well," snapped Harding. "Want to tell me what the hell you thought you were doing with that girl?"

"I'm sorry it happened so, so clumsily—"

"Clumsily! That's a polite way of putting it."

"I know it must have been a shock."

"A shock. Jesus Christ."

"She does have the right to know." Vicky took a sip of coffee; it burned her lip.

"Know *what*? She thinks I'm her father!" Harding took the spoon out of his cup and tossed it with a clatter onto the table.

Was he going to deny it now? "She's Rachel's daughter."

"She may be Rachel's daughter, but she sure as hell isn't mine."

"Of course she is. You admitted you were the father of her baby. Surely it must have occurred to you that person could show up some day."

Harding began to laugh. He leaned back in his chair until it tipped dangerously, and he laughed, so loudly the young woman behind the counter, who had been engaged in her own conversation on the phone, looked up in alarm. Tears formed in Harding's eyes. His laughter seemed wild, out of his control.

At last he stopped, wiped at his eyes, leaned forward across the table towards Vicky. His face was red.

"The pregnancy I was responsible for," he gasped, shaking his head, "happened only a few months ago."

Vicky stared at him. "You mean ... Rachel was pregnant when she died?"

"Yes. God, you didn't know. I admitted it to you and you didn't know." He kept shaking his head, as though if he didn't the laughter would erupt again.

"But ... I don't understand. Jacob Cornelius said ... At least he implied ..."

She tried to remember his exact words. He hadn't explicitly said Harding was the father; he'd mentioned Harding's name in a strategic and misleading way, that was all, letting Vicky draw her own conclusions and not contradicting them. And he'd managed to not quite lie to Kristin, either, had just told her to ask the helpful Mrs. Bauer.

"The old man was always good at implying," Harding said. "And I'm sure if he could imply something about *me* he'd be particularly pleased. He never did have any use for me, and he certainly never forgave me for supporting Rachel against Dennis." He picked up his glasses, jammed them onto his face, hard; Vicky could see his eyelashes touch the glass. "What Jacob Cornelius likes most in life is to make trouble between people. He has a gift for it. God-given, probably. Too bad you didn't figure *that* out."

"I wasn't completely gullible. I was suspicious of what he told me. It was only when you admitted being ... the father that I really believed it. And it did seem to fit. When I told you about those pictures Rachel was getting and I mentioned the Hammond School, you said you didn't know anything about it, but I had the feeling you weren't telling me the truth. And Junior, I mean Vance, knew about it."

Harding took a sip of his coffee. "It was none of your business," he said bluntly. "Why should I have talked to you about it? It was a horrible time in her life, she was never the same after that. She had the right to her privacy, to try to forget."

He had a point. "Well, I'm awfully sorry," she said. "About the mistake. Jacob Cornelius tricked me."

"Yeah. The old bastard."

"I didn't want to tell Kristin about you. But Cornelius said that if I didn't he would, and that he'd make it much uglier than I was likely to."

"He'd have stopped short of actually naming me. He's a God-fearing man, after all. He'd stop just this side of an outright lie."

"And if he outright lied he would've had to Make Right the lie and apologize."

Harding looked at her, surprised. "How do you know about that stuff?"

"Kristin. Her adoptive parents are in the same church."

Harding grunted. "Of course they only Make Right to each other. Lying to people outside the church is probably just fine."

"Who was Kristin's father, then?"

"I don't know—some neighbour boy, I think. If she wants to go find him, good luck to her. Just tell her to stay away from me."

"I will. I guess it'll be up to Cornelius whether or not he gives her the right name next time."

"I doubt if he knows it. Rachel would likely have been too afraid to tell him. That bastard," Harding said, shaking his head again. "That bloody bastard."

"So Rachel was pregnant when she was living with me." Why didn't she *tell* me, Vicky wanted to demand, but she had already heard the answer Harding would likely make. It was none of her business. She felt a sudden flare of anger at Rachel, as though she, like her father, had played Vicky for a fool.

Maybe Harding could tell what she was thinking because he said, "You have to understand that Rachel was a very private person. You probably noticed how she didn't like to be touched."

"That didn't apply to you, obviously."

He shrugged. "That was sexual. At other times, well, she was just as likely to pull away from me, too. She just ... didn't want anybody to get too close. In any way. She probably didn't confide in me much more than she did in you. And she'd only just found out herself she was pregnant. She'd have told you eventually. She was just waiting to let the stuff with Dennis settle down."

"I doubt if it would have settled Dennis down to hear she was pregnant with your child. Or would he have assumed it was his?"

Harding gave a rather stiff smile. "He might have. But I don't think you understand. Everyone thought she was infertile because she had this disease—"

"Endometriosis."

"That's it."

"Or I wondered if that sadistic doctor, Angeletti, might have tied her tubes when she had Kristin."

"No, no. Not be fruitful and multiply? Rachel wasn't the one unable to have children. It was Dennis."

Vicky gaped at him. "Dennis? Mr. Stud?"

"The doctors said Rachel should be able to get pregnant, that the endometriosis wasn't preventing it. They wanted to test Dennis, but of course he refused. Everything had to be Rachel's fault. Well, Rachel really wanted to have a child. Was desperate to. At first it was just to please Dennis, but then it was for herself."

"And you were only too happy to oblige."

Harding shifted impatiently in his seat. "Think whatever you want. I know it's hard to believe that timid little Rachel could have initiated this affair, but that's how it was. She was prepared to have Dennis think the child was his, although by the time she died she didn't care what Dennis thought, she didn't want him to have any connection, any hold, over her any more. She was happy just thinking about herself and the baby. And she would never have wanted me to leave Linda for her. The idea appalled her. She wasn't in love with me. Not like ..." He turned his head aside, as though he couldn't face the words. "... I was with her."

They sat not looking at each other, toying with their coffee cups. A young couple with a toddler came into the shop and took the table beside them. The child grabbed hold of the strap of Vicky's purse hanging on her chair back. The mother laughed.

"Don't you go bothering the nice people now," she said, making no effort to retrieve the child.

Harding stood up abruptly and headed for the door. Vicky, managing quickly to extricate her purse from the child, who began screaming at the loss, followed him.

"I ran into Linda and Jun— Vance the other day," she said as they went out. "He said he was getting a place of his own."

Harding seemed in such a hurry that she wondered if he would bother answering her. But he paused, fumbling in his pocket for his car keys, then said, "Yeah, well. He never should have moved back in with us. I think Linda babies him. She thinks I bully him. Maybe we're both right." He pulled out his keys, hefted them in his hand. "But Vance is ..." He hesitated, frowned. Then he said bluntly, "Vance is weak."

Fathers and sons, Vicky thought, feeling a sudden sadness for both of them. *There's no love lost between those two*: it was something her father used to say of people, and it was always a phrase that confused her, because it seemed to say the opposite of what it meant.

Harding turned, snapped a brisk look at his watch, and headed for the blue Mercedes parked carelessly enough to take up two spots in the lot. Their eyes met as he backed out, but they both looked immediately away, as though they were strangers who had glanced at each other by accident.

Vicky sat in her car for some time, watching the street down which Harding had disappeared.

He wasn't Kristin's father. But he and Rachel had recently conceived a child. Rachel wasn't infertile.

Vicky closed her eyes. The more she found out, the more confusing it became. She had thought of Rachel as this innocent, a victim in need of protection, but she was far more complicated and resourceful than Vicky had imagined. Maybe it shouldn't bother her to find out how much Rachel had kept from her, but it did.

She'd have told you eventually.

Yeah, right. When she couldn't hide it any more. When she had no more use for you. When she moved out, moved on.

Survive and reproduce: the two great Darwinian imperatives. Rachel had certainly managed the latter, and she must, on some level, have concluded her chances of the former were better if she kept Vicky in the dark. And maybe Rachel had been right. Maybe she'd understood that Vicky's support depended on Vicky's continued perception of her as weak and passive. Would she be alive now if she'd told Vicky the truth? If, as Vicky wanted to think, telling her wouldn't have made any difference, Rachel would still have died.

What was the use of all this conjecture? A headache was settling in at the back of her head. Vicky started the car and drove home, where she ran a bath and lowered her headache into it. The phone rang, and when the machine took the call she could hear Kristin's voice. She tried not to listen. When she got out of the tub and played the tape back she wasn't surprised at the message, although she had expected Kristin to be more angry.

"So what should I do now?" Kristin concluded plaintively. "Do you think Mr. Harding was telling the truth? Should I go back to Mr. Cornelius? Would you ask him for me?"

Vicky had to smile at that one. "Fat chance," she told the machine.

Kristin had said she was going out in half an hour, so Vicky waited a full hour before calling back, praying to get a machine, but Kristin's mother answered.

"Just tell her Mrs. Bauer called, that I'm sorry about the misunderstanding," Vicky said with careful casualness, parrying the woman's curiosity.

Maybe, she thought after she'd hung up, she should have talked to the woman a little longer. She still had the feeling there was something, something about the photographs, that Kristin was keeping from her. But since her mother had probably known nothing about them, and given Vicky's record lately of getting things wrong, it was just as well she hadn't stuck her nose in deeper.

She called Amanda, but there was no answer. And then

she made herself call Clark. It was time, she decided, to tell the police everything she knew. They may not have cared about what happened to Rachel all those years ago, but what she had discovered now was more relevant. If Dennis had found out Rachel was pregnant by another man, it would have given him more reason than ever to want her dead. That she would also be implicating John Harding was something she didn't want to think about.

She reached Clark at the station and asked him to come over as soon as he could, adding, before he could think it was a personal call, that she had some information about Rachel's case.

There was a sound like static on the line, other voices, a rustling of papers, the clicking of a printer, and then Clark said, "Okay. Is five o'clock soon enough?"

"Sure. I have a tutoring student before then, anyway," Vicky said, just remembering. "Do you want ... Should I make us something to eat? Nothing fancy." Why had she asked that? She hadn't wanted this to become social, didn't want him to think she might be engineering another date. Although why shouldn't she? She had as much right to invite him out as he did her.

"I can bring over some take-out," he said.

"Better yet."

After she hung up, she ran the vacuum cleaner quickly around the living room. "You know how important a clean house is to Travis," she told the cat.

When Travis arrived, the cleanliness of the carpet was clearly the last thing on his mind. He seemed so preoccupied and unprepared for his session that Vicky decided crankily she would not even show him the carrot cake.

"Sorry," Travis sighed, dropping his pencil and slouching back in his chair, which at the sudden shift of weight tilted nervously onto its back casters. "I can't concentrate."

"You haven't been getting enough sleep, have you? And I suppose you've been skipping school, too."

Travis rubbed at his nose, which seemed to have accrued several more scars. It took him several moments before he answered. "You'll be mad when I tell you this."

"What?"

"I'm going to quit school after this year."

"Oh, Travis, you can't! You were doing okay—"

"I can always pick up my Grade Twelve later."

"The odds are you won't, and it would be ten times harder than it would be now!"

"Well, it's my dad's idea. He says I have to go for the hockey career while I can, and school is keeping me from playing or practising as much as I should. Plus he thinks this team in Colorado has me lined up as one of their bantam draft picks. And they're not supposed to, under the League rules, to offer me more than just living expenses, but my dad thinks he can get them to cough up maybe an extra ten thousand. Ten thousand *US*."

"So this is about money? About bribery?"

"No, no— I mean, sure, my dad could use the money, but ..."

"So it goes to him, not you? And it's all just speculation? You might not even get picked. Why not at least wait until you know?"

"Because I can practise in the meantime, get myself into really good shape."

"Oh, Travis. You should think about this really seriously."

"I have. I'm going to drop out." He was staring at the zipper of his jacket. His fingers fumbled with the tab, ran it up and down. Zing, zing, zing. Vicky wanted to slap at his fingers.

"Drop out and I won't give you any carrot cake."

Travis could barely manage a smile. "I'm sorry. I know you're disappointed in me."

"It's not about me. Look, do you want me to call your father? I could—"

Travis sat up, his face tense with alarm. "No! Please. It would just make things worse."

Butt out: she could hear the father's words already.

"Okay," she said. "I won't interfere." She could see him relax a little, sink back.

"It's just, you know, complicated."

"Everything is complicated," Vicky sighed. She went into the kitchen, took the carrot cake out of the refrigerator and set it on the table.

◆

Clark had brought Chinese food, enough to feed half the city. She should have told Travis to stay. But the chop suey tasted of stale cooking oil, the deep-fried prawns were overcooked into brittle chunks, and a Szechuan vegetable dish was so hot she couldn't eat it at all. Clark didn't seem to blink at any of it. They had started eating at the coffee table, sitting cross-legged on the floor. It was a posture Vicky was comfortable in but one Clark clearly had trouble maintaining. There was something undignified, she realized, in having a policeman in uniform sitting on the floor.

"Let's go to the table," she said again.

"This is fine." He unhooked his right leg, stretched it out straight under the coffee table, and propped himself up with his left hand. His knee under the coffee table was only inches from hers. She tried hard to keep her eyes from it and even harder to keep her hand from running itself up his thigh. Alien hand: she thought of Jacob Cornelius. The memory was enough to quell any erotic impulse.

She set down her chopsticks. "I have to tell you what I found out about Rachel," she said. "Turns out one of the students I was tutoring is the daughter she gave up at birth, and she's the one who sent out the pictures—"

Clark raised his eyebrows. "Really?"

"Anyway, that's a whole other story, but what you might find more relevant is that Rachel was pregnant when she died. And it wasn't by Dennis. It was by John Harding, her boss, who was at one time married to her aunt."

"How did you find that out?"

"Mostly by accident. I was accusing Harding of something else, of being this student's father, actually—oh, it's too bizarre to go into—and he admitted he was the father of the baby Rachel was carrying now."

"Well. That's very interesting. The DNA tests showed Dennis wasn't the father, but we didn't know who was."

"What? You *knew* she was pregnant?"

"Of course. We did an autopsy."

"Why didn't you *tell* me?" She wanted to jab a chopstick into his leg. "I mightn't have gone rushing around making a fool of myself."

"I couldn't. It was—"

"I know. It was none of my business." She stabbed her chopsticks at a brittle prawn. It skidded away, onto the floor. Why couldn't they just have used bloody *forks*? Clark picked the prawn up, set it carefully on the coffee table.

"I'm sorry," he said. "But you're right."

"If nothing is any of my business, why am I still in the middle of all this?" She was sounding whiny. Besides, she knew he could answer, quite reasonably: because you choose to be. She said in a more agreeable voice, "I feel as though I've been stumbling around stupidly in the dark. Like Woody Allen in *Shadows and Fog* when he protests, 'I don't *know* enough to be incompetent.'"

"I wouldn't call you incompetent," Clark said.

"Exactly. I don't know enough."

Clark gave her a little smile for that. "You probably know more than you should."

"Anyway," she said. "So Rachel was pregnant. I suppose it gives Dennis another reason to want to kill her."

"It's part of the prosecution case."

"What about Harding? Will his affair with Rachel have to be made public?"

Clark shrugged. "Probably." He stretched his left leg out straight, pulled in his right. His knee cracked, and he winced.

"The way Harding tells it, it was Rachel who initiated the affair. I'm not sure if I believe him, but in any case this could destroy his marriage."

"That's a rather classic motive for murder."

Hearing it expressed so baldly made Vicky flinch. "I've thought about that. Harding just, well, doesn't seem the type."

"You'd be surprised at who can be the type."

Vicky sighed. "I guess I just wish they could get the trial the hell over with and find Dennis guilty. Somehow he ... deserves to be found guilty. I remember seeing an interview with a prison warden who said that most of the men in his prison were guilty of what they'd been sentenced for and the rest were guilty of *something*."

"With those criteria I could arrest everybody."

"I suppose so," she said.

"Well, they probably will convict him. Although the defence might make some hay with the fact his wife was pregnant by another man."

"It's funny, in a sick kind of way," Vicky said. "Dennis, this big stud who gave Rachel such abuse because she couldn't get pregnant: and here it turns out to be *his* problem."

Clark looked down at his cleared plate and didn't answer, and Vicky realized she might have sounded a touch vulgar. She rearranged the cardboard food cartons and asked briskly, "Want any more?"

"No thanks."

"How about some carrot cake for dessert? I was using it to bribe a student, but since the wretched boy is going to drop out of school he was too ashamed to finish the whole panful."

"That would be nice."

"Come to the table," Vicky said, getting up. One of her knees cracked worse than Clark's had, and she laughed.

She pushed the CD play button on her way into the kitchen, then brought the carrot cake to the table. They ate it, saying "mmm" and "ummm," crumbs dropping from their mouths. She had thought the CD she'd left in slot one was Vivaldi, but it turned out to be Zamfir. She hoped Clark liked panpipes. If he was still here in an hour he'd get the Vivaldi, too.

"What?" Clark asked.

Vicky realized she had been staring at his cheek, where a bit of the cream-cheese icing was sticking. "A bit of the cake," she said. She reached over, wiped it off with her forefinger.

Clark caught her hand, took her finger into his mouth, sucked off the icing.

Vicky closed her eyes. Yes.

Clark put his mouth on her palm, then lowered her hand to the table. "We have to talk," he said quietly.

Vicky's eyes snapped open. *We have to talk*: was there ever a more ominous phrase? He was involved with someone else. He was gay. He was a priest. All of the above.

"Okay," she said. She swallowed the cake in her mouth without chewing, pulled her hand from where it lay under his, and laced her fingers together in front of her on the table.

Clark cleared his throat, but then said nothing. Vicky sat still, waiting. It's going to be a brush-off, she thought; for whatever reason, I'm getting the brush-off. Suddenly Clark pushed back his chair, got up, strode to the living room, stood with his back to her looking out at the street. It was dusk, that time when the waxy western light made long dendritic shadows on her lawn from the branches of her elm tree. The houses across the street had already pulled their curtains, turned on their lights.

Vicky went to the window, pulled the drapes closed. Only after she had done it did she realize how rude it must have seemed, like the cat walking on her newspaper as she tried to read, saying, don't look at that, pay attention to me.

"Sit down," she said. "Tell me." She turned on the floor lamp beside them.

Clark sat down on the sofa, leaned forward, clasping his hands between his knees. When he answered he seemed to be addressing his hands or the floor, not Vicky.

"Okay," he said. "God. I had no idea this would be so difficult. I guess, well, it's the first time I've ever had to tell anyone."

What, for heaven's sake, she wanted to yell, but she made herself sit quietly and wait. The lamp beside him had begun its slight flutter, probably because she had too many appliances overloading the circuit. She considered turning it out but was afraid to do anything to distract him.

Clark cleared his throat again. "I, uh, I've developed this condition. This physical condition. It's an endocrine imbalance. It's made me unable to ... to have sex."

"I see." Whatever revelation she had expected, this wasn't even on the list.

"Are you saying you can't ..."

"Perform."

She was dismayed to feel herself flush. *Perform* was up there with *frigid* as a word she would ban from the sexual lexicon. "You can't ... get an erection?"

"That's right."

"Is this, well, are you getting treatment? Is it something permanent? I thought there was this miraculous new drug now." *Priapica*, Amanda had called it, shuddering, after a particularly unfortunate date, but Vicky had the sense not to try make jokes about it now.

"Not miraculous enough for me. But it may not be a permanent condition. I guess I haven't ... Well, there hasn't been anyone for a while with whom I've, you know, had a relationship."

She knelt beside him, put her hand on both of his, which he had clenched into a white-knuckled knot. Under her fingertips she felt the strong and steady pendulum of his pulse.

"It's okay. It's nothing to be embarrassed about."

But it was, wasn't it? She remembered what she had just said about Dennis, her derision at how it had been *his* problem, not Rachel's, and that Clark had said nothing. She'd been so inadvertently cruel, even though Dennis, she assumed, was sterile whereas Clark just couldn't get an erection. Just. It would matter to her.

"Easy for you to say."

"Making love is about more than, you know, intercourse."

"Easy for you to say."

"Look. If this is your only reason to stop seeing me, well, it's not good enough. I was expecting something like you were gay, or seeing someone else. I won't pretend I wasn't looking forward to having sex with you, but, well, we can deal with that."

If he said *Easy for you to say* one more time, she thought, she would smack him. But what he did say was, "Isn't it pretty to think so?"

She frowned. What was that supposed to mean?

Clark slowly loosened his clenched hands. "*The Sun Also Rises*. It's what Jake says to Brett when she says they could have had such a damned good time together. But they couldn't, of course, because Jake has this ... war wound."

"Yes, I remember." The things he knew kept surprising her. "Well, I'm not Brett Ashley. And you don't have a war wound."

He was quiet for a while, and then he said, "I'm no bargain."

"Neither am I."

They sat the way they were for some time. The lamp beside them was still fluttering. Finally she got up and turned it off, and then she sat down on the sofa beside Clark, in the darkening room.

I'm no bargain. Neither am I. Solemn as wedding vows. She did like this man. Maybe she even liked him more now than she had half an hour ago. It should have been, but was not, reassuring.

CHAPTER FOURTEEN

S HE HAD A RESTLESS night, tossed with elliptical dreams, of fear and flight, of dangerous sexuality. At least, she thought, getting up, still tired, at ten o'clock, she was no longer dreaming Rachel's unfinished dream. It had started to seem like some nocturnal parasite, some incubus. Or perhaps she *was* still having the dream; how could she know for sure?

She made the coffee and sat down with the day's paper, but it was hard to think of anything other than what had happened with Clark last night. She wished she could call Amanda and talk to her, but she knew she couldn't tell her about Clark's condition; it would be too big a betrayal, and she could already hear Amanda saying, "What? Superman can't fly?"

So now she had another secret to keep. She was sick of secrets, and of the lies that had to be told to protect them.

Lies: nearly everyone connected with Rachel, including Rachel herself, had told her untruths or half-truths. When it was convenient for them, they manipulated her, and when it was inconvenient they told her it was none of her business.

Well, it was over now. She would just have to hope that Dennis would be convicted. He *had* to be guilty. What had made her doubt it were the loose ends about the pictures and Angeletti, but she knew the truth about them now. It had been nothing more sinister than a confused teenager wanting to find her mother. And John Harding? She couldn't believe he would harm Rachel. Besides, he was probably still at work when she was hit.

She gave up on reading the paper and assembled an over-due load of laundry which she tossed into the washer. On her way upstairs she almost stepped on the cat, who had taken to sleeping in front of the door to what had been Rachel's room. Vicky had begun calling him Greyfriar's Tabby.

She realized that she had not been in the room since she and Junior—Vance—had packed up Rachel's things, about two weeks ago now. Well, it was time to reclaim the room, to open the window and let in the fresh air. She nudged the cat aside, took a deep breath. *Here be dragons.* Get real. She opened the door.

She wasn't sure what she had expected, but there was a musty desolation to the room that pressed a lump into her throat. She swallowed, made herself go inside. She wrestled open the small window and immediately felt the cool outside air push in. The cat jumped onto the dresser, meowed querulously.

"I know," Vicky said.

She heard the washing machine grunt into another part of its cycle. All right, she decided, she would strip the bed and wash the bedding next. She shook the pillows out of the pillow-cases, shoved the comforter off the end of the bed, and began to unhook the fitted sheet.

She was undoing the third corner when she found it.

The sheet was on so snugly that she'd had to lift the mat-tress slightly, and her fingers brushed against something rigid that she knew immediately should not be there. She lifted the mattress higher, carefully. Lying on the boxspring was a beige file folder, thin, holding no more than a dozen papers.

Vicky lifted the folder out, lowered the mattress carefully, sat down on it. She could feel her breathing quickening. What she had found must be important if Rachel had needed to hide it.

On the tab of the file was written, in what was almost certainly Rachel's careful half-printed writing, one word: *Vance.*

She opened the file. The first page was a photocopy of what looked like a bank form, confirming the electronic transfer of $9,480 from an account at a trust company to an account at the Royal Bank in Vance Harding's name. The second page was a copy of a brief handwritten memo, with the logo of a Vancouver delicatessen at the top, saying, "Okay, Vance—I'll clear it through your account first." The third page was similar to the first, a record of an electronic transfer, this time of $4,000, to Vance's account.

What did it mean? There must be something illegal involved.

Maybe he was smuggling Freon. She remembered his cynical remarks about his father's environmentalism. Maybe, as she'd suspected, it *was* himself he was talking about. Smuggling Freon was profitable, she knew, because although CFCs were being phased out they were still manufactured and were much cheaper than their more environmentally friendly replacements. Canada, she had heard, was an easy conduit for CFCs from other countries to the US.

She turned to the next page, eagerly, looking for something more clearly incriminating, but it was only another bank form indicating a deposit to Vance's account from a credit union in Burnaby.

It wasn't until the next page that she figured it out. This page was not a photocopy, and it was crumpled, as though it might have been retrieved from a wastebasket. It held two rows of pencilled, handwritten figures, the left column with no heading and the other, which had been often erased or crossed out, saying simply, "Dad's." On both the right and left side of each entry were jotted other elliptical bits of information: "June 10, Roger's," "cash, ML Co," "Gran. Isl. Meats: leave alone." The amounts in the first column, except in cases with the pencilled notation "Leave alone," were several thousand dollars higher. Vicky glanced down the approximately twenty entries in both columns and calculated the difference to be at least $30,000. The dates seemed to cover about a six-month period.

In a year, then, Vance could have skimmed sixty thousand dollars from his father's company.

Vicky made herself look at the remaining few sheets. Three of them contained photocopies of cancelled cheques, four to a page, some payable to Vance Harding and others to Harding Refrigeration. It seemed likely that these were confirmations of the discrepancies on the sheet she had just read.

The last page was different. It was an original, on a lined page with "Harding Refrigeration: Internal Memo" printed at the top, and it was divided in half, the upper part labelled "message" and the lower labelled "reply." The first section was in Rachel's handwriting, and it said, "Vance—*please* tell him. You've got to tell him! The auditors will *know*." Vance's reply, in a thick felt pen, said, "Don't worry, okay? I just need a little longer. The auditors *won't* know."

Vicky lowered the file to her lap, closed it. Junior. Vance. Vicky remembered him in the Safeway parking lot, his pleasure at having his own place. Paid for with embezzled funds. That Rachel had assembled the file and hidden it here meant that she must have been distrustful of him. It seemed likely, indeed, that the auditors would have uncovered a fraud this clumsy, but perhaps Vance had cooked the books more smoothly in places it mattered, or bribed someone. And it was a family business, after all. Who would suspect this of an only child destined to inherit the company?

An only child. But Rachel was pregnant. Vance would not have been his father's only child for long.

Vicky closed her eyes. She thought of Vance here in this room with her, cleaning out Rachel's things. The way he had cried. The way he had said that he missed her, that he had been able to talk to her about his father, that he might have been falling in love with her.

She wanted a drink. Her hands began to shake, and she shoved them between her knees. She couldn't give in, because it would not be just one drink, just one to drive the ugliness from her brain, it would be another and another, and soon she would no longer know or care about what she should do next.

She took the file upstairs, called the police station, asked for Clark. He was out, the receptionist said, and wouldn't be back until five-thirty.

"I'll meet him there," Vicky said. "Tell him to wait. It's important."

Five-thirty was only a few hours away, but it felt to Vicky like days. She would start to do something, then wander away, circling always around the file lying in the centre of her coffee table.

It all felt slightly unreal. What sordid things would she discover next about the Hardings? Perhaps soon she would find something incriminating about Linda. Why not? If Linda had found out about her husband's affair, wouldn't she have had a motive to kill Rachel, too? Maybe it was all three of the Hardings, a conspiracy. Vicky gave a bitter laugh, picked up the file. It was Vance; it had to be. She was holding the evidence in her hand.

She thought of Dennis, suddenly. Would what she had found mean he would go free now? What about the black car Birdy had seen in the alley? Could Dennis have been there, too, brooding in his car?

But there was something else about the car that was nagging at her, some thought that had skipped across her synapses like a stone across water several days ago and that she must try to find again.

Although it was raining, and early, she set out for the police station, which was only a few blocks away. She stopped in the alley, stood looking down it, frowning, trying to remember what had tapped at her memory that night she had stood here with Clark after the poetry reading. She thought about the hole in the centre of everything people saw that the brain paved over with portraiture borrowed from the surrounding visual field, a deception exposed if, for example, they looked through a telescope at night: dim things disappeared if looked at directly. Astronomers combated the effect by looking slightly away. Averted vision. Vicky looked off to the side, at her neighbour's green fence, willing some revelation. Nothing.

She slid the hood of her jacket over her head and trudged on through the rain. On impulse, she stopped at the corner grocery, made photocopies of everything in Vance's file, and shoved them into her purse.

It was only quarter after five when she got to the station, but she told the receptionist she would wait in the tiny lobby. She read every pamphlet in the wire racks, learned that shoplifting is a crime and that she should beware bicycle thefts and get-rich-quick schemes and that disobeying a subpoena could cause her to be arrested. Then she counted the number of officers (twenty-two) in the large photograph of the White Rock City RCMP Detachment taken on the beach in front of the eponymous white rock. The officers were dressed in their fancy red jackets with the pouchy black pants and brown boots, and they were lined up on both sides of the one officer on horseback. Vicky wondered if they felt as uncomfortable as they looked. She supposed Clark was in the photograph, but she couldn't tell from where she sat since the picture was behind the counter.

At last the door to the main part of the building opened and Clark came out, wearing his uniform, the blue windbreaker draped over his arm. He looked a little flushed, and Vicky wondered if he had been embarrassed to be told she was waiting.

She stood up. "Corporal Kent." She was afraid to call him anything less formal here. She felt her own face warming slightly, and tried not to think of what had happened between them last night.

"Vicky."

"I've got something to show you. Something that's going to surprise you."

He raised an eyebrow. "Let's go out," he said, pushing open the main door. "There's a cafe across the street."

The restaurant was large and bright. They took a table at the front, although Vicky might have wished for a more private and dimly lit spot. In the movie, she indulged herself, they would be huddled at the back of a dark, smoky bar; she would slide the folder furtively across the table, her eyes nervously scanning the room.

Clark read through the file, slowly, carefully, going back and reading pages again. Outside it was getting dark, street-lights coming on. Vicky was twitchy with impatience. She ran her front teeth under her thumbnail until it was in danger of snapping off, and drank three cups of coffee. Clark hadn't touched his. The waitress didn't offer her another refill. From the way she was looking at Vicky, she was probably thinking Vicky was about to be arrested.

"And you found this under her mattress?" Clark asked finally. He reached for his coffee, his eyes still on the last page in the folder. Vicky moved his cup closer to where his fingers were groping.

"Yup."

"You'd make a good detective."

Vicky smiled. "Yup."

"And this is John Harding's son, right? The one they call Junior? I think we took a statement from him."

"Yup."

Clark closed the file, looked at her. "It certainly changes things."

"So what happens now?"

"We talk to him again. I assume he'll be at work as usual tomorrow?"

"I expect so. Why?"

"We prefer to confront suspects at their workplaces if it's a serious crime. They don't expect it, and they're less likely to become violent." He tapped his forefinger on the file. "When we show him this he'll be pretty rattled. Maybe he'll confess to more than embezzlement."

"Will you charge him with murder?"

Clark took a swallow of coffee, which must have been barely tepid by now. "That's not up to me." He paused, looking off through the windows. "We'll obviously need to do some rethinking. Dennis is still the prime suspect. There's compelling evidence against him. His girlfriend's testimony, his history with Rachel, your neighbour's testimony about the black car ..."

The black car. What *was* it that had nudged her brain about that? She frowned, staring at the tabletop.

"Well," Clark said briskly, pushing his chair back. "I better go." He picked up the file. "This is going to stir up a lot of interest." He stood up, pulled his jacket from the back of the chair, put it on. "You need a ride back home?"

Vicky was staring at his jacket.

"Vicky? What's wrong?"

"I remember!" she exclaimed. "There was something, I knew there was something— Look, okay, yes, give me a ride home. I'll show you."

"Show me what?"

"You'll see."

"Will it take long? I want to get this to the sergeant." He tapped the file.

"Just five minutes."

"Okay. Wait here. I'll get a car and pick you up."

Vicky watched him trot across the street to the station. What if she was wrong about what she remembered? But, no, she wasn't, she was sure of it. The waitress, now that it seemed clear that Vicky was not under arrest, came over, smiling, asked if she wanted anything else.

"No, nothing, thanks," Vicky said, watching the street. "I'm just waiting for a ride. Oh. I almost forgot to pay." She took out a five dollar bill, handed it to the waitress.

"You don't have to pay for *his*," the waitress said, nodding out the window.

"Sure I do," Vicky said. "Can't have them running a protection racket, can we?"

The waitress looked dismayed, and Vicky's laugh seemed to do little to reassure her. Clark pulled up in front then, and Vicky snatched up the change the waitress gave her, not caring whether she had paid for two cups of coffee or one.

It was dark now, but not cold, and the rain had stopped. Vicky got into the police car, and Clark drove quickly down Pacific, used to the respect the vehicle commanded, expertly rounding the mini-traffic circles the city had installed apparently to encourage people to crash into a disguised pile of concrete in the middle of the road. A substantial number of citizens had obliged.

"Go down the alley," Vicky said, "past Mrs. Birdsell's, and park in my driveway."

Clark made what might have been a sigh of impatience, but he did as Vicky asked. He got out of the car and started for the house, but Vicky grabbed the sleeve of his windbreaker.

"Wait here," she said. "I'll be right back."

"What are you—"

But Vicky was already running up her back steps, jamming the key into the lock. She left the door standing open, galloped through the kitchen into the living room, snatched up the phone.

If Birdy wasn't home, she was thinking, she would take the spare key Birdy had left with her and do it herself—

"Birdy! It's Vicky. I'm glad you're home. Look, would you do me a favour? Turn on your outside light.... No, don't come out. Just turn on your outside light. I'll explain later."

She hung up, dashed back out to where Clark was standing in her driveway, looking impatiently at his watch.

"Vicky, I really don't have time to—"

"Come with me." She grabbed his arm, pulled him into the alley. "Okay. The black car was parked about here, Birdy said." She drew Clark along with her. Birdy's light blazed at them, making them squint, turn sideways to it.

She looked at Clark. She'd been right.

"What colour's your jacket, Clark?"

"It's blue, of cou—" He stared at it. "Jesus Christ."

"I should have realized it sooner. But the first time something rang a bell was when we were walking back from the poetry reading. You were wearing that blue jacket, and suddenly the light hit us and I aware of us being so stark, somehow. Of your jacket being black."

Clark shaded his eyes, looked towards Birdy's house. "She must have some sort of high-pressure sodium light, or metal halide."

"The Hardings have a blue Mercedes. John Harding drives it most often, but Junior, I mean Vance, uses it, too. And I'll bet that if we parked it over here Birdy would identify it as the car she saw that night."

Clark looked back at her. "I wouldn't be at all surprised."

"And now we have an explanation for why the car was probably here such a short time. Dennis wouldn't have known Rachel was working late that night, but Vance would have."

"So would John Harding, probably."

"Well, yes," Vicky allowed. "And maybe even Linda, and they all drive the Mercedes. But Vance was embezzling money. He knew Rachel had the file—that's what he was hoping to find when he came to collect her things—and he knew she disapproved enough of what he was doing to expose him. He's an ambitious man. He was expecting to inherit the company. Rachel's alliance with his father would have destroyed him."

"You may be right."

♦

It took Vicky a while to get over her excitement. She found herself walking back and forth across her living room, itching to call Amanda, but she'd promised Clark to keep quiet until the police decided what to do.

She slumped on the sofa, cajoled the cat into her lap. She thought about Junior. Vance. It was easier to think of him as Vance now: some other person, some Mr. Hyde. She thought for the first time of what it would be like for John and Linda Harding, realizing how he had betrayed them, realizing he must have killed Rachel.

The phone rang.

As though he had known she was thinking of him, John Harding was on the line. Vicky sat up straight, dislodging the cat.

"Hi," she said, wondering if a single word could sound guilty.

"Sorry to call you, but, you know." He sounded drunk, his words spaced out too far. "I was just sitting here feeling like shit. And I wanted to ask if you told the police about, you know, about me and Rachel."

"Yes. I'm sorry, but I thought I had to."

She expected him to be angry, but he only sighed. "It's like ... I sit here and wait for them to come and arrest me. They probably think I killed her."

"I'm sure they don't."

"Like waiting for a firing squad. Waiting for your life to just, to just end."

"I know the police don't think you killed Rachel ..." *Because your son did, your son who was robbing you blind.* Vicky squeezed her eyes shut.

John Harding began to cry. Vicky bent over, pressed her forehead to her knees. Oh, please don't, she wanted to plead, but she just sat there, forcing herself to listen, telling herself it was only what she deserved.

"It'll be all right," she said, miserably.

"Come and meet me tomorrow, Vicky. Come and have lunch with me. You're the only one I can talk to about Rachel. You're the only one. Please."

"Oh, I don't know, I can't, really—" She sat up.

"Please, Vicky. You're the only one. *Please.*" He blew his nose. The line suddenly crackled and clattered, as though he'd dropped the phone. "That stupid girl called me again, you know."

"What stupid girl?"

"That one. The one who thought she was my daughter."

"Kristin? God, I'm sorry. She shouldn't keep bothering you. What did she want?"

"To see if I know who her father is. Why does she have to harass *me* about that? Why didn't her boyfriend tell her? If he knows who the mother is he probably knows who the father is."

"Wait a minute. Kristin's *boyfriend* told her about Rachel? She said she stumbled across her birth certificate in a safe deposit box."

"Well, I don't know," Harding said crankily. "She was so excited when she came to the house I don't know what all she said. But I'm sure she told me this guy called her out of the blue one day and said, 'Want to meet your mother?'"

"I see." *Damn* Kristin. Vicky had been right. There *were* things in her story that didn't add up.

"So tomorrow. You'll come meet me. One o'clock. Come to my office. We'll go somewhere nice. Thanks, Vicky."

"Yeah, sure."

She was barely registering what she had just agreed to. All she could think of was how Kristin must have lied to her. The Make Right policy didn't apply to people outside the church, Harding had said. How convenient, she thought angrily; Kristin had to tell the truth to people like Jacob Cornelius, but not to her.

Her fingers were shaking as she dialled Kristin's number. She didn't care who or what answered the phone, she was going to say some very pissed-off things.

"Hello?" It was Kristin.

"This is Mrs. Bauer. And I want the truth now, the whole goddamned truth. Who told you Rachel was your mother? Tell me or you'll be telling the police."

When Kristin's voice finally answered it sounded as frightened as Vicky could have wished. "I'm so sorry. I'm so sorry." It was barely a whisper.

"Tell me. Right now." Vicky didn't want to give her time to gather her wits.

"He was just trying to help me."

"How did he find out about Rachel? Was it his idea to send her those pictures? Why did you go along with it?"

"I don't know how he found it all out. He just ... knew. He'd gotten my birth certificate somehow. Or a copy of it. He knew Rachel didn't remember, he knew about Mr. Cornelius, he knew that sending her those pictures was the best way to make her remember."

"He knew all that, did he?" Vicky demanded. "And you believed everything he said?"

"Yes. I did. He was right about how she didn't remember. Mr. Cornelius confirmed that she didn't, so I thought he was right about the rest, about the best way to, to proceed."

"Okay. So he gets you to steal the pictures from Jacob Cornelius. He takes the one of you in Bellingham and the one outside my house. What about the one of the staff at the Hammond School? Is he the one who stole it from the church in Blaine? Is that even where he got it?"

"I don't know. He just had it. He circled the doctor's face and told me what to write."

"God, Kristin. This guy—he calls you out of nowhere, with this bizarre scheme, and you just do everything he *tells* you to? Who is he, anyway? What's his name?"

There was silence on the line. Vicky could imagine Kristin trying desperately to manufacture another convincing lie. "Well?" she said threateningly.

"You know him. Rob."

"*Rob?* The Rob I tutor?"

"Please don't tell him I told you. *Please.*"

Vicky was too stunned to say anything. Rob. Nothing was making sense. "Why?" she asked finally. "Why would he do this?"

"He wanted to help me. He wanted me to find my mother. He'd just found his own birth mother, and he was so happy. The perfect reunion, he said it was."

"I remember him telling me about it."

"We didn't want to hurt anybody. I didn't think it would hurt anybody. You have to believe me. And the tutoring—well, it's not as though I didn't need it, right? Rob suggested it, but my mom and my teacher thought it was a good idea, too."

"All right," Vicky said, letting her voice soften a little. She sighed. "Well, I'll talk to you later. By the way. Don't phone Mr. Harding again. I mean it. He doesn't know who your father is, and he's got enough to worry about."

Rob, she thought, putting down the phone. Rob. Why would he care about Kristin finding her mother? How would he know so much about all of them? His tutoring, she realized, would have been manipulated just as Kristin's had been, not because he needed it but because Vicky was living with Rachel.

She had to talk to Rob. Now. Before Kristin did. Before he could prepare more lies for her. *We didn't want to hurt anyone,* Kristin had said. That was probably true. But Rob still had a lot of explaining to do. She remembered the way he would look at Rachel. She had thought it a simple sexual attraction to a beautiful woman, but it was obviously more complicated.

No answer. Damn.

She had the urge to drive to his apartment, bang on the door, and demand some answers. As though that would make him be home. He was probably out for the evening; she would have to wait until tomorrow.

Tomorrow. Good grief. She had agreed to meet John Harding. What was wrong with her *brain*? How could she have lunch with him and say consoling things when she knew that soon he was going to get even more devastating news?

And what would Clark say about her appointment? She would have to tell him. Tomorrow he was intending to go talk to Vance, maybe even arrest him. Clark would hardly be pleased to hear that Vicky would be on the scene, too.

She called his home number, hoping he wouldn't be back yet and that she would get his machine. She did.

"I just thought I should tell you," she said, "that I got a call from John Harding, and he was, well, pretty depressed, and I seem to have let him talk me into having lunch with him tomorrow. I'm supposed to meet him at the plant at one o'clock. I know you wanted to talk to Vance tomorrow, so I thought I should clear this with you? To make sure I won't be in the way? Well. Call me if it's a problem."

She hung up, hating the way her voice had sounded, the raised inflections at the ends of her sentences, a teenage girl asking permission from Daddy. Still, this was a murder investigation; if Clark ordered her not to go it wouldn't be a question of someone trying to bully her.

She was in the basement trying to shake wrinkles out of the laundry she'd forgotten in the dryer when she heard the phone. She ran up the stairs, grabbing the receiver just before the machine would have cut in.

"Got your message," Clark said. It was hard to tell how annoyed he was. "What's this about your going to see Harding tomorrow?"

"He just sounded so ... needy, I couldn't say no."

"It's not the best timing, Vicky."

"I know."

"The situation is dangerous. And I haven't forgotten, in case you have, that Rachel was wearing your jacket the night she was killed. It's not a complete impossibility that you were the intended target."

A chill went up her neck. She *had* forgotten, actually.

"But I won't even be seeing Vance. I'll just go to Harding's office and then we'll go out. There are dozens of people around all the time. Why should anything happen to me now when nothing's happened to me there before?"

Clark sighed. Vicky could hear him tapping something against a hard surface. "Okay, look," he said. "You're meeting him at one. I'll give you half an hour to get out of there and then we'll go in and pick up Vance. It might be just as well to have his old man out of the way. But I don't want either of them to know we're coming."

"Yes, sir."

"This is no joke, Vicky."

Vicky sighed. "I know."

"It won't be easy meeting with Harding and not telling him what you know about his son. Are you up to that?"

"I'll have to be."

"All right, then. We'll wait outside, in an unmarked car. We don't want to spook either of them. After you've left we'll go in and see to Vance."

"What if he's out?"

"I'll call in the morning, say I'm a new customer, make an appointment."

"Are you going to arrest him?"

There was a pause. "Don't ask," he said.

Don't ask? What kind of answer was that?

After she'd hung up, she demanded of the cat, who was dozing beside her, "*Am* I being foolish?" He slit open one eye. "I don't need a lecture," she said, getting up and pacing around the house.

Finally she called Amanda.

"Yes. You *are* being foolish," Amanda declared. "You don't owe Harding this pity lunch."

Vicky winced. "Well, I did help to screw up his life."

"Don't flatter yourself. He screwed it up himself. Besides, this is police business. How do you know Harding isn't just luring you there? How do you know you can trust him?"

"He just ... Well, if he's faked everything with me so far he's a better actor than Olivier."

"Everyone above ground is a better actor than Olivier."

"You're supposed to be reassuring me, not quibbling with my verb tenses."

"Yeah, yeah. Well, look—just call me as soon as you've had lunch. If I don't hear from you by two-thirty I'm phoning Superman."

"Okay. Two-thirty."

"I really don't know why you still want to be involved with these people, Vicky. Do you feel you still owe it to Rachel somehow? You know she just used you."

Vicky had to think about it. *She just used you*: perhaps she had, but it wasn't that easy to stop caring about her. Besides, hadn't Vicky had used Rachel, too—to give herself some sense of usefulness, to drive away the loneliness from her house?

"Loose ends, maybe," Vicky said finally. "I don't like loose ends."

Amanda snorted. "Sounds like some bathroom joke."

"And ... simple curiosity, I suppose." Vicky remembered the cartoon of the cat belly-up outside Ye Olde Curiosity Shoppe.

"The only simple thing here, my dear, is you."

"'Simplicity is the result of profound thought.'"

"Duh. What idiot said that?"

"Another dead Englishman."

CHAPTER FIFTEEN

VICKY PARKED AT THE FRONT of the building. Around the side she glimpsed Vance's red truck beside the blue Mercedes. Good. They were apparently both here. Maybe she had hoped they wouldn't be. Why had she agreed to this, this cloak and dagger lunch, she asked herself morosely for the hundredth time. Maybe Harding had been so drunk that he wouldn't even recall asking her to meet him. She remembered such episodes in her own life, opening the door blearily to people and barely recognizing them as they exclaimed, "Aren't you ready?"

And what if she ran into Vance? Could she convincingly pretend not to know both what he had done and what was awaiting him?

It was ten to one. She supposed she had to make sure Clark had arrived before she went in, so she sat uneasily in the car, wishing she had come a bit late. It would look odd now if she drove off and came back in ten minutes. If she'd had a cell phone, which Amanda kept urging her to buy, she could at least have called Rob again. There'd been no answer all morning.

Then she saw Clark in the rearview mirror, just pulling up across the street. There was another man in the passenger seat. The car was an unmarked sedan, but the men were both in uniform. The vehicle was chosen, she assumed, so as not to alarm Vance, and the uniforms were to do the opposite. She resisted the urge to wave. The cloak wasn't supposed to wave to the dagger.

She got out of her car, went to the front door, pulled at the handle. The door didn't move. She put her hands up to the glass, peered inside. There was no one at the reception desk, but she could see a small sign propped on it saying, Back In Twenty Minutes. Oh, great. Now what should she do? She could see the door to Harding's office, but it was closed. He probably wasn't even aware the receptionist was away.

She glanced across the street at Clark, hoping he could see what had happened. She was about to return to her car when she heard someone say, "Hey, there!"

It was one of the two men wrestling a refrigerator into a truck at the side loading bay. Vicky went over to them. The one who had spoken eased the dolly he was wheeling to an upright position, took off his work gloves, and wiped his face with the back of his hand. He was barely five feet tall, but so muscular that he seemed larger than his gangly, six-foot companion.

"Hi," Vicky said. "The front door seems to be locked."

The man rolled his eyes. "Must be that new girl. She don't know what she's doing."

"I had an appointment with Mr. Harding," Vicky said. "I don't suppose you know if he's in his office?"

"Expect so. Saw him around here a minute ago. You know how to get to his office from here?"

"I—"

"Just go through this workroom, through that door at the end, see, and straight through the showroom to the front."

"Thanks," Vicky said. "I appreciate your help."

"No problemo." The man put on his gloves again, started moving the dolly along the ramp into the back of the truck, where his co-worker had already disappeared.

Vicky stepped up into the workroom, a large warehouse-size area stacked with piles of what were probably parts of freezers and refrigerators. A row of barrels stood against one wall; another wall was hung with huge hoses and pipes, which she assumed had something to do with the coolants. About twenty walk-in freezers of various sizes and states of assembly formed a crooked aisle, down which she headed towards the door at the far end.

A machine suddenly started up somewhere, a compressor perhaps, something loud and large enough to make the floor tremble. She shivered; there didn't seem to be any heating in the room. That made sense, considering the nature of the business, but she could imagine it made working conditions less than pleasant.

She tripped over a plank, stumbled against the side of one of the freezers. Her purse fell to the floor. As she knelt to pick it up, she glanced at the door through which she had entered. She could still change her mind, make a dash for the policemen across the street and say this was too hard, she'd learned her lesson, from now on she just wanted to mind her own business—

She straightened, slid her purse strap determinedly over her shoulder, and stepped over the plank.

And suddenly she was falling, forward and to the right. Something had pushed her from behind, and, even as her hands flew out instinctively in front of her to break her fall, she knew they would be too late. Her foot had caught on the slightly raised sill of the freezer door beside her, and she fell, hard, onto her left knee and then sideways, onto her right shoulder and her chest, into the freezer. Her head cracked against one of the metal shelves, and, as she felt herself pulled into the grey whirl of unconsciousness, she heard the freezer door slamming shut.

◆

She blinked, again and again, her pupils opening and opening and finding not even the tiniest fragment of light. Her head was throbbing, and she felt something wet on her forehead and on her cheek. There was an acrid, sour smell in her nostrils.

It took her several moments to remember what had happened, where she was. How long had she been here?

She struggled to her hands and knees, fighting against the dizziness and the pain shooting into her temples. Breathe, she told herself, just breathe, in and out. Each inhalation brought a surge of pain to her head. When she clenched her teeth against the throbbing, she realized they had been chattering, that she was shivering uncontrollably.

Cautiously, she groped to one side, found what must have been a vertical support rod for the freezer racks and tightened her fingers around it, then slowly pulled herself to her feet.

It was the blackness that was most terrifying. She had never experienced such complete darkness.

She made note of where her feet were and then tried to turn herself ninety degrees. Now, she hoped, trying to remember how she had fallen, she should be facing more or less in the direction of the door. There would be a handle, a light switch—

And even as she thought, but the light won't work because the freezer isn't plugged in, thank God at least for that, she heard a sound that made her rigid with horror. The sound of a motor.

Panic clawed at her. She extended her arms in front of her and stumbled forward. She touched a wall, moved her fingers sideways along it, scrabbling, clawing, looking for a crack that might indicate a door. She could hear her pulse booming as though someone had turned up the volume.

"Help! Help!"

She began beating on the wall with her fists.

Could anyone possibly hear her? The freezer was well insulated; perhaps that would make it soundproof. She thought of the machine that had started up outside just before she had been pushed into here; it would muffle her cries even more.

It was getting colder. How long would it take before the

temperature would be below freezing? Perhaps it was there already. She was wearing jeans and a lightweight jacket, nothing that would really keep her warm. Northern Alberta where she had grown up was a part of the world where the possibilities of freezing to death were all too real; every child was taught the dangers, every parent knew the cautionary tales. A fiery hell was a southern fiction; hell, for her, was cold.

Her whole body was shaking. That was good, she remembered: shivering was helping to maintain her normal body temperature. But it was something the body couldn't continue indefinitely; she would keep losing heat, a degree every few minutes. When the shivering stopped it would mean the heart was slowing down, limiting blood flow to the limbs to maintain the core functions. And how long before the heart stopped, before the final coma? Twenty minutes? Half an hour?

Clark said he'd give her half an hour. Maybe he had already started looking for her. How long before he found her?

She flattened her body and arms against the wall, moved sideways, feeling for any irregularity that could be a door seal, a hinge or handle, a light switch, a thermostat. It wouldn't be long before she wouldn't be able to touch anything with her bare fingers, before they would freeze to any metal they encountered.

"Help!" she shouted, pausing to pound on the wall. It seemed to be getting harder to breathe. Maybe shouting was pointless; maybe she should be conserving oxygen. From the glimpse she'd gotten of the interior before the door was slammed shut, she had a sense of a room smaller than her bedroom. How long would it take to deplete the oxygen in such a space? Surely not less time than it would take her to freeze to death.

"Help!"

The wall was starting to feel colder. She was wasting her

warmth spread-eagling herself against it like this. But her only hope was to find the door handle. Was she up against the wrong wall?

She continued moving sideways, faster now, every part of her body straining to feel something other than the sleek, smooth coldness.

A corner. Maybe she had been on the wrong wall. Should she go back, or try the wall she had just come to?

She took the new wall, began inching along it. She stepped on something hard and jagged and kicked it aside. Her outspread fingers touched metal; she could feel a sticky burning, and she jerked away, pulled her hand inside her jacket sleeve and fumbled for the metal again. It felt like the supporting pole holding the wire racks, perhaps the one against which she had fallen. Where was she? Was she back where she had started? Where was the damned door?

She moved back to the corner, felt her way along the wall she had been against before. Another corner. She turned, felt her way along this third wall. She was making a noise in her throat, a kind of moaning, something she couldn't stop. Her fingers were growing numb; they felt like insensate claws at the ends of her hands. The wetness on her cheeks, which could have been either blood or tears, was freezing. She had to keep blinking to stop the moisture in her eyes from turning to ice.

Something jabbed her suddenly in the ribs. A hard flat oblong embedded in the wall. She felt it move as she pulled back from it. It was a lever of some kind. A handle.

She pulled her hand higher up into her sleeve, fumbled for a grip, jerked down on the handle. She could hear something grate in the lock, something release. She held the handle down as far as it would go, pushing with her whole body. Nothing. She pulled inwards on the handle. Nothing. The door seemed to be jammed from the outside. She tried again and again, screaming wordless, frantic syllables into the darkness.

There wasn't anything more she could do. If the freezer had any emergency safety features she hadn't found them. Maybe they hadn't been installed yet. Or maybe whoever had locked her in had disabled them.

She pounded her fists against the door, feeling the impact now only in her shoulders, and sank slowly to the floor.

"Help! Help!" The air she was drawing in seemed to be hardening in her throat. She knew that if she could see it when it came out it would be a white cloud, turning into fine crystals settling on her arms.

She pounded on the door. "Help me," she said, in a whisper now. "Please help me."

The door opened.

She fell forward, over the sill, in a heap on the warehouse floor. The sudden light was overwhelming; she squeezed her lids shut, tucked her head closer to her chest.

"Vicky! My God! Are you all right?" It was a woman's voice.

"Thank you," Vicky said. Her tongue had trouble forming the words.

"My God! How long have you been in there? What happened?"

Vicky slit open one eye, looked up. The overhead lights blinded her, and she closed it again. But she had recognized the woman. Linda Harding.

"What time is it?" she asked. She could look at her own watch, but it would mean opening her eyes.

"Almost one-thirty. Oh, Vicky." Linda knelt down, began rubbing Vicky's hands between her own. "I thought I must be imagining things when I walked past and heard something inside. How long were you there? You might have frostbite. I'll get John, or Junior—"

"No. No, it's okay." She made herself sit up, squint an eye open again at Linda. It was less difficult this time. "Outside. There's someone ... Never mind."

Linda kept rubbing her hands. "Are you sure?"

Vicky stumbled to her feet. "It's okay. I'll just go. I should keep moving."

Two workmen in denim overalls had come over and stood staring at her.

"She was in the *freezer*?" one of them asked.

"Yes," Vicky said, shoving clumsily past them, to the open door through which she'd entered. "She was in the damned freezer."

◆

The hospital wanted to keep her overnight, but when the X-rays came back she insisted on going home.

"No frostbite, no concussion. I'm fine," she said.

"You should have someone stay overnight with you then," the doctor said, tapping his clipboard as though he were only following its instructions.

"I'll stay with her," Clark said.

"It's not necessary," Vicky said. "Really."

"It may not be absolutely *necessary*," said the doctor impatiently. "But I'd advise it."

Vicky's voice seemed to have trouble deciding on submissive or irritated. "Okay. Fine," she said. The "okay" sounded submissive and the "fine" sounded irritable.

She let Clark escort her out through the lobby. People in the waiting room put down their magazines and stared. With her patched-up forehead and rumpled clothes and police chaperon she must have looked like someone who'd been in a barroom brawl.

"You really don't need to stay overnight," she said. "Even the doctor said it's not necessary. And Vance has been arrested, right? A whole herd of police were galloping up to the warehouse as we left. I'm hardly in danger any more."

"It's a precaution."

"It's not *necessary.*"

"You might not be the best judge right now of what's best for you."

She started to make some sarcastic reply when she realized that staying was something Clark needed to do, because he felt guilty and angry with himself. No matter that she'd protested that it had been her idea to meet Harding, he'd set his mouth grimly and said, no, it was his fault.

"All right," she said. "If you really want to."

The car was still standing in the ambulance zone. They got in, headed south to White Rock. They passed the street Dulci Warner lived on, and Vicky tried to remember when her next tutoring session with her was, but it seemed almost comically irrelevant. Tomorrow, next week, who cares? They had given her an injection of something, and it seemed only now to be taking hold, making her spacy.

It was getting dark. Time flies when you're having fun, she thought, pushing the heater slide up to maximum. She hadn't felt warm since she'd left the warehouse. She wrapped her arms around herself, tried not to shiver, knowing Clark was casting disapproving glances at her, wondering if he should turn around and have her strapped into a hospital bed.

She smiled at him. He had a very handsome profile, all nice crisp angles, his asymmetrical nose looking perfectly straight from the side. She wanted to reach out and press her palm against his forehead, like an iron smoothing away the worried wrinkles. "I'm okay, Clark, really," she said. "A headache, that's all. Maybe a lingering phobia about frozen food."

"You could have been killed. If Linda hadn't come by just then ..."

"Well, she did. It's over. Besides, who'd have imagined Vance would do something like that?"

Clark shrugged. "He must have suspected Rachel had told

you about him, or that you'd found the papers. Maybe he heard you tell the workmen you had an appointment with his father, and he panicked, had to stop you from talking to him, or to us. Suddenly he sees you walking past the freezer, just pushes you in, anything to stop you. Who knows exactly what he was thinking? Of course he's not admitting anything."

"I guess his father and Linda have been ... told about everything by now." It made the pain in her head worse to think about them, what they must be facing. Linda had saved her life, and this was her reward.

"I suppose so. I've asked to be taken off the case."

"Why?"

He stopped at the light at 16th, the boundary between Surrey and White Rock. He took his time before answering. "I made an error in judgement."

"How? What?"

"You."

"An error in judgment. I've been called worse."

He frowned. "You know what I mean."

"I don't, actually. You can't blame yourself for something I chose to do."

The light went green; he accelerated, fast. "I'm blaming myself for what *I* chose to do," he said.

"Which was?"

"I chose to get personally involved."

She considered several replies but decided against all of them. They started down the slope towards the beach, Semiahmoo Bay bursting into view and reflecting the shards of sunset. He turned on Pacific, then down her alley and into her driveway, parking close behind her car. If she wanted to get away she'd have to do it on foot. She could imagine Birdy twitching aside her curtains for a better look, could imagine what she would say the next morning when Clark's car would still be there.

I chose to get personally involved. Going up the stairs she thought suddenly of Conrad. If he were here none of this would have happened: she wouldn't have invited a stranger to stay in their house, she wouldn't have had to see her die, she wouldn't have met any of the woman's confusing relatives, she wouldn't have had anyone try to kill her today, she wouldn't be coming home with a policeman who chose to get personally involved.

Clark stood on the top step, as though he needed to be invited inside. "Well, come in," she said, her voice chipped with more *brusquerie* than she'd intended. "Unless you want to sleep in the car."

He ran his hand up and down the railing. "I don't have to stay. If you really don't want me to."

She didn't know whether to laugh or scream. "For Pete's sake. Come in."

She turned on the stereo and left him reading a magazine while she took a shower. Even under the hot water spells of shivers gripped her, and she stood rigid, trembling, her eyes squeezed shut, feeling the water turning to ice. When she reached out to turn it hotter, she snatched her hand back, her mind shouting, no, it's metal, your skin will stick to it.

Finally, she kicked the bathtub plug into place and let the tub fill, lay back in it. She knew only by looking at the steam and her reddening skin that the water must be hotter than she was used to.

She tried to make her mind empty, to let what had happened to her soak away into the water, but her thoughts kept finding their way back to the moment she had been pushed, kept imagining Vance standing there. He must have been desperate, Clark said. Still, she had known him and liked him, and all the while he must have been wishing her dead, as he had wished Rachel dead.

She wondered if Rachel had seen who hit her, if in that split second she had thought, too, no, Vance couldn't do that to me. Had he killed her only because she knew of his embezzlement, or was it also because he knew she was pregnant with his father's child? Was he jealous, not just of the child but of Rachel? He had loved her, he'd said. What would it feel like to find out a woman you wanted was sleeping with your father, especially a father you resented? Money and sex, the commonest motives for murder.

Vicky was still shivering. With her feet she turned the tap as hot as it would go and felt the water surge around her calves.

She remembered reading about an experiment on frogs who when placed in hot water struggled to escape but who when later placed in cool water that was gradually warmed sat peacefully until cooked. Why do that to poor frogs, she'd thought, when we already know people would cheerfully cook themselves to death in hot tubs?

Her own tub took the precaution now of running off most of the new hot water, gulping and snorting, into the overflow pipe. She wouldn't be able to cook herself peacefully to death today.

There was a rap at the door.

"Yes?"

"Are you okay in there? It's been quite a while."

"I'm getting warm, finally. I've had ice, now I want fire. 'Fire and Ice.'" The poem, as she recalled, was not as much about fire and ice as about hatred and desire.

"Robert Frost," Clark said, surprising her.

"Right," she said.

"I've ordered a pizza. I hope that's okay."

"Good idea. Will I have to get out of the bath to eat it?"

"I could slide some under the door."

She laughed. The man had made a joke, an actual joke. To be sure, she glanced at the door to see how big the crack under it was.

"Give me a minute," she said.

She was glad he was here. The knowledge came so suddenly that she sat up abruptly, slurring water over the edge of the tub: it's simple, I'm glad he's here.

The pizza had arrived by the time she'd put on her robe and come into the living room. The whole house was steamy, the windows fogged over. The cat lay in the corner, dazed, his legs in the air as though he'd been chloroformed. Tina Turner was playing, low, on the stereo. Vicky wondered if it was the CD she'd left in or whether Clark had chosen Tina's belligerent "We Don't Need Another Hero."

The pizza was actually three, in case, Clark said, there were toppings she didn't like, but she was suddenly ravenous, ready to eat all of them.

"There was a phone call while you were in the shower," Clark said. "I probably shouldn't have answered, but I did. It was your friend Amanda."

"What did she say?" Oh, please, she thought, let it not have been anything insulting.

"She asked me if I was Superman."

"Oh, God. I'm sorry."

"It's all right," Clark said. "I'm used to it."

"I didn't tell her much about you. Just, you know, your name, how we met."

Vicky wondered if he believed her. Men always suspected women of gossiping about them. Probably because it was true.

Clark took a bite of pizza, wiped his fingers on his napkin. They left a red smear. He was sweating, she noticed, which was hardly surprising considering the humidity in the room.

"I'm sorry if I sounded so ... uptight earlier," he said. "I was just angry at myself for putting you in danger."

Not this again. "Well, we pesky civilians *will* keep getting in the way."

He didn't smile. "Maybe I'm too old for this job."

"Yeah. Right."

"I'm serious." He ran his hand through his hair. "Age is a big factor in work like this."

"You're not exactly a weedy old man."

"I don't mean physical conditioning. My brother does some Formula racing and he told me drivers over forty are considered a disadvantaged class. I assumed it was because of slower reflexes or eyesight, but it's because they have more fear."

"Fear puts one into a disadvantaged class?"

"Apparently. But evolution must have had a reason to make the young more willing to take risks."

Vicky told him about the frogs in warming water. "The point being," she concluded, "that animals, including humans, don't sense danger if the risk is slow and familiar. We don't anticipate what we can't perceive. But, hey, maybe old frogs would have been more afraid and suspicious to start with."

"So you *can* teach an old frog new tricks."

She laughed, louder than she'd expected to. Clark had made another joke. Life was good.

"If fear is a trick," she said, reaching for another slice of pizza.

"*Not* having fear might be a worse trick. Anyway, the fear I could do without is the kind you get later, when you remember the danger. Retroactive fear. The 'what if.'" Clark balled up his napkin and set it beside his plate.

Vicky smiled wryly. She couldn't argue with him about the paralyzing perniciousness of the great What If.

There was enough pizza left over to last her for a week. She couldn't persuade Clark to take any, although she supposed she could ask him again in the morning.

She wrapped the leftovers in wax paper and reached into the refrigerator to jostle some room. The sudden current of cold air made her gasp, stumble away, slam shut the door. She stood backed up against the sink, astonished at her reaction.

Clark had come into the kitchen carrying his plate. "Are you okay?"

She made herself laugh, not convincingly. "Just ... feeling that cold from the refrigerator all of a sudden."

"That's a normal reaction, I imagine, after what happened." But he was still staring at her.

"What's odd is that the memory wasn't of being trapped in the freezer, but of a day when I was a kid, one of those grey, minus-forty-degree January days you can get in northern Alberta. I was walking home from school. I was still small and light enough to walk on top of the drifts hardened by the wind. Suddenly I broke through the crust and plunged in, right up to my armpits. It seemed to take half an hour to struggle free, and I could feel the numbness moving up my legs, the wind freezing my breath and my tears to my face. Funny, I haven't thought of that in twenty years."

"It's the way things work, I guess. You experience A and it reminds you of B."

"Associative memory," she said.

"Retroactive fear," Clark said.

They went into the living room and Vicky turned on the TV, something safe, so they wouldn't have to talk. They watched *Jeopardy*, whose answers, she was disconcerted to discover, Clark was quicker at than she was, and then a movie full of car chases and impossibly constructed women. Clark sat beside her on the couch, his arm loosely around her shoulders. She wondered if she should get dressed, if he might consider the robe with nothing underneath it provocative, but then she thought, what the hell, if he wants to spend the night he gets what he deserves.

Being so close to him was making her nervous and itchy with desire. How could she feel like this? She had narrowly escaped death and here she was a few hours later wanting to have sex. Maybe it was *because* she had narrowly escaped death, her body now clamoring for life, the old *carpe diem*.

A trembling passed through her. Clark tightened his arm around her shoulders.

"Sorry," she said.

"It's all right. You still feel cold?"

"The house must be ninety degrees. It's you."

"Me?"

"Where do you want to sleep? On the couch or in my bed?"

It took him a long time to make any response. Then he slid his free hand slowly inside her robe, onto her breast. It made her shiver again, the skin of her whole body reaching for him. She closed her eyes, caught her breath.

"I'll disappoint you," he said. "You know that."

"No, you won't. I have retroactive hypothermia. It's like retroactive fear, only colder. I just need you to lay your naked body beside me and make me warm."

He ran his fingers lightly across her other breast. "It sounds almost like my duty," he said. "One of those serve and protect kind of things."

"There you go."

CHAPTER SIXTEEN

*C*LARK WAS GONE by the time she got up, but she found a note on the kitchen counter.

"Vicky," it said, in a rather stiffly upright and half-printed script. "Sorry I have to leave so early." There was the beginning of a word, crossed out, and then, "Thank you for letting me stay."

She smiled. Thank *you*. Obviously it had been more fun for her than for him, but she realized it hadn't exactly required a lot of skill to satisfy her. It embarrassed her now to remember how aroused she had been; he'd barely needed to touch her. Something to do with what happened at Harding's, some get-it-while-you-can biology.

She made herself coffee, let the cat in and out, in and out, checked her calendar for tutoring sessions. Ajit: two-thirty. She would have forgotten.

She felt more dazed and sluggish this morning than she had last night, and her temple, where she had fallen against the racks in the freezer, was throbbing. When she peeled the bandage back for a look she grimaced. Maybe she should have let the doctor put in a stitch. Maybe there would be a scar for the rest of her life, reminding her of Vance, of Rachel, every time she looked in a mirror. Associative memory.

She sighed, pressed the bandage back into place, and called Amanda, knowing she'd still be at work, not wanting to have what Amanda called the full-Nanaimo conversation until the weekend, when they were meeting for a movie.

"Yes, he did stay overnight," she told the machine. "And if

you call him Superman again I'll give him permission to shoot you. I mean it."

She had just hung the phone up when it rang.

"Hello?"

"Hey. Vicky."

Her hand clenched on the receiver. "Dennis?"

"Yup. They let me out today. My lawyer says it had something to do with some papers you found. So thanks, eh?"

What could she say? She *had* helped him get released. The words *you're welcome* formed automatically on her lips, but she bit them back. The thought of Dennis being grateful to her, for anything, made her slightly nauseous.

"I see," she managed, trying for neutrality.

"So it was one of those damned Hardings." He laughed. "I might have known. Those fucked-up relatives."

"Well." Did she dare just say goodbye and hang up?

"Maybe I'll call you sometime, Vicky. Give us both a treat, eh?"

"That's not a good idea, Dennis."

"Why the hell not? I'm not good enough for you?"

"There are legal implications." Would he buy that? She held her breath, waited for his answer.

"Yeah, well, whatever. I gotta get back to work now. Those bastards tried to take my job away, but my lawyer, he's a real kick-ass guy, he's making them give it back."

"Okay. Goodbye then, Dennis."

Her hand was shaking when she replaced the receiver. Please, God, she thought, don't ever let him call me again. She realized that if she had to choose between being alone in a room with Vance or with Dennis she would choose Vance.

Well, it was unlikely she would ever need to make such a choice. Dennis, Vance, they were history. She had a life to get back to. She glanced at the calendar, circled the time Ajit was coming.

The phone. She let the machine take the call, in case it was Dennis again.

"Vicky? This is Rob. Look, Kristin told me that you—"

She grabbed the receiver. "Rob." How could she have forgotten? Yesterday morning she had been calling his place every half hour, chafing at not being able to talk to him, to sort out the perplexing things Kristin had confessed. Her mind snapped alert, retrieving her anger at his duplicity.

"Kristin told me you found out. About ... You know. How I helped her."

"Helped her. You certainly did. Helped her to lie and deceive and upset Rachel with those damned pictures."

"I'm sorry. I didn't mean—"

"And me. You didn't want tutoring at all, did you? You were just using me."

"Hey," Rob said bluntly, "you got paid, didn't you?"

Vicky took a breath, held back her reply. If she wanted Rob's co-operation she would have to cut her anger with civility. Either that or threaten him with the police, which she would prefer not to do.

"Look. I just want an explanation. Why did you get involved in all this? How did you know about Rachel, about Kristin being her daughter, about the Hammond School and Angeletti?"

There was a long pause. She was about to say "Well?" when he answered, "Okay. I didn't tell Kristin everything. I didn't think I needed to. I'm at the college now, I've got a class in three minutes. I can come over after that."

Come over. Vicky glanced out the window, envisioning his black Camaro pull up. Black. Under Birdy's lights, blue turned black, but black would remain black, wouldn't it?

She looked away, tried to scoff at herself. It's Dennis! No, it's Vance! No, it's *Rob*!

But she couldn't laugh away the chill of fear. The last time she had imagined herself safe she had almost died.

"I have to go out," she said. "I'll meet you at the college after your class."

He hesitated. "Okay. Meet me in the cafeteria at eleven. I have the stuff in my car."

"The stuff."

"To show you."

"Okay. Eleven. The cafeteria."

The day was unseasonably warm, spring pulling cherry blossoms into bloom from the trees along the street that led to the college. Vicky was perspiring in her sweatshirt and jacket as she walked across the small campus to the two-storey building housing the cafeteria. Students in shorts were sunning themselves in the quad.

The last time she had been here it had been to meet Rob's History professor, to get his instructions as to how much editing he would accept from her on Rob's papers. It annoyed her to think about it now, how Rob had just been wasting her time. Perhaps he had even made mistakes deliberately, to make her think she was being useful.

She went up the stairs to the cafeteria, which took up the whole second floor. A group of students blocking the turnstiles and laughing at something in a magazine gave her an odd glance as she squeezed by: perhaps she was too old to carry off the bandage-on-the-forehead look. She got a coffee, went into the large seating area occupied now by only about a dozen people. She was early, so she didn't expect Rob to be here yet, but there he was, against the far wall, with a cardboard storage box sitting on the table in front of him. He waved at her, rising slightly from his seat. As though he might actually be happy to see her.

She went over to the table, sat down. Rob pushed the box to the side so they could see each other. His usually amiable face looked tight and pinched, and his hair had an odd uncombed sprout at the top of his head. Half a bran muffin was on a plate in front of him; crumbs speckled his grey T-shirt.

Rob, her favourite student. She had to remind herself of what he'd done, to make herself be angry.

"All right. Tell me."

"I just wanted to help Kristin. And Rachel."

"Sure. You get Kristin involved completely over her head in some absurd scheme. And you send Rachel pictures to terrify her."

"They weren't meant to terrify her—"

"Right. Kristin explained all that. They were supposed to make her *remember*." Her voice put a hard edge on the word. "I can't believe you were part of this mess, Rob. Kristin, okay, she's young and silly, but you—I'd have imagined you as the level head here. Surely you could have approached Rachel in some more direct way. Why this bizarre charade?"

Rob ran his hand through his hair. The bit sticking up at the top had enough of a knot in it to snag his fingers. "Okay, I agree it might have been ... excessive. But, well, I have this Psychology prof—Psych is my major, remember—and she's really into all that Freudian stuff, the unconscious and all that. And what was going on with Rachel sounded as though it was all about the unconscious. I figured we could start with that."

Vicky sighed. "A little learning is a dangerous thing."

"And then maybe the ... the intrigue of it all took over. I know you think it's all my fault, but Kristin was the one who really got into it."

"She was the one who stole the first pictures from Rachel's father, I assume?"

Rob nodded. "I admit it was my idea to send them to Rachel one by one. But taking them in the first place was Kristin's. She was enjoying it. Visiting the old guy. Pretending. I was just along to drive her. I'm sorry about the phone call, by the way."

"What phone ca—?" Then she remembered. "That was *you*? *You're* the one who called from the retirement home to warn me off? For God's sake. You frightened me half to death!"

"I'm sorry. I really am. But ... we arrived that day just as you were leaving, and we got scared, thinking you might be finding out too much, that you'd figure out it was Kristin who was the church woman coming to see old Cornelius."

Vicky sighed. "I wasn't anywhere close." Was that a small twitch of satisfaction on Rob's lips? If so, it was gone almost immediately. "And the pictures that weren't from the album. The one of Kristin, and the one outside my house. You were the photographer, I suppose."

"Yes."

"And the one from the Hammond School?" She hadn't even a wild guess for an answer to that one.

Rob reached into the box and took out a photograph. "This one?" He slid it across to her.

It was, except for the missing circle around Angeletti's face, the same as the one Rachel had gotten, the one Bitsy had exclaimed over at the church.

Rob was smiling now, trying to hide it, but smiling. She pushed the picture back across the table to him, didn't answer. She knew he would explain, that his smile was the eager kind that preceded a revelation.

"Do you know what's most important to me about this picture?" he asked.

"I've no idea."

He pointed at one of the women, in a long dark dress with a cameo brooch at the neck, seated in the front row. "Know who that is?"

"No." Could it be Bitsy? She'd said she was in the picture, hadn't she?

"That's my mother."

Vicky stared at him. He was rubbing his forefinger on the

stud he wore in his ear, and Vicky remembered him telling her he'd had it put in to celebrate finding his birth mother. When Rob saw her looking at the stud he took his hand away, but with an almost coy gesture that suggested he might have been fondling it deliberately, either to give her a clue or to give himself some private amusement at its significance.

He laughed, a little wildly, picked the photo up, stared at it. "Finding her was the best thing that ever happened to me. She was as happy as I was when I got in touch. It ... explained things. Things my adoptive parents never knew. I wanted Kristin to have that same chance, that same experience."

"But ... how did you get the picture in the first place? And circling the face of the doctor, Angeletti—how did you know about him? Did your birth mother tell you?"

"My mother," he said, still looking at the picture, "just confirmed what I already knew."

Vicky swallowed back her impatient questions. He would tell her; she would just have to wait.

He reached into the box, took out a handful of file folders, each containing perhaps a dozen pages, and fanned them out across the table. The folders looked old, a darkened brown, the edges frayed. A slightly musty smell rose from them. On each was printed a woman's name. Lucille LeClaire. Patricia Jewinsky. Ann Ferris.

"These are Angeletti's," Rob said. "There are over fifty of them."

"And one of them," Vicky said, a shiver prickling the back of her neck, "had the name Rachel Cornelius on it."

"I told Kristin to say that if anyone asked where she got her birth certificate she should say she found it at home some-where. But everything was in here." He put his hand on the box. "The good doctor kept impeccable files. Everything about the girls, their parents, the babies, the adoptions—"

"The names of the fathers?"

"Some of them. Not in Rachel's case, though. But Angeletti kept updating the files whenever he learned something new, for ten years, twenty years—some of them practically to the day he died. I had current addresses for everyone connected to Rachel, just as I had on the others."

"The others?"

"Just two so far. I chose the first ones because they lived in the lower mainland."

The first ones, Vicky thought coldly: my God, he was intending to contact everyone in the files.

"But Rachel ..." Rob hesitated. "She was more of a challenge."

"Challenge."

If Rob heard the distaste in her voice he gave no sign of it. "Angeletti had written 'No Contact' in her file on several pages, and the notes made clear that she apparently didn't remember, that she had been traumatized. Not surprising. She'd had a horrible labour. Angeletti specialized in horrible labours. You should see the things he wrote about these girls, the details about the deliveries and how he had ways of making the labour last as long as possible, how he made the girls pray and repent and suffer."

Vicky shuddered, tried not to think about Rachel, about Lucille LeClaire and Patricia Jewinsky and Ann Ferris and all the others whose young lives Dr. Angeletti had punished and then stored up like dirty memories for his old age. She looked at the box. Over fifty files.

"I still don't understand," she said, "how you got these files. Did you steal them from the church?"

"I don't have anything to do with the church. They were sent to me."

"Why? By whom?"

Rob paused, making her wait. "Haven't you guessed?"

"I haven't a clue."

Rob pushed the picture of the Hammond School staff across to her. "My mother's in this." He paused again. "And so's my father."

Vicky stared at him. "Angeletti. He's ..."

"My father." There was less satisfaction in his voice at her surprise than she would have expected. "My mother admitted it was a tad ironic that she started out as a staff member and ended up as an inmate." He took the picture, looked at it again, dropped it into the box. "This was my inheritance. The box arrived one day along with a letter from a lawyer, saying Angeletti had left it to me. The son and heir." He laughed bitterly.

"Why ... why do you suppose he did that?"

"So I could learn who I was and continue his work, maybe." He raked up the files on the table and threw them into the box.

"And ..." Vicky chose her words carefully. "Maybe that's what you've been doing."

An uneven redness rose into Rob's cheeks. "Is that what you think? That I did this out of, out of sadism?"

"Not ... sadism, maybe. But this meddling in other peoples' lives, seeing them as some kind of challenge. Frightening people. It's ... voyeurism, at best. Whatever you might tell yourself about how you're helping people." She gestured at the box. "And you intend to go on with this? Go through every file and religiously—so to speak—look up every mother and child?"

Rob laughed, a coarse, humourless bark. "Why shouldn't I? I *am* my father's son." He pushed his chair back, hard, so that it might have fallen if it hadn't hit the wall, and stood up. "Why do you think I brought these here?"

"I don't know."

Rob took a large bite of the dried-out muffin on the table. He swallowed, apparently without chewing. "So *you* can play

God, too, Vicky. You've at least as much potential as I do." He turned and strode away.

It took her a moment to understand.

"Wait." She stumbled to her feet, ran after him. The cafeteria was crowded now, almost every seat taken. The students around her looked up, startled, as she grabbed at Rob's sleeve. "You can't just—"

"Of course I can. I didn't ask for them, either." He nodded at the table, where two students were already appropriating the empty chairs. "Or you can just let the box sit there. And walk away." He pulled loose of her fingers. And walked away.

◆

The box sat on her coffee table. When Amanda dropped over after school the next day and Vicky explained what was inside, Amanda popped off the lid and said, "Come on, Pandora. Aren't you at least curious?"

Vicky slapped Amanda's fingers away, closed the box again. "Of course I'm curious. But I don't have the right. I'd be as bad as Rob."

"Okay, then." Amanda picked up the Yellow Pages, flipped through them. "Here we go. Paper Shredders. A whole page of them. This one's ad says, 'We Know How To Keep A Secret.'"

Vicky sighed. "I don't know if I have the right to do that, either. These may be the only records of who the birth mothers are, of what happened to their babies. I can't just destroy that."

"Well, then tape the damn thing up and store it in the basement. Just think carefully about whom you leave it to in your will."

"Maybe I'll leave it to you."

"Huh. I'm going first, smart-ass." Amanda kicked off her

shoes, propped her feet on the coffee table. "So. They've arrested Junior."

Junior. Amanda had changed conversational lanes again without signalling. Vicky picked up a banana, began to peel it slowly. "Apparently. The car had been carefully washed, but the police found some cloth fibres on the underside of the bumper that matched Rachel's jacket. My jacket, actually." She took a bite of banana. "I still wish it had been Dennis. He was such a creep. Is such a creep."

"If he calls you again, don't talk to him."

"He probably won't call. I'm not his type. He'll look for someone like Rachel, someone meek and passive and easy to intimidate."

"Rachel wasn't all that meek. Most battered wives would be scared to death to have an affair. Even if it *was* just to get pregnant."

Amanda was right: Rachel had not been as meek and passive as she appeared.

The last bit of banana had gone black. Vicky folded the peel over it and set it on the end table.

"Well, I should go," Amanda said, getting up. "You seeing Superma— Clark again this weekend?"

"Yup."

Amanda grunted. "I'm really getting sick of being jealous of you and your boyfriends."

"I could see if he has a friend. Constable Bruce Wayne or somebody."

"Oh, please. The one time I went out with a cop he brought his Doberman along. I got more action from the dog than from the cop. No, wait. Maybe that wasn't a date. I seem to remember a jail cell."

When Amanda had gone Vicky peeled another banana, ate it while wandering around the house. Her eyes kept being drawn to the box on the coffee table. The shredder or the basement? Finally she pulled two big strips of masking tape across the lid and down the sides, to keep herself out as much as to protect the files, and carried the box to the top shelf of the closet in the room that had been Rachel's. That seemed to be where it belonged, for now.

For now. She doubted she could keep her nose out of it indefinitely. But there was a third choice, she thought, as she went up the stairs. She could give the box to some Social Service Agency, let them decide if or when it should be unsealed.

She stood at the front window for a while watching two crows build the inevitable spring nest in her elm tree. While one inserted twigs expertly into the loose weave, the other flapped away into the west. Vicky watched it until it was out of sight. But it would be back, to finish its nest and raise its noisy crow babies and have its crow life.

When Ajit arrived for his session, he pointed at her head and exclaimed, "You have injured yourself!"

"That is the active voice of the verb. Try the passive."

Ajit frowned. "You ... have *been* injured," he pronounced. "By person or persons unknown."

Vicky laughed. "Good," she said.

Persons unknown. It was a good description of everyone she had met because of Rachel. Persons unknown. They had come into her life like a tornado, whirling their lies and secrets and half-truths. Now it had passed. There was more debris than she had first imagined, but it was not hers, not in any lasting way. She could set upright the things that had fallen over, and resume her life. It wouldn't be like that for the others.

She sat down opposite Ajit at the kitchen table. "So, what have you decided about getting married?"

Ajit raised his eyebrows and pulled his lips back in an expression she couldn't decipher but assumed meant he was uncomfortable.

"We have found a compromise," he said. "I have told the

girl the truth, that I am not ... all she might desire in a man. But she still wishes to marry me. She wants so badly to leave her unpleasant parents. And I will get the money to go to medical school. Everyone will be happy."

Vicky sighed. "This seems to me like a recipe for making *nobody* happy."

"We will care for each other, in our own ways. And does not the recipe for romantic love also have unsavoury ingredients? My parents had an arranged marriage and were very happy. My aunt married for love and he beat her."

"But isn't it better to trust oneself than one's parents?"

"When one is in love one isn't oneself."

Vicky laughed. "What an old man you are. Are you afraid of love?"

Ajit smiled. "Of romantic love? Of course. It is a very dangerous thing."

"Nonsense. You're young. And the young, I am told, have no fear."

"That is a very romantic view," Ajit said.

◆

She was just turning away from the window where she had waved goodbye to Ajit when she saw a car pull up in front of the house. A yellow Tracker.

"Good Lord," she whispered to the cat. "It's Linda Harding."

The freezer, the blackness, the intensifying cold: the memory swept over her. Linda suddenly, mercifully, releasing her into light.

Linda got out of the car. She was wearing a thigh-length beige jacket, a slightly darker beige dress, and beige pumps. Her thick black hair looked as though it had just been done, in a careful French braid with wispy curls around the ears and temples, and it was the only thing about her today that did not look deliberately beige.

"Linda! How good to see you!" What did you say to someone who had saved your life? Vicky simply stood there, holding the door open. She considered giving the woman a hug, but her appearance seemed to discourage physical contact.

"I should have phoned first," Linda said. "Is it okay if I come in?"

"Of course, of course. Come in, sit down. Can I take your coat? Would you like a coffee?"

"No, I'm fine. I won't stay long."

Linda sat down, her spine straight and not touching the back of the sofa. She pressed her legs together, laid her beige purse on her lap and clasped her hands on top. Around her cuticles was a faint trace of red, as though she had recently removed the polish from her nails.

"I'm sure I never really thanked you properly," Vicky said. "You saved my life."

Linda didn't answer, appeared not even to have heard. Her face seemed glazed and stiff, even her eyes incapable of movement, staring straight ahead, not quite at Vicky, who felt an urge to move her chair over a foot to put herself in Linda's line of vision.

She would still be in shock, Vicky reminded herself. Her son was a thief and a murderer. Having opened the door to a freezer, no matter what was inside, would probably not be uppermost in her mind.

"Are you sure I can't get you something? Tea, maybe? Something to drink?"

Linda shook her head. She fumbled in her purse and, without looking, took out a slim, silver case. She extracted a cigarette, lit it from a lighter she might already have been carrying in her other hand. At any other time it would have surprised Vicky that she hadn't asked permission to smoke. Vicky took the oranges and bananas out of the bowl on the coffee table and set it beside her guest. As an ashtray it was ridiculously huge, but Linda said, "Thank you," absently, and tapped her cigarette into it.

Why had she come? Vicky fidgeted in her chair, avoiding looking at that pale, rigid face. What was the best thing to do, to say?

"I was thinking of Rachel," Linda said suddenly. "When I was driving here. I was thinking of the first time I ever met her." She took a deep pull on her cigarette. "Do you know who the father of her baby is?"

Vicky tried to keep her expression neutral, unsurprised. Which baby? she had to stop herself from asking. Could Linda know about her husband and Rachel? Surely not. Still, Vicky would rather not lie unless she had to. She owed Linda that much.

"What do you mean?" she parried.

"I just wondered if she told anyone else."

Anyone else. It must mean Rachel had confided in Linda. So they must be talking about the first pregnancy.

"And ... you know who the father is?" Vicky's voice sounded more eager than it should have. What difference did it make now? No matter who it was, she was *not* going to tell Kristin.

"He raped her. She came to our door afterwards, the night it happened, how she got there I don't know, but I was the only one home and she told me. She made me swear not to tell anyone. She never spoke of it again. And neither did I."

"God. Poor Rachel. Did her father know?"

"I don't think so. Surely even he wouldn't have been cruel enough to make her marry the man."

It took Vicky a minute to understand. "*Marry* him? You mean ... You mean it was *Dennis*?"

"Yes."

Vicky's head was throbbing. None of this made any sense.

"But … did he know she'd had his child?"

"No. She was so ashamed, as though it had been her fault. I sometimes wonder if she made herself forget—about the rape *and* the baby—because it was the only way she could stand to live with him. Or maybe it was some kind of revenge, not letting him know he had a child when he wanted one so badly."

"I thought Dennis couldn't have kids."

Linda laughed unpleasantly. "As far as I know there's nothing wrong with him in that department. Rachel had this disease—"

"Endometriosis."

"—and she used it as her excuse for not getting pregnant. But as soon as she married Dennis she went on the pill. I found the pills, the first time she ran away from him and stayed with us."

"But I thought she wanted children."

"She did. But not his."

"I'm … amazed," Vicky said.

Had she known Rachel at all? What a complicated life she had made for herself in order to survive. John Harding had told her Rachel hadn't confided much in him—it certainly sounded as though she hadn't told him that she'd been on the pill when she was with Dennis. Did she think that Harding would be less likely to begin the affair, to help her conceive, if he knew Dennis wasn't infertile? Vicky thought of the convoluted scheme Rob and Kristin had concocted, and then of how Rob had said bitterly, "I'm my father's son." If a preference for the convoluted was the criterion, Kristin was certainly her mother's daughter.

In any case now, whatever else she did, Vicky had to keep Kristin from finding out who her father was: a rapist. It was a secret Rachel had spent most of her life protecting. And Linda had kept the secret, too. But would she continue to do so now that Rachel was dead? She didn't know about Kristin; she might think there was no longer any point. She had just told Vicky, after all.

"I suppose we should respect her wishes on this," Vicky said. "I mean, to keep her secret. Maybe you shouldn't even have told me." Why had she said that? It sounded clumsy, a reprimand.

Linda's mouth pulled tighter. She stubbed her cigarette out in the bowl, making it skid a few inches on the end table. "What does it matter now?" she said harshly. "She's dead. They think Junior killed her."

Vicky winced. Linda's blunt words had been flung across the room like an accusation. "I'm sorry. It—"

"Junior didn't kill anyone. The idea is ridiculous, completely ridiculous! He was a kind and loving boy, and he's a kind and loving man."

Vicky licked her lips, tried to think of what she should say next, what it was that Linda wanted from her. "I know it must be hard to believe," she said carefully. "That he was stealing from the company and that—"

Linda laughed, a hard, unnatural sound that hardly caused her lips to move. "Stealing! He wasn't stealing!"

"But there *is* evidence—"

"The money was his. He worked like a slave in that place, and John, all John thought he was worth was some little *allowance*. Like you give a child. You don't know. What could you know? You think John is this nice, charming man. You don't know how selfish and stingy he is. I couldn't stand to see him make Junior beg for every penny. It was my idea for him to set up his own account."

Vicky's eyebrows went up. "You knew about it?"

"Of course I did. I kept the books. Junior couldn't have done it by himself. He didn't know anything about accounting. Neither did John, fortunately."

Vicky's heart had quickened its beat. "Did you know Rachel had found out about this ... account?"

The spiritless and drugged look that had been on Linda's face was gone now. Her eyes were wide, staring at Vicky so intensely they seemed to be pushing her back in her chair.

"I knew something was going on, that she was pressuring Junior. He was getting so jumpy. But he didn't want to worry me, he was like that, he never wanted to worry me." She lit another cigarette, her motions quick but steady. "I think he was suspicious about that appointment on Wednesday, maybe he even knew they might be coming to arrest him, but he went in anyway, and he wasn't even supposed to go to the office that day, he was supposed to be out on a job in Burnaby. But he didn't tell me, he didn't want to worry me, that's how he was. If I'd known he was at the plant, I would never have—"

"Never have what?" Vicky's hands were clenched onto the arms of her chair. She went cold, icy cold.

"Never have pushed you into that freezer. And that's why I came here. I came yesterday, but you were out. I need to ... well, to settle things. To apologize. I didn't mean to hurt you." She gestured vaguely at Vicky's bandage. "I didn't know you'd get knocked out. I thought, I'll keep the door jammed for ten minutes or so, and then I'll pretend to find you." Her voice was unwavering, as though she might be explaining the uses of Tupperware.

"But *why*? Linda, my God, why?"

Linda took a long pull on her cigarette, gave Vicky a little smile. It made Vicky feel even colder. "I know why you went there. To meet John. To go off for a nice little lunch and talk about Rachel. And then there'd be another lunch, and another, and, oh, John would be just so appealing, the way he'd be needing somebody to confide in and feel sorry for him. Oh, I know all about that, that's how it was with me after his first wife died—"

"But—you thought I was after your *husband*? That's why you locked me in a freezer?" Vicky had to stop herself from laughing hysterically. "My God, Linda, I'm not interested in him, good grief—"

"Maybe you even really do believe that you aren't, but it would have happened, he would have made it happen."

"So locking me in the freezer was, what, some kind of a *warning*?"

"I'm sorry. It was— I was upset and angry. I went there to ask you not to go out with him, and suddenly, well, there was this opportunity. I wanted you to think it was John who pushed you. Even if you didn't suspect him, surely the police would, I thought. It never occurred to me that they would think it was Junior. He wasn't even supposed to *be* there. But the police would be suspicious of John already, I thought. I know you told them he was the father of Rachel's baby."

Vicky swallowed. Her mouth tasted of chalk. "You knew about the baby."

"Of course I knew. He would phone her from home, like he phoned you. As though I would walk past his study with my hands over my ears, as though I'd be too stupid to pick up an extension."

Vicky took a deep breath. "So it was you. You were driving the Mercedes that night."

Linda pressed her fingers against her forehead. Her voice went quiet, so low Vicky had to strain to hear. "I hadn't intended to kill her. It was ... like with you, I suppose. A warning. I wanted her to think it could have been John. She wasn't wearing the right coat, I remember, and for a moment I hesitated, thinking, what if it wasn't her, and then she turned around and saw me, and ..."

Through the long silence in the room Vicky could hear the tiny sounds within it, her watch ticking, a fly fumbling at the kitchen window, the cat scratching at the front door, a jogger's shoes hitting the pavement as he passed on the street.

"Why are you telling me all this now?"

A look of impatience crossed Linda's face, the kind of look that meant, *Haven't you been listening?* "They've arrested Junior. They think *he* killed her, that *he* could have done it. I never dreamed they could suspect him, never thought she would have hidden away some *file* on him."

"And of course you couldn't let him go to prison for what you did."

"Of course not."

"You'd have let Dennis rot in jail, though, for the rest of his life."

"Dennis. Why should I care about Dennis? He's a nasty man. It was his fault Rachel got involved with us in the first place. He's a horrible man." She stubbed her cigarette out, hard. "Why should I have felt bad keeping him in jail? It would have been a favour to the next woman he's going to abuse."

Maybe I'll call you sometime, Vicky. Give us both a treat, eh?

Vicky made herself release her fingers from the arms of the chair. The tips began to tingle. She rubbed them along her thighs, the gesture of wiping something away.

"You must have ..." She paused. "You really hated her. Hated Rachel."

"Yes," Linda said. "I did. I liked her at first, you see. Everybody did. Little waifish Rachel, she's had such a hard life, she needs our help, and she's so sweet and grateful, poor thing— And then you find this person you've ... opened your home to, your feelings to, has betrayed you. I think you hate somebody like that worst of all, because you liked and trusted them once."

Vicky could feel herself nodding, stopped abruptly. "And then you find out she's threatening to expose Vance ... Junior."

"She was threatening to tell John, but not because she

thought Junior was doing something wrong. I don't think she cared about that at all. It was because she was ... allied with John. Sleeping with him." Her fingers wrapped themselves tighter around her purse strap.

"I don't think he'd have left you for her."

"Of course he would. All she would have had to do was snap her fingers and he'd have gone."

"So why did you kill Rachel and not your husband?"

Linda laughed. It sounded genuine, amused and surprised. "Maybe I should have. But I didn't want him dead. I just wanted him back."

Vicky looked at Linda, the last person anyone could expect to have done what she had done, an ordinary, beige woman, incapable of the red passions that led to murder. But even the small secrets Rachel had kept from Vicky had upset her; what if the secrets, the betrayals, had been so much larger? What would it take to become Linda?

"It's just hard to believe," she said finally. "That you could kill anyone."

"Why? Because I'm a woman? It was easy enough for you to believe Dennis capable of it, or Junior. Are women just supposed to get depressed and suicidal?"

She had a point, Vicky thought. "It was as hard for me to believe it of Vance," she said, but it wasn't true. "You both seem like the kind of people who should have had ... other answers."

"Well, you were wrong."

"What are you going to do now?"

Linda stood up, in the quick, smooth motion of a body that had been only perched on the edge of its seat. Vicky tensed. It had not until this moment occurred to her to be afraid, to think that Linda might have come here not just to confess. Vicky's eyes dropped to Linda's purse. Was it large enough to conceal a gun, a knife— If she leapt up now, she could dash into the study, thrust the back of the chair there under the doorknob, snatch up the phone—

But Linda was turning away, to the front door, smoothing her dress down along the back of her right thigh, frowning slightly as though reprimanding the fabric for wrinkling.

"I'm on the way to the police station. I would have gone yesterday, but there were things I needed to do, to straighten out. You're the last. I wanted to say I was sorry. About the freezer. That you had to be in there so long."

But not for putting me in there in the first place, Vicky thought. She stood up. The movement made her head start to throb again, and she reached up to the bandage, then dropped her hand, not wanting Linda to see, though she wasn't sure why.

"It's important ..." Vicky said, and then hesitated, because she wasn't sure what she meant to say, what was, finally, important. "It's important that you show remorse. About killing Rachel. They expect that. Do you, do you *feel* remorse?"

Linda was reaching for the doorknob. She drew her hand back slightly, stood for several moments staring at where it had been. "No," she said.

She opened the door. "Your cat just came in," she said. "I hope that's okay."

Your cat just came in. I hope that's okay.

It seemed like the most bizarre thing Vicky had ever heard, and she knew that, in spite of herself, a time would come when she would be telling someone about this conversation, and she would say, "And then as she was leaving she said, 'Your cat just came in. I hope that's okay,'" and whoever she had told would say, "No!" or "You're kidding!" and there would be laughter, cheap and obliging, and the thought of it now made the tears come to her eyes, but for whom she couldn't say.